Foundation

MISSION ROAD

RON CORBETT

A FRANK YAKABUSKI MYSTERY

Published by ECW Press
665 Gerrard Street East
Toronto, Ontario, Canada M4M 1Y2
416-694-3348 / info@ecwpress.com

Cover design: Michel Vrana
Author photo: © Julie Oliver

Get the
eBook free!*
*proof of purchase
required

Purchase the print edition
and receive the eBook free.
For details, go to ecwpress.com/eBook.

LIBRARY AND ARCHIVES CANADA CATALOGUING IN PUBLICATION

Title: Mission Road / Ron Corbett.

Names: Corbett, Ron, 1959– author.

Description: Series statement: A Frank Yakabuski mystery

Identifiers: Canadiana (print) 20200190733
Canadiana (ebook) 20200190741

ISBN 978-1-77041-396-2 (softcover)
ISBN 978-1-77305-468-1 (PDF)
ISBN 978-1-77305-467-4 (EPUB)

Classification: LCC PS8605.O7155 M57 2020
DDC C813/.6—dc23

The publication of *Mission Road* has been generously supported by the Canada Council for the Arts which last year invested $153 million to bring the arts to Canadians throughout the country and is funded in part by the Government of Canada. *Nous remercions le Conseil des arts du Canada de son soutien. L'an dernier, le Conseil a investi 153 millions de dollars pour mettre de l'art dans la vie des Canadiennes et des Canadiens de tout le pays. Ce livre est financé en partie par le gouvernement du Canada.* We acknowledge the support of the Ontario Arts Council (OAC), an agency of the Government of Ontario, which last year funded 1,737 individual artists and 1,095 organizations in 223 communities across Ontario for a total of $52.1 million. We also acknowledge the contribution of the Government of Ontario through the Ontario Book Publishing Tax Credit, and through Ontario Creates for the marketing of this book.

PRINTED AND BOUND IN CANADA   PRINTING: MARQUIS   5 4 3 2 1

MIX
Paper from responsible sources
FSC® C103567

For Millie Patten
And the adventures ahead

AUTHOR'S NOTE

This is a work of fiction. All places and characters are imagined. While the story takes place somewhere on the Northern Divide, there are no literal depictions of any city or town on the Divide.

I
MONEY

CHAPTER ONE

Frank Yakabuski looked at the man seated the other side of the kitchen table and couldn't decide what to think of him. Calvin Jayne. He wore grey sweatpants and a ribbed t-shirt that had slid up his stomach far enough to reveal three rolls of pale mid-winter skin and tufts of sweaty black hair. It was too hot in the apartment. He was overcompensating, although he wasn't the only one. Winter had been late arriving on the Northern Divide, but when it came it was bitter cold. The salt trucks couldn't run most days because of the cold, and there was black ice everywhere. Highway fatalities were common. So were morning sightings of animals, standing in some distant field with fog swirling around them — scrawny black bear, teetering moose, awoken from their hibernation and not sure what to do next.

It was a winter of ill-fated wonders. The first fortune hunter arrived the second week of February. His name was

Jason McAllister, and he was a postgraduate mathematics student from Syracuse University who checked in to the Grainger Hotel after arriving on a direct flight from Toronto. Because he showed no sign of needing to be in Springfield — he didn't check in with the gear of a hydro worker or a tree-marker; didn't seem to be looking for work at the sawmills or the truck yards — he was noticed.

During the next two days, McAllister was seen shopping at Murphy's Sporting Goods, where he purchased packets of dehydrated food and some propane tanks, and Stedman's department store, where he purchased wool socks, long underwear, and several toques. He used the business suite on the second floor of the Grainger several times, where there was free Wi-Fi. Many of the staff in the hotel recalled him working on a laptop.

On his third day in Springfield, he checked out of the hotel and took a cab to Mission Road, a hiking trail west of the city. His mother reported him missing two days later.

Calvin Jayne — forty-eight years old, drove a cab for Shamrock Taxi, was a mill-hand before that — said he remembered the fare. McAllister gave him a twenty-dollar tip, but he claimed he would have remembered the fare even without that. "I told the kid he was nuts, no one did the Mission Road trail in the middle of winter, especially not a winter like the one we're having. But the kid said he'd done Mount Robson last year, and he knew what he was doing. That's what he told me. He'd done Robson."

"Did you see him start down the trail?"

"Yeah. I still thought he was nuts, so I waited to see if he was going to back out. I think it was minus forty or something that morning with the wind chill."

"You watched him for how long?"

"Till I couldn't see him."

"Then you drove home and didn't think about him again?"

"No. I kept on working."

Yakabuski glanced around. Jayne lived in a one-bedroom walk-up on Derry Street. No signs of a wife or children. Cases of Old Milwaukee stacked by the back door.

"Did you think you should have told someone about him? Like you said, it was forty below that morning."

"Kid knew how cold it was."

"He was alone. Not from around here. Might have been nice if someone knew he was out there. That never occurred to you?"

"Might have been nice? Do you want my list of might-have-been-nice, Detective? Look, I'm sorry the kid is missing and everything, but have I done something wrong here?"

Yakabuski thought about it a minute. "Criminal negligence? I know you can't cut off a person's hydro in weather like this. Maybe you can't drop anyone off in the middle of the bush either. Did McAllister tell you what he was doing on the Mission Road trail in minus-forty-degree weather?"

The cabbie looked surprised by what Yakabuski had asked. His eyes narrowed a bit. "No. He didn't say anything about that."

"What did you *think* he was doing?"

"Well . . . I didn't give it much thought. He was just another fare, you know?"

"No thought at all?"

"Not at the time, no. Some people like winter camping? What the fuck do I know."

"What do you think now?"

The cabbie gave Yakabuski another stare that lasted a second longer than it should have, a man lacking the wit to conceal what he was doing. Deciding right then just how truthful he needed to be. "Well, knowing what I do today, sure, I guess I've got an idea."

"What's come to you, Calvin?"

"The kid might have been out there looking for those missing diamonds."

"There's a thought. Did you tell anyone, after dropping him off, that Jason McAllister might have been doing a thing like that?"

The cabbie started to speak, but before he could Yakabuski held up his hand to silence him. He left his hand there for several seconds before saying, "I'll canvass the taverns. I have you pegged for O'Keefe's, so that's where I'll start. You would have been there last Tuesday night. Maybe Wednesday . . . though I figure you couldn't wait to tell someone about it, so Tuesday."

The cabbie was starting to look sick. His head was resting in his hands and he was making small sounds that might have been moaning, might have been prayer, Yakabuski wasn't sure. If there hadn't been more than a billion dollars in lost diamonds hidden somewhere in Springfield, Calvin Jayne could have stayed under the police radar the rest of his life. Never quite honest. Never crooked enough to notice. Those diamonds were almost entrapment for people like Jayne, though Yakabuski supposed you could say that about any kind of greed, and maybe that wasn't saying much.

"Get your coat," he said, having come to his decision. "Let's finish this conversation downtown."

"You're arresting me? On what charge?"

"Not the right one, I'm willing to bet, but I'll think of something. Do you have a coat, Calvin, or are you going outside in that shirt?"

CHAPTER TWO

Six weeks earlier, the largest armed robbery in history had taken place in Springfield — $1.2 billion in uncut diamonds, stolen from a De Kirk Mines cargo plane sitting on the tarmac of the Springfield International Airport.

It happened a week before Christmas, and it still seemed like fantasy to a lot of people. Or a thing that was both real and unreal, if that made any sense. People saw that diamond robbery the way you see some distant date. Real enough — but so far away it seemed hard to imagine, almost implausible.

It stayed that way well into the new year, a shared sense of disbelief in Springfield, an odd calm in the city, as though people were waiting to see if the jewellery heist had been a seasonal fable, some shining star in the east that was no longer there.

It was hard to tell exactly when that changed. When the penny dropped and people realized, with surprise, that the story was true. One-point-two-billion dollars worth of uncut, untraceable diamonds had been stolen in Springfield and the police had not a clue what happened to them after that.

"Soon as Christmas is finished, people are going to start thinking about those diamonds, and not in a good way," George Yakabuski had warned his son.

"I know that."

"Whole town could go mad-trapper crazy this winter, if you don't find them."

"We're looking, Dad."

Yakabuski, senior detective with the Springfield Regional Police Service, had come to the conclusion diamonds made a robbery investigation worse in every way possible. If a dozen Van Gogh paintings had been stolen, Yakabuski couldn't imagine someone like Jason McAllister coming to Springfield to try and find them, because what were you ever going to do with a dozen Van Goghs? Set up a private viewing room in the back of your garage? Give them away to close friends and family?

Same deal with money. Most people would figure paper currency was marked and they'd get caught if they tried to spend it, so what was the point in trying to find it? And they'd be right. Not to mention the square footage of $1.2 billion in paper currency would be a problem logistically. Even Saddam Hussein couldn't make off with that much cash when his son rolled up with a tank brigade to make a last-minute withdrawal from the Central Bank of Iraq the day before the Second Persian Gulf War started.

But a billion dollars in diamonds? That was different. You could throw that in the trunk of a Cadillac and be on your way.

Store them in your garden shed. Ship them to friends in some FedEx boxes. Those diamonds weren't cut, and Yakabuski figured that made a difference too. They weren't banknote paper or priceless works of art. They weren't stamped gold bars. They were stones you could have found yourself if you were lucky enough to be walking in the right place at the right time and stubbed your toe the right way.

Ownership seemed different for a thing like that. More fluid. More open to debate. "Why shouldn't those diamonds be mine? Christ, I've worked hard enough." A lot of people needed only a small amount of rationalization and self-deception to start asking that question.

So the penny dropped, maybe two weeks ago. That was when Yakabuski started to notice people on the street looked different somehow. A bit dreamier. Lost in thought. Middle of winter so that wasn't unusual, but they didn't have the lethargy you normally see that time of year. If anything, they were more animated. Hopped up. The foot traffic in Cork's Town had increased probably tenfold since the start of February, and there was no good reason for it. People were walking the home turf of the Shiners, just hoping to hear something, hoping to get lucky. It wouldn't be long before they were doing more than that.

He looked at Calvin Jayne in the back seat of his Jeep, staring sadly at his handcuffed wrists.

Maybe they already had.

CHAPTER THREE

Yakabuski left Jayne in a holding cell in the basement of the Centretown police detachment, telling the duty sergeant to hold him until he could come back and do the paperwork.

"What's the charge?" asked the sergeant.

"I'll give you one when I come back."

"Have to write it on the intake form, Yak. Can you give me something?"

"How about aiding and abetting in a possible disappearance."

"Is that even a charge?"

"Should be. Just write it down, Barry. I'll clean up the paperwork this afternoon."

The sergeant nodded and didn't ask any more questions.

Yakabuski took an elevator to the third floor, where a criminal investigations departmental meeting was underway. It was a special briefing, with two Correctional Service officers in attendance to get the latest on what around the police station these days you only needed to call "the investigation" and everyone knew what you meant. Inspector Mick Lawrence, head of criminal investigations, was addressing the room when Yakabuski entered.

"We have more than the normal amount of ground to cover this morning, and some guests from Correctional Service here, so let's keep our comments on point, please. Don't want to be here all bloody day."

Lawrence motioned with his hands for the lights to be dimmed, and the video screen in front of the conference room filled with the black-and-white image of a plane's cargo door. There were loud groans.

"That's exactly what I'm talking about, people," Lawrence said. "I know we've all seen this before. But we're going to run it right from the start. Maybe today is the day we solve this motherfucker."

Laughs this time instead of groans, and Lawrence didn't reprimand anyone. Yakabuski guessed it depended on the interruption. Mick Lawrence was in his late fifties and had blond hair that was long but not too long. He wore wire-rimmed glasses, the colour of which changed a few times a week.

"What you're looking at is the cargo door of the De Kirk plane robbed of $1.2 billion in diamonds while sitting on the tarmac of the Springfield International Airport last December seventeenth."

Lawrence spoke directly to the strangers in the room, conspicuous in their grey prison-guard uniforms in a room full of plainclothes cops. Onscreen, the cargo doors open and a pilot appears, pushing a wheeled storage bin. A black Econoline van with covered licence plates pulls up to the plane. Two men get out, wearing fishermen caps and black balaclavas, leaving no skin exposed. One man, with long hair sticking out the bottom of his balaclava, disappears into the plane with the pilot. The other man loads the bin into the back of the van.

The man with long hair reappears with two more storage bins and pushes them to the cargo door. The men load the bins into the van and drive away. The elapsed time is two minutes fifty-six seconds. The pilot is never seen again.

"Because of events occurring in Springfield at the time of the robbery," said Lawrence, stopping the video and motioning for lights to be turned on, "we believe Shiners were the ones who stole those diamonds. As most of you know, they're a homegrown embarrassment, a gang of Irish thugs that got their start busting up bush camps along the Springfield River in the eighteen hundreds.

"We believe the man driving the van is Sean Morrissey, leader of the Shiners. We have not been able to ascertain the identity of the second thief. We believe Morrissey was in partnership with Gabriel Dumont, a Métis leader who lived near Cape Diamond, where De Kirk has its mining operation. He belonged to a group called the Travellers. The pilot was Dumont's man.

"The pilot was killed on the plane, and Dumont was killed at his home the same night as the robbery. Morrissey was picked up the day after and held on a three-day material-witness warrant. The night before he was to be released, he punched the duty sergeant in the holding cells and got himself charged with assault. He pled guilty at his first court appearance and was sentenced to eighteen months. With two-for-one credit for time in the cells, and the standard two-third reduction we give to crooks in this country just for showing up, he'll be paroled in ten weeks. Is that correct, Mr. Gallagher?"

"Yes," said the older of the two men in grey uniform. "The actual release date is April thirtieth. That works out to four months served."

"How has Mr. Morrissey been since he got to Wentworth?" asked Lawrence.

"It's been less than a month, but no incidents so far. The sentence is so short he won't be in any of our programs. My guess is he'll do his time quietly."

"Any visitors?"

"His lawyer, Tyler Lawson. Twice. That's been it."

"May I ask a question?" It was the second corrections officer, sitting with his hand in the air, a much younger man.

"Go ahead," said Lawrence.

"The assault on the jail guard seems deliberate, a way for Morrissey to stay behind bars. Is that what you believe?"

"It is. We don't know if it was improvised or something he had planned all along. We also don't know why he did it."

"But you believe Morrissey killed Dumont?"

"We believe he hired it out. The assassin's name was Cambino Cortez, a business partner of both Dumont and Morrissey. Hasn't been picked up yet. He's from Mexico, a little village called Heroica, not far from the Brownsville, Texas, border crossing. The last sighting we have for Cortez was Sioux Falls, the morning of the heist."

"He's still in the area?"

"We believe so."

The corrections officer leaned back in his chair with a satisfied smile. The clever kid had just asked some clever questions. Yakabuski knew there were going to be more now.

"As far as theories on what Sean Morrissey might have done with those diamonds after he stole them," continued Lawson, "I'm not sure if there is a theory I have not heard. A journalist from South Florida called me this morning wanting to talk about possible extraterrestrial involvement."

Laughter from everyone in the room. Again, Lawrence let it go.

"I like to keep things simpler than that. In any robbery, you follow the money, which in our case is that Econoline van. I'm going to turn the meeting over now to Constable Donna Griffin."

Donna Griffin had, for all practical purposes, been permanently seconded to Major Crimes following the diamond heist. A patrol officer Yakabuski had asked to do some computer research, she had provided the best clues in the investigation so far.

"I'll start at the airport, for the benefit of Corrections," she said, and the lights dimmed again. A still-frame of the Econoline van passing through the commercial-hangars gate of the airport appeared on the screen. She hit play, and the van started moving.

"We've put this together from eighty-seven security, closed-circuit, and red-light cameras that caught the Econoline somewhere in Springfield that night. It left the airport at 12:46 a.m. and we have continuous eyes on it for the next eight minutes, thirty-seven seconds. It then drives into this parking garage on Doucet Street. It's a three-storey, enclosed garage, and the van is inside for eleven minutes, fourteen seconds. Here it is leaving." She paused the video on an Econoline van of a different colour and trade, a plumbing service now, exiting the garage.

"So they gave the van a quick makeover," said the young corrections officer, not bothering to raise his hand this time. "Why not just steal one and have it waiting in the garage?"

"We don't think our thieves wanted to run the risk of some bad-luck traffic stop," said Griffin. "The Econoline wasn't stolen. It was registered to a man who died in Cork's Town twenty years ago."

"Nice trick."

"Yes it is."

Griffin hit play and the van continued down Doucet Street. "We have steady eyes on the van for the next sixteen minutes and twenty-three seconds. Not one second of that is black. The van leaves the garage and takes Highway 7, heading east. It takes the Mission Road exit at 1:20 a.m. and is spotted on a CCTV camera at an Irving station three minutes later. That's the last we see of the van for forty-seven minutes."

She fast-forwarded through the video and stopped at a still-frame of the Econoline engulfed in flames. She hit play and said, "The van was found burning in the alley off Belfast Street by a waitress at O'Keefe's at 2:10 a.m. She shot this video with her phone. No diamonds in the van. No Sean Morrissey and no second thief. Forensics has turned up exactly zip on the vehicle, and that won't be changing anytime soon."

She turned to look at the young corrections officer. It was time for him to ask a clever question.

"Forty-seven minutes," he said, as if on cue. "You can practically drive from one end of Springfield to the other in forty-seven minutes. Those diamonds could be anywhere."

"Not exactly," said Griffin, and she smiled when she said

it. It had been several days now since she had been patted on the back for what was about to appear on the screen.

"Security cameras not only tell us where something is, they also tell us where something is *not*." As she spoke, a street map of Springfield appeared on the screen. "If you take away all the places the van wasn't spotted during our forty-seven-minute gap, and do the math to figure out how far it could have gone and still be back at Belfast Street by 2:10, this is what you're left with."

The map began to fill in, as though ink were spilling down the streets, washing over the city parks, the rivers, rolling through Cork's Town and the French Quarter, wiping out the entire North Shore, leaving in a few seconds only thin veins of white.

"These are the places that van could have gone during our forty-seven-minute gap. As you can see, we have the lower half of Albert Street, an off-road trail by the Springfield River, and most of Mission Road."

"You were able to rule out Cork's Town?" said the young corrections officer.

"More cameras in Cork's Town than any other part of the city."

"You're still looking at a lot of ground."

"We are," said Lawrence. "I'll let Senior Detective Frank Yakabuski take it from here. Thank you, Donna."

Yakabuski waited for her to sit down, and then he leaned forward in his chair. He didn't bother to stand. He had no visual aids. He looked directly to the young corrections officer and said, "We've had that map for about two weeks. For various investigative reasons, our search is now focused on Mission Road."

"Why there?"

"Because the search of Albert Street and the off-road trail didn't turn up anything. And because Mission Road is an area well known to the Shiners."

"How can you be sure Morrissey didn't pull a sleight of hand during those forty-seven minutes? He could have passed the diamonds off to a third person. Maybe they're not even in Springfield anymore."

Yakabuski took a good look at the corrections officer. He didn't give him much past thirty. Probably under. He had barbed wire tattoos on both wrists. Hair shorn as short as it could go, so you could see the bone formation of his skull.

"Because we didn't find any more bodies," he said.

The corrections officer didn't say anything. There was a different tone to Yakabuski's voice than there had been with Mick Lawrence. He feared asking a stupid question, but after an awkward amount of time had passed and he realized Yakabuski had given him no other choice, he said, "What do you mean, you didn't find any more bodies?"

"I mean there were only five people who knew about this heist. That's the entire inner circle for the largest armed robbery in history. Two of those people are dead, two are in the wind, and one is sitting in Wentworth Correctional Facility. There wouldn't be someone else in play because Sean Morrissey wouldn't have wanted someone else in play."

"Just how concerned should we be about Mr. Morrissey, Detective?"

It was Officer Gallagher speaking. The first good question from Correctional Service. The younger officer's had all been for show. This was practical: how will this affect my workday?

"I suspect you're right about Morrissey wanting to spend his time quietly," said Yakabuski. "We'll be there when he walks out, sir. We'll staff it with whatever is needed, right up to a full tactical team. You'll need to coordinate with us the week of his release. And you should let us know right away about any incidents or threats to Mr. Morrissey. There's been nothing like that so far, you say?"

"Nothing."

"He's in general population?"

"He is."

"And no incidents. That may be a good sign. We've been looking for a few of those. They're about as easy to find as diamonds."

This time Yakabuski got the laughter, a little louder than it had been for Lawrence, and he knew that would annoy the inspector. He wasn't surprised when the meeting came to an end shortly afterwards, Lawrence thanking everyone for coming, now let's go solve this motherfucker. Lawrence spit out the profanity like a man who rarely swore but figured he should from time to time so he could be one of the boys. The sort of insincere, unctuous swearing you hear coming from executive offices everywhere.

As Yakabuski left the room he passed the young corrections officer, still staring at the map of Springfield. He stared at it with him for a second before saying, "Yep, it's a regular treasure map."

"I wasn't thinking that."

"Sure you were. It's what everyone thinks the first time they see it."

CHAPTER FOUR

Mission Road was an old colony road running down a south-racing ridge of the Northern Divide, about a mile from the Springfield River. It was named by evangelical Mormons who settled there in the 1880s, travelling from Salt Lake City with dreams of building an agricultural utopia. The provincial government granted the Mormons one thousand acres, and there were ten families that came, a little more than a hundred people.

Both the settlement and the road the Mormons built were given the name Mission, and they were built far enough away from the Springfield River that the clanking and hissing of the sawmills was but a distant sound, the sulphur of the pulp mills a passing scent that came only on days with an easterly wind. For decades there was virtually no contact between Springfield and the Mission settlement.

The first thing the settlers built was a split-log tabernacle.

After that came the barns and silos, the multi-winged log cabins, the hundred acres of cleared land for cash crops — wheat, hay, hemp — another twenty for potatoes, beets, and carrots, stored in root cellars for the winter. Because of their hard labour, their faith, and the hard currency they brought from Utah, it was several years before the Mormons realized they were not growing enough food to survive.

Like every farmer lured to the Northern Divide with promises of government land grants, the Mormons had been tricked. To their shock and dismay, the settlers came to realize the land they had been given, that they once believed so bountiful, a gift from God, was nothing but a deceit. A top loam of rich black soil, but the loam was shallow and lacked peat, sat atop a rock face of granite and gneiss, so that after a few years of being tilled the loam turned to fine sand and blew away.

Yakabuski never understood the farmers who stuck it out after that. The stubborn ones who hung on for generations, never admitting they had been duped. The ones who lasted the longest were now considered founding families in all sorts of small villages along the Northern Divide. They had been given street names and brass plaques. A few had chapbooks written about them that you sometimes found for sale in hockey arenas and four-corner gas stations. Yakabuski felt the honours were poor compensation for passing deprivation and hardship down through five generations of your family. He knew others saw it different.

The Mormons were some of the stubborn ones. They stayed another thirty years after realizing they had been tricked. They prayed in their tabernacle for rain, sun, peat, whatever might save them. And when they weren't busy praying, they worked their stone fields. Near the end they had stopped sleeping, stopped eating, rolled in the dirt talking in tongues, lived in a world of feverish delusion and faith, but not even this was enough to save them.

In 1919 the sheriff of Springfield County came to evict them for unpaid land taxes. Having no money to leave the Divide, the men found work in the mills, where they were beaten for the clothes they wore, while the women got jobs as scullery maids or pot washers or whores in brothels owned by the Shiners.

Yakabuski wondered why the Mormons never figured it out after all that praying. Bad land is bad land. God never feels any different about it.

❖ ❖ ❖

Inspector Fraser Newton was waiting for Yakabuski at the trailhead to Mission Road. It had snowed the night before, and the spruce trees ringing the parking lot were capped with white cones. A light mist was swirling through the upper boughs, along with cold exhaust from idling police vehicles and the breath of men working somewhere down the trail.

"Hear you've got a missing kid," said Newton when Yakabuski was standing beside him in the parking lot. The men stomped feet and blew into gloved hands while they spoke.

"Jason McAllister," answered Yakabuski. "Twenty-two years old. Graduate student at Syracuse. He came up here a week ago and hasn't been seen since."

"We've been here five days."

"Have far in are you?"

"Less than a mile."

"Seen any signs of people on the trail?"

"Plenty. Trail gets used all year long. Crazy, if you ask me, coming out in weather like this." Newton looked down the trail, covered by tall white pine and thick spruce stands, the trailhead looking like the entrance to a dark, cold tunnel.

"Have you had the crime-scene tape up the whole time?"

"Yep. We're starting to get gawkers. Don't know if anyone's told you that."

"What are you telling them?"

"Since this morning we've been telling them we're looking for your missing kid. Before that, we said it was part of a homicide investigation."

"Taking some liberties there, Newt."

"Really? You don't think there's a body or two buried somewhere on Mission Road, Yak?"

Yakabuski didn't answer, although he understood the inspector's argument. The forest did not reclaim the farming community of Mission, or the road the Mormons built to get there. The original settlement, twenty miles east of the trailhead, was now a gated community with some of the most expensive homes in Springfield.

As for the colony road, it turned out there was a purpose, a waiting utility, for an abandoned road high in the hills overlooking Springfield. The Shiners ran stills and juke joints along Mission Road for decades. Conscription dodgers hid out during both World Wars. Some members of the Ma Racine gang lived in the caves along the Mission Road when the Mounties were hunting them back in the '30s.

Before the turn of the last century, twenty miles of the road had been converted into a hiking and biking trail, but Newton was right. Any cop could show up at the Mission

Road trailhead, say he was investigating an historical homicide, and he wouldn't be lying to anyone.

"With an actual missing person, the story will be an easier sell," Newton continued, "but I'm still expecting to see a television van up here before long asking questions about those diamonds."

"And how are we doing with that?"

"Not great, Yak. Don't know what else to tell you. The Shiners know these hills better than anyone, so there's no end to the places Morrissey could've stashed them."

"Has Griffin worked up any math for you?"

"She has. She figures Morrissey would have had between fourteen and sixteen minutes up here, max."

"So what does that give you?"

"Gives me three miles down the trail, and the diamonds would need to be hidden right there. You back up the time and distance, and the search area at the trailhead is eleven hundred yards in either direction."

Yakabuski squinted as if trying to see it. "So, three miles in distance, starting at twenty-two hundred yards and ending in zero."

"Are you going to try and do the math in your head?"

"Two-point-three square miles."

"You are a freak some days, you know that, Yak? But yeah, that's the number."

Yakabuski had always been good with numbers. Sometimes he looked at homicide investigations as geometric patterns that needed to be put together. Looking for the missing variable. It was down that trail somewhere.

"Big search area," he said.

"With big assumptions. How sure are we that Morrissey even came up here?"

"You want sure? At your age?"

"Not filling me with confidence."

"What can I tell you? You look at the map of where Morrissey could have gone that night, and if you had to pick only one place to search, this is where you'd come. Now we have a kid missing who seems to have thought the same thing. Nothing is telling us to stay away."

"Well, maybe we'll get lucky," said the Ident inspector, not sounding like a man about to get lucky. "Are you sending a major crimes team up here to look for the boy?"

"Don't see the sense in it. You're already here. I'll have a canine unit come up later today but that'll be it."

They didn't say anything for a moment. It was mid-afternoon but it felt like dusk, with a white winter sun hidden behind a thick bed of clouds, the temperature already dropping, the mist from exhaust pipes and expended breath circling the girth of the forest.

"So, just the dogs?"

"I figure."

"I wish diamonds had a scent."

"We all do, Newt."

CHAPTER FIVE

By the time Yakabuski got back to the holding cells, the sun had gone for the day. Springfield was built where three northern rivers met, at the skirt of the Great Boreal Forest, and in mid-February the sun was late to arrive and early to leave. On the coldest and bleakest of winter days, it was little more than a mysterious presence. A sort of shading to the day that kept the world from complete blackness.

The holding cells were in the basement of the main detachment in Centretown, called that even though it was nowhere near the actual centre of the city. It was the name the wealthy of Springfield gave to the neighbourhood when they built it over a century and a half earlier. The English lumber barons and Scottish forward-steerage merchants wanted nothing to do with the sawmills on the river, or the French and Irish mill-hands who worked there, so they moved inland and built a neighbourhood of fine brick homes and stately stores and

26

gave it a fictive name. When you own the city, you can do things like that.

The cells were built at the same time as Centretown, although the detachment above was a modern building. It had been constructed twenty years ago. Defence lawyers were disgruntled at the time, when they first saw the plans for the building, but when an interview room was added to the main floor, a place where the lawyers could wait while their clients were brought up from the cells, they stopped complaining.

The holding cells still had stone walls and forged metal bars and a smell Yakabuski figured must take a hundred and fifty years to get just right. A stale stink that was overbearing yet subtle, as though a thousand bad little smells had crawled up in a corner somewhere and died. He found Calvin Jayne sitting on his metal cot, holding his head in his hands and pinching his nose.

"Rough day, Calvin?"

The cabbie took his hands away from his face and looked up at Yakabuski. In a sad voice he said, "You're giving the Concorde Motel a run for its money with rooms like this, Detective."

Yakabuski chuckled. It wasn't a bad line. He watched the special constable unlock the cell door, using a key big enough to hammer nails, then he stood aside as the bars creaked open.

The constable walked away, and Yakabuski entered the cell. How could a scent be stale yet overpowering? The Concorde Motel had a smell that came close. The cabbie was right about that.

"It smells better in Dorset," said Yakabuski, leaning against the stone wall and looking down at Jayne. "I'd still prefer a quick visit to the holding cells in Springfield."

"You telling me those are my choices? The Dorset Pen or here? You haven't even told me what I've been arrested for."

"You're not thinking clearly. Has this been a lifelong problem for you?"

"So there's no charge. You're just rousting me."

"Calvin, if you dropped a puppy at the Mission Road trailhead last Tuesday, I could arrest you. I could charge you with cruelty to an animal, failure to provide the necessities of life. You think a boy matters less to the law than a dog?"

The cabbie didn't say anything. Yakabuski crossed his ankles and leaned harder into the stone wall, wondering if there might be a sweet spot somewhere. He stood six-foot-four and weighed 250. Maybe when he was a young man stone walls didn't mean much to him, but with his fiftieth birthday come and gone only two months prior, a stone wall was never going to be a friend.

"It ain't the same thing," the cabbie said finally. "That kid knew what he was doing. A kid ain't no dog."

"Some people might think that makes it worse. Tell me something, Calvin, do you consider yourself a lucky man?"

"What do you mean?"

"I just want to know."

"Lucky enough, I suppose."

"That's good. Because I think you're going to need some of that luck. Maybe you're right about people not caring that you treated that boy worse than an animal, but I sure suspect they'll have a problem with the rest of it."

"Ain't no rest of it. I took that kid to Mission Road. I dropped him off like he wanted. He paid me. That's all that happened."

Jayne straightened his back and gave the detective a hard

look. Yakabuski knew what the cabbie had been doing in the holding cells since he'd seen him last. Jayne had spent his time convincing himself that Yakabuski was bluffing about going to O'Keefe's. Then, he'd convinced himself the bartender would cover for him. He'd tipped him enough over the years. In one giddy moment of near-hysterical lucidity just before Yakabuski returned, Jayne had probably even convinced himself it never happened.

But the hard look faltered within seconds. The cabbie looked at the floor of the cell and said in a quiet, resigned voice, "You don't even know what happened to that kid. He could have given up and checked in to a motel. He could be anywhere. You don't know."

"Calvin, that's the first smart thing you've said. We don't know."

He looked up hopefully. "Then why am I here?"

"So I can offer you one of those lucky breaks you get all the time. That's what you said, right? You're a lucky man?"

Jayne looked more hopeful. Hopeful and hurt at the same time. Which Yakabuski figured was just about right.

Yakabuski stepped toward him. "Here's what you need to understand, Calvin: if Jason McAllister turns up dead, and you did nothing to help me find him, you're in a whole lot of trouble. If the boy was murdered, you're looking at aiding and abetting. If he froze to death, it's criminal negligence. You're looking at felony charges either way. For a lucky man like yourself, it will come as quite a shock to learn just how fucked you'll be."

Yakabuski didn't swear often. When he did, his words had the extra timbre and resonance of a man who's normally in control but was getting annoyed. He gave the cabbie a taunting look to go along with what he'd said, and then he waited. If Jayne wanted to give him the information he needed while in an unthinking anger about wounded pride, Yakabuski could work with that. He waited until it was obvious the cabbie wasn't going to say anything and continued. "Of course, if you help us in our investigation, if Jason McAllister turns up in that motel like you said, well, you'll be a bloody hero, Calvin. Even if McAllister is dead, you still did the right thing, so, no harm, no foul. Do you see the difference?"

Jayne's gaze came up. He nodded.

"Because it's a big difference."

"I see that."

"Local hero or ten years in Dorset," Yakabuski said. "Don't know if a difference can get much bigger than that."

"What do you want to know?"

❧ ❧ ❧

Yakabuski stretched his back and looked at his watch. Seven minutes and twelve seconds. Just about everything he had just told the cabbie was fiction, but hard-luck people always assumed bad news was true. Didn't even question it. Dangling any sort of lucky break in front of someone like Calvin Jayne was like dangling a mickey of single-malt Scotch in front of a drunk.

Now that the cabbie was ready to talk, Yakabuski realized he wasn't sure what he wanted to ask him first. A lot he wanted to know, but what was the first question? Jayne was still staring at his feet, no longer pinching his nose. He'd given up on trying to block the smell.

"How much did you get from the Shiners, for telling them about the kid?"

"I got nothing."

"What were you hoping to get?"

"I hadn't thought about that."

"So why did you do it?"

The question seemed to surprise Jayne. He shook his head a few times, tilted it once in what Yakabuski guessed was supposed to be a gesture of careful consideration, before saying, "I didn't want to get left behind. Does that make any sense to you? Someone is going to find those diamonds, and someone is going to get rich when they do. Why can't I get a taste of that for once?" He shrugged his shoulders after saying it. Then he looked embarrassed and looked back down at his feet.

Another victim of the age, thought Yakabuski. Raised to want things he was never going to get, always feeling a little bad about that, a little cheated, dreaming and scheming of ways to change it, without putting in any heavy lifting — like many people these days, it was only when Calvin Jayne was forced to speak about his hopes and dreams that they became foolish to him.

"What did you think the Shiners were going to do when you told them about that kid?"

"I sure as fuck didn't think he was going to disappear."

"You never considered that a possibility?"

"Swear to God, no. When I went down to O'Keefe's, I thought they might run the kid off. Give him a good scare and that'd be that. Maybe they'd remember me down the road, when Morrissey gets out. That's all I was thinking."

Yakabuski recrossed his feet and straightened his back a few times. Thinking about what the cabbie had just said. Wondering what wasn't right about it. When it came to him he said, "That's what you thought when you *went* to O'Keefe's. What did you think when you *left*?"

The cabbie hesitated and Yakabuski swore a second time. He pushed himself off the wall and knelt so he was eye-level with Jayne. "Calvin, this is your last chance. Why did you leave O'Keefe's thinking bad things were going to happen to that kid?"

"I didn't know that for a fact, it was—"

"Calvin!"

"All right, all right. But I'm telling you the truth. I didn't know what was going to happen to that kid. I *still* don't know what happened to that kid."

"So why are you scared?"

The cabbie opened his mouth and started to speak, then he stopped, bowed his head, and said, "Because of what happened when we left O'Keefe's. The Shiner I went there to find—"

"His name?"

"Billy O'Donnell. He's at O'Keefe's all the time. I've played pool with him before. I bought him a beer and told him about the kid. He was interested in the story. Said I needed to tell it to someone else. I asked him why. I'd just told him. He said that wasn't good enough. Someone else needed to hear it."

"Did he take you somewhere?"

"Strathcona Park. By the water fountain."

Yakabuski stood up. Nothing about this was sounding good. "A public place, surrounded by woods. Tell me you wondered about that."

"Wondered? Fuck, I thought I was going to get shot."

"Did you see any guns?"

"O'Donnell had one. He showed it to me when he said we needed to leave O'Keefe's."

"Who was waiting for you in the park?"

"Detective Yakabuski, has anything changed between us, about this being my lucky day and all that?"

Yakabuski pushed. "Who met you in the park, Calvin? Did you get a name?"

"I didn't need to get a name." He laughed and looked at Yakabuski with the first sign of defiance he had shown since being taken to the holding cells. "I knew who it was the second I saw him, and for your sake you better be a cop with good luck too. It was Bobby Bangs."

Yakabuski tried not to let anything show on his face. *Bobby Bangs*. Like it was the name of one of his neighbours in the Queen Elizabeth Towers, or a character in the novel sitting on his bedside table. *Bobby Bangs*.

"Bobby Bangs hasn't been seen in Springfield in years," he said quietly. "Are you sure it was him?"

"I'm sure. I know the stories. I know the song. The man in the park was Bobby Bangs." He laughed one more time. "Good luck, eh."

CHAPTER SIX

Yakabuski left the holding cells and went to his office. He waited by the printer in the middle of the desks lined up in the Major Crimes Department as it spit out the eighteen-page criminal record for Robert Allen Bangles. He printed off the most recent surveillance photo for Bangles, taken from a CCTV camera in Manhattan two years ago, Bangles standing with Billy Adams in front of a nightclub. The most recent booking photo was two years before that. Yakabuski printed copies of both photos and left the detachment, heading to the North Shore.

He already knew most of what was in the files. Robert Allen Bangles was born thirty-two years ago in Burk's Falls, a village a hundred miles upriver from Springfield, where there was still old-growth pine, wooden dams, and rivers no one had fully navigated. He was raised in an original settler's cabin with the white mortar chinking and single window, a home that would have had the shadows and feel of dusk to it no matter the time of day. He was one of thirteen children, slept with his six brothers in a curtained-off area of the living room.

Just about every family in Burk's Falls was Irish, and just about every adult male was a brushman working for O'Hearn Forestry Products. Brushmen worked the partially logged fields and thinned out forests that the clear-cutters had left behind, gathering the detritus — the deadfall and bramble, the stunt-pine and lightning strike. At the end of each workday, the brushmen sold what they had gathered to an O'Hearn timber agent who had a lumber scale set up in back of the depot store.

Yakabuski had been to Burk's Falls many times, and he knew what the workday was like for the men who lived there. In winter the brushmen worked while a cold mist swirled around their bodies and ice dangled from their chins. In spring they trudged through leafless, desolate forests in mud up to their knees, pulling their brush carts behind them. In summer they stripped to the waist, worked under a searing sun, and left the woods at the end of the workday with skin torn and sliced, rivulets of blood running down their arms and chests.

The tale of Bobby Bangs had been told in song and story, in police reports and last-call drunken bets, and it was a mishmash of truth and folklore, although some facts were more or less agreed upon. He'd started working as a brushman when he was eight, so small the tree branches that slashed the other men's chests slashed his face, leaving scars he still carried. The spring mud swallowed him not to the knees but to the waist. The winter fog did not hang below his head, as it did for the other brushmen, so the boy had to work as though blind, crabbing his way across the forest floor, reaching his tiny hands through the mist, and pulling out whatever he touched, in the hopes it was something he could sell.

One winter's day in early February, Bangles was working a field on the south shore of the Racine River. He was twelve years old by then, working in a thick fog, on his belly with his arms outstretched, rooting beneath the stump of a fallen white pine, when his hands touched something cold and metallic.

The boy's fingers bunched around the object and he pulled it out. When it was clear of the stump and the fog, Bangles stared in wonder at the Colt .45 in his hands. He had never seen a handgun. He'd seen plenty of other guns: .22-calibre hunting rifles, duck guns, a few other shotguns that weren't for duck hunting, but this gun was nothing like those. It was beautiful to look at, with wooden grips and pearl inlays, not worn down and held together by tape and bailing wire. It felt good in his hands, too, comfortable and reassuring, probably about as right as it was possible to feel about a weight in your hands.

This was a weapon not to be used against duck or deer but against another person, and when that thought occurred to the boy it exploded in his brain like a busted aneurysm. What he was holding could change the fate of a man. The man who stood in front of the gun. And the one who stood behind. Change. That's what he was holding in his hands.

Bangles brought the gun home, keeping it a secret from his family. He hid it in an inside pocket he cut in the lining of his parka and waited, carried it with him for three months, never leaving the coat out of his sight. Waited until spring had come and the snow was out of the bush, when the road into Burk's Falls was about as firm as it ever gets, and he would soon need to put away the parka. It all worked out to the first Friday in May.

On that day, Bangles went to a field not far from Burk's Falls. He worked only a little and made sure to be one of the first men back to the depot store. Fourth in line. His cart not even a third full. The men gathered around the boy stared at him strangely, but no one spoke.

After they'd waited thirty minutes, the timber agent came in the back door of the depot store and walked to the scale. He was a big man dressed in a long beaver coat that smelled of BO and whisky. When it was Bangles's turn, the boy pulled his cart to the scale, dropped the yoke, and put his hands in his pockets. The O'Hearn agent stared at him.

"You need'a load it, boy."

"Not today."

"Not today? Are you whacked? I sure as fuck ain't loadin' it for you."

"You don't need to weigh it. I already know what it's worth."

"You already know . . . listen you fuckin' pissant, if you don't want your wood weighed, then fuck off and go home. There's men waitin' behind you."

There was an awkward silence. The men in line turned their eyes to the ground. The agent stared at the boy until his eyes began to bug out. He was starting to move toward him when Bangles pulled the .45 from his parka.

"Today, I think this wood is worth what I say it's worth. And I say it's worth every dime you've got."

The agent stopped and stared at the boy in disbelief.

"What the fuck are you doin'?"

"I'm robbing you, you dumb fuck. Now go to that till and hand me everything you've got inside it."

"Are you crazy?"

"No. I just figure it's time to get the fuck out of Burk's Falls, and I figure you owe me. Are you heading to that till, or do I have to shoot you?"

The agent did as he was told, and Bangles was given $1,122. Before leaving, the boy got the agent to step on the lumber scale, and when the weight arm stopped moving, he muttered, "Two hundred and forty-three pounds of shit," and shot him. When the man fell to the ground, Bangles shot him two more times.

The murder was never solved, as the police never found a witness. Every brush worker they interviewed said he'd had his back turned at the time of the shooting. One old man even suggested that maybe the timber agent had committed suicide. The cop asked him why he thought that. The old man said the O'Hearn agent might have become overcome with guilt after making so much money off the busted backs and scarred bodies of Irish brushmen and killed himself. The cop said if that were true, where did the money go? The old man said you didn't need to know every detail to every story to know when you were hearing a true one.

Bangles fled to Springfield and lived with his uncle Tommy for a couple years, then started doing jewellery heists and bank stick-ups in upper New York State. He never came back. Billy Adams brought him to Boston when he was nineteen and put him on his top crew. It was said Bangles was there when an armoured truck left idling in front of the Tiffany flagship store in Manhattan was robbed a few days before Christmas, 2012; and in Northern Ireland when a badly botched mail-train robbery left four cops dead. There were other sightings. Other stories.

A few years after leaving Burk's Falls, a fiddle player from the Upper Divide wrote a song about the weigh station robbery that became a regional hit. It was still a tavern favourite, and you could hear it just about any weekend in Cork's Town, at any club with a live band. The song was called "The Ballad of Bobby Bangs."

CHAPTER SEVEN

Yakabuski had been in Rachel Dumont's apartment so many times he could notice small changes. A new painting by her daughter, Grace, taped to the fridge. An African violet on the windowsill, no longer in bloom. A vanilla scent today, instead of the cinnamon that was here last week.

Dumont's father had been leader of the Travellers, a criminal gang that was part Métis, part Gypsy, with lineage that went all the way back to the sixteenth century, the steppes of Poland, and the French port of Brouage, where the Travellers first embarked for the New World. Gabriel Dumont had worked with the Shiners to steal those diamonds, staging a fake war between the two gangs that left most of Springfield hiding behind locked doors.

The apogee of the fake war was the kidnapping of Gabriel Dumont's granddaughter. She was taken three days before the robbery and that was the tipping point, the act that put the city on the verge of what seemed like a full-blown gang war, what let a cargo plane with more than a billion dollars in diamonds land practically unnoticed at the Springfield airport. Grace had been released the day after the heist and came home with a diamond in her pocket worth more than $150,000.

Not many people knew about that diamond. It had been kept out of news reports and most police reports. Yakabuski had insisted on it, fearing for the girl's safety. Now that Jason McAllister had gone missing, he wished he had done more. Or never told anyone about that diamond after Rachel Dumont had phoned him.

Now, he sat at the kitchen table, drinking sweet cedar tea. Rachel sat beside him, Grace the other side of the table. She was still dressed in her school clothes. White shirt under a grey sweater, pressed jeans, long black hair in braids. She was twelve years old now, and her grade seven photo from Northwood Elementary had run on the front page of the *Springfield Sun* for more than a week. There were still elderly ladies who lit candles and prayed for her, knowing she had been safely returned, but liking the habit of praying for an innocent soul that looked like her. Yakabuski took the photo of Bobby Bangs from his pocket and slid it across the table.

"Have you ever seen this man, Grace?"

She looked at the photo a few seconds and then shook her head. "I don't think so."

"You don't think so?" Yakabuski took the photo back and looked at it. It was the mug shot from four years ago, and it showed a man with long blond hair and a face you would remember. There were scars on his cheek that made it look like a small animal had attacked him. His most noticeable facial feature, though, was not the scars but a full-neck tattoo, green and red for the most part, snakes and Celtic crosses running across his Adam's apple.

"You're not sure if you've seen this man?"

"No."

"This man?"

"Lots of people have tattoos, Mr. Yakabuski."

He showed the photo to Rachel Dumont. She looked at it, and after a few seconds had passed she said, "Grace, Mr. Yakabuski thinks this man may be one of the men who kidnapped you. He's right. I would remember this face."

"I'm sorry, Mom, but I don't."

"The man who first abducted you, the one you only saw that one time, has anything come back to you about him?" asked Yakabuski.

"No. Just what I've already told you."

"Large man, black hair greased back, spoke like someone from Cork's Town."

"Yeah."

Yakabuski stared at the girl but didn't say anything. A description that could have been Sean Morrissey. Could have been half the men in Cork's Town. And for her second kidnapper, the man who held her prisoner for three days in some apartment the police had been unable to find, who cooked her meals and watched television with her, all of which she freely admitted — less of a description than that.

What was going on? Yakabuski had been wondering since his first interview with Grace, when it became obvious she wasn't telling the whole story. He stared at her and didn't say anything, because sometimes that's what you did when someone had just told you a story implausible to the point of absurdity. You waited. To see what they'd say next.

But Grace did nothing more than stare back at Yakabuski, and before long he knew the next person to speak would be him.

"Well, I appreciate your help, Grace. May I speak to your mother for a minute?"

The girl got up from the table and left the kitchen. When they heard her bedroom door close, Rachel Dumont said, "Bobby Bangs? I thought that was just a song."

"No. He's real."

"I don't know what's going on with her, I really don't."

"Is she scared?"

"I don't see any sign of it. She's sleeping well. Her marks are good. I sometimes wish she would act more scared. That would seem normal to me."

"She's a tough kid. Is it possible she's blocking it out?"

"I don't think so. We talk about what happened that week. She doesn't avoid the subject." Dumont took a sip of tea and looked around her kitchen. There was worry in her eyes, and Yakabuski knew she had given the mystery of her daughter's recollection of those three days as much thought as he had. No, that wasn't right. She'd given it more.

"She never talks about her captors?"

"Never."

Yakabuski sat there and wondered again what might have happened in that apartment. After a while he looked at Rachel Dumont and said, "I'm told someone has taken your father's place as leader of the Travellers."

"That's right. Linus Desjardins."

"Do you know him?"

"I knew him when I was a kid. He's much older than my father. He'd be in his seventies now, I think."

"Seventy-three. Has he been in touch with you?"

"He's phoned a couple times. There were papers I needed to sign. Apparently I own a house in Cape Diamond."

"So you can get a message to him?"

"Yes."

"I'd like to know what the Travellers are planning to do when Sean Morrissey gets released. Can you arrange a meeting between us?"

"I don't know where he lives, or if he ever comes to Springfield, but I can ask."

CHAPTER EIGHT

"Do you believe the cabbie?"

Yakabuski looked at his father, sitting with a paper plate on his knee, his sister's backyard skating rink framed nicely in the bay window behind him. Nearly a week had passed since his interview with Calvin Jayne, the cabbie being released early the next morning without charges, complaining as he left the station about the cops wasting his time, and where was that big son of a bitch? He doesn't even come by to apologize?

Beat cops had gone through Cork's Town showing Robert Bangles's mug shot in nightclubs and taverns, the Blue Bird diner, the St. Bridget's community hall, making sure to go on euchre night, when there wouldn't be an empty seat. They had turned up nothing so far. Quite a few people had asked the beat cops if they could take a photograph of the mug shot, as they had heard the song but never seen a photo of Bobby Bangs.

Yakabuski was attending a fourteenth birthday party for his nephew, and there was a large crowd gathered around the rink. He could see his sister, Trish, and her husband, Tyler Lawson. See the birthday boy, Jason, playing shinny. Somewhere in the crowd cheering the boys as they raced up and down the ice would be his niece, Julie.

"I don't know why he'd make up a story like that," said Yakabuski, turning to look at his dad. "Something scared that cabbie. He's still scared. Bobby Bangs standing in the shadows of Strathcona Park might do that to a person."

"Fuck, I guess so. How come you didn't know he was back in town?" His father was older now, but still thought like the cop he'd once been, and asked honest questions without giving them much thought.

"He hasn't been seen at the Silver Dollar, Dad. Hasn't been seen in Cork's Town or anywhere else in the city, and we've been canvassing a few days now. We've received no alerts about him from the FBI or Interpol."

"Any outstanding warrants?"

"Nothing. He was never charged with the weigh station killing. He's been charged twice down in the States, felony murder both times, and he's been acquitted both times."

"So he doesn't have to hide. He's choosing to do that. He's here because of those diamonds."

"I think he's been here a long time because of those diamonds." Yakabuski took a photo from the pocket of his parka and handed it to his dad. George Yakabuski took a pair of glasses from the pocket of his cardigan, studied the photo a few seconds, and said, "Christ. Bobby Bangs is your second thief."

"I think so. A nephew of Tommy Bangles, that's someone Sean Morrissey would have trusted. That's been the problem up to now, Dad. Everyone we looked at for the second thief, we asked, 'Would Sean Morrissey trust you with the biggest score of his life?' And we kept getting no for an answer. The Ident guys were convinced he was wearing a wig. I'm going to enjoy showing them this photo."

His dad adjusted a blanket over his knees and turned his wheelchair so he could see out the bay window. George Yakabuski had been a cop in High River for nearly thirty years, until the day he went into Stedman's to pick up mosquito netting for his hunt camp only to be followed in a minute later by a stickup crew from Montreal. He spotted the crew and was approaching two men making their way to the back office when he shouted, "Cop, put your hands where I can see them!"

Thinking that's all you needed to say when you were a cop and you'd caught someone red-handed. Old school like that. Didn't have his service revolver, hadn't called for back-up, probably about as surprised as he'd ever been in his life when the robbers, rather than obeying him, turned and pulled sawed-off shotguns from beneath their coats and shot him.

The robbers took off with $68,000, only to be caught later that night at a tavern in Montreal. George Yakabuski never walked again.

"Do you think Morrissey knew how big a score it was going to be?" he asked.

"No. I think it surprised him."

"That's why he put himself into Wentworth for the winter. Lay low so he could figure out all the angles."

"I suspect so. Thieves usually have a pretty good take on how money works. They're not fooled about it like most people. He knew people would be coming." Yakabuski stared at the hockey rink outside, but he had trouble following the game.

"He'd be an idiot if he didn't know that," said his dad. "Sean Morrissey may be a lot of things, but idiot isn't one of them. How worried do you figure he is about that guy from Mexico?"

"If I were Sean Morrissey, I'd be damn worried."

"What's the latest on him?"

"No confirmed sighting since he was caught on security tape at the Algoma Ferry Station the night before the heist. He was probably at Sioux Falls the next morning, and he's probably the one who killed Gabriel Dumont the next night, so he was up at Cape Diamond. Nothing since."

"Two months now. Maybe he went home."

"Maybe he went anywhere. We don't know, Dad. But I think he's still here."

"Waiting for Morrissey to be released."

"Yeah. They have unfinished business."

"How does your missing kid play into all this?"

"He was looking for the diamonds. Griffin tells me he belonged to some Facebook group that's been trying to figure out where they are. She says there's nearly twenty of them out there, websites or online groups."

"Searching for those stolen diamonds? Like it was some sort of a game?"

"Exactly like that. Pokémon Go, with a real prize at the end."

"How stupid can you be?"

"There's money on the table, Dad. Stupid has nothing to do with it. That group McAllister belonged to was only open to postgraduate math and science students at tier one schools in the States. Anyone can see it all right, but you needed to be logged in with a student number before you could post anything. Griffin's calling it the 'smartie-pants boys-and-girls group.'"

Frank Yakabuski looked back out the window. Jason's birthday party had attracted quite a crowd. He saw two city councillors and a deputy crown attorney. The man who owned the Junior A hockey team. Several well-known defence attorneys. His brother-in-law was a lawyer, and in a strange twist of fate, his biggest client was Sean Morrissey. Tyler was working his way through the crowd, pouring mulled cider from an oversized thermos. Yakabuski wondered how many of the people gathered around him actually had children at the party.

"Do you think I could be wrong, Dad?" he said, still staring at his brother-in-law. "Could Morrissey have shipped those diamonds out of Springfield somehow? We've been looking a long time, and we don't have much to show for it. Some sort of a treasure map. That's about it. I had a dream last night that people a hundred years from now were using that map and still not finding anything. It was some world-famous wild-goose chase. Like Oak Island. Or D. B. Cooper."

"You're not wrong, Frank. Morrissey is a Shiner, and Shiners bury what they steal. I've never known any Shiner to bury something more than a day's drive from where they lived."

Damn right. That was true gen. Yakabuski just needed to hear it.

Just then there was a large cheer from outside, and people were clapping. Then they started walking back toward the house. It looked like the hockey game was finished.

"Are they coming?" said his father, who had turned his wheelchair around and was reaching for the mulled cider he had left on a serving table.

"They are."

"Anyone in that bunch you can arrest? I'm getting a little bored."

"Couple city councillors."

"That'll do it."

Yakabuski's sister swept into the room carrying a thermos. Trish was dressed in black stretch pants and a white cashmere sweater. Tyler followed, his head tilted toward the city councillor walking beside him. It was a favourite pose of Yakabuski's brother-in-law, head tilted toward someone who was talking to him, eyebrows furrowed in concentration. The lawyer at work, giving you his complete attention. The councillor, though, was a notorious bore, and Yakabuski doubted even Tyler was going to be able to tilt his head for much longer.

"Frankie, there you are," shouted Trish, and she ran toward her brother. When she hugged him, the thermos bottle hit his back hard. "Why weren't you outside watching the hockey game? Would you like a drink?"

"I've got some cider, Trish, thanks. Thought I'd keep Dad company."

"Well, aren't you the considerate one."

She leaned down and gave her dad a peck on the cheek. George Yakabuski kept his hands up, in case she stumbled. Just then Yakabuski's phone chimed. He looked at the incoming number and saw the call was coming from the Centretown detachment.

"I have to answer this, Trish."

"I swear, Frankie, I think you have that phone programmed to ring two minutes after I see you."

"Just a second."

It was Bernard O'Toole, chief of the Springfield Regional Police Service. Not the voice Yakabuski was expecting.

"Yak, you better get down here right away. Jason McAllister has just posted something to his Facebook group."

"Just now? That means he's alive."

"We can't say that. Griffin tells me the post was programmed to go up today. McAllister set it up ten days ago, the same day he went to Mission Road."

"What did he post?" Yakabuski turned his back to the crowd and pressed the phone closer to his ear.

"Our search map."

CHAPTER NINE

O'Toole was furious. About as mad as Yakabuski had ever seen him, and he'd once seen O'Toole punch a tactical vehicle. He and Donna Griffin sat the other side of his desk. It was Saturday afternoon, and they seemed to be the only ones on the third floor of the detachment.

"Our search map, Donna? How the hell did McAllister get our search map?" He was yelling, but not swearing as much as Yakabuski would have expected. Because Griffin was there, he suspected. Still, O'Toole was angry, and when a loud man with a body that looks like a brick outhouse with an add-on is angry, he gets your full attention — no swearing needed.

"Did someone in major crimes leak this?" he continued. "I swear to God, if that's what happened, I'm going to hang the bastard off the roof of this detachment."

"I don't think there's been a leak, Chief," said Griffin. "If you look at the map closely, it's not *exactly* ours. It's close, but there are differences. It looks like he didn't have all the cameras."

"How did he do it? Hack the camera feeds?"

"I think so. Most of the cameras are owned by the city, so one hack there and he would have had plenty of information."

O'Toole took the big, beefy hand that had been slapping his desk and started stroking his chin. The possibility that McAllister's map was the result of a city mistake — lousy firewalls in their IT department — seemed to calm him. He understood city mistakes well enough. No mystery there. Good to know the provenance of the map couldn't be traced to some misguided, or greedy, detective working in his Major Crimes department. One problem gone. A whole lot remaining.

"Do I have this right, Donna?" he said. "This McAllister kid didn't have all the cameras, didn't have all the variables, but he figured out our search area?"

"What can I tell you? The kid is damn good. He figured out the time gap somehow. That would have given him one variable — forty-seven minutes. A good topographical map would have given him distance. That's two variables and you could work something up with that. It's impressive work, but I can see how he might have done it."

"That map needs to be taken down right away."

"Too late, Chief. Since noon, when the map was first posted, McAllister's Facebook group has had more than a million hits. It crashed forty-five minutes ago. People are posting screen grabs now."

"Shit."

"Yeah."

They sat in silence for several seconds, a silent office on a silent floor, no one sure what to say. It seemed like a green room, where people waited to be called before the cameras. Before long Yakabuski heard the chiming of elevators, and car tires rolling over the hard-packed snow in the parking lot below O'Toole's window. News of the search map being posted online was starting to spread. The executive floor might stay quiet the rest of the day, but Yakabuski knew the desks in Major Crimes were starting to fill up.

◆ ◆ ◆

The following day Yakabuski got a meeting request from Piers Grund, Senior Vice President, Operations, for De Kirk Mines. Yakabuski parked his Jeep on a side street near the Baton Rouge and found Grund sitting at a table in the back of the restaurant. He had a scowl on his face so pronounced and malevolent it looked like he had scared away everyone except the maître d', who was hovering around his table like a dog wondering where the next kick was coming from. At the sight of Yakabuski, the maître d' gave a quick look of relief and pulled out a chair.

"Detective Yakabuski, so nice to see you," he said. Then he turned and almost ran away. Grund stared at his retreating back as though staring at a battlefield deserter.

"That man knows you?"

"Looks that way. I don't know him."

"It's because of Ragged Lake."

"I suspect."

"He calls himself a maître d'. In Johannesburg he would not be allowed to scrub pots."

"Good thing we're not in Johannesburg."

"Is that an attempt at humour, Detective? I see nothing humorous about people not being able to do their jobs."

"What did he do wrong?"

"He came to me and apologized after I sent back my Manhattan. Worst Manhattan I have ever tasted. Do you know how much time I wish to spend hearing the apologies of a fuckin' maître d'?"

Grund had been in Springfield since the day after the heist, flying in from Johannesburg on a private jet. When he arrived, he went not to a hotel but to the Centretown detachment to demand a meeting with O'Toole. When he got his meeting, Grund asked the chief why he had left the Springfield airport "as unprotected as a slut at the beach."

Yakabuski was at that first meeting and figured it was jetlag talking, or fear, but Grund's demeanour had never changed. He would start conversations with a threat and end them with an ultimatum. He was profane and aggressive, probably in his mid-sixties, a tall, blond-haired bully who walked with the chest-out, crotch-kicking gait of all bullies.

Yakabuski had found ways to avoid Grund, and the other De Kirk executives who soon followed him, most of whom resembled their boss in some strange way, but he couldn't avoid the man completely. He was a senior VP for one of the biggest employers in the region, one that had just been robbed of more than a billion dollars, so he could request a meeting with the lead detective on his case and get one.

Yakabuski waited until Grund stopped glaring at the spot in the restaurant where the maître d' had once stood and then he said, "Why did you want to see me, Mr. Grund?"

"So you can tell me where my fuckin' diamonds are. Why the fuck do you think I wanted to see you?"

"I could have given you an update on the investigation by telephone."

"I prefer face to face. And I prefer talking with a Manhattan in my hand, if your bartender can fuckin' figure it out. So tell me who the fuck this kid is that's gone missing."

Yakabuski had figured that's what the meeting request was about. "His name is Jason McAllister. Postgraduate student at Syracuse University. Some sort of math whiz, I'm told. He's been missing nearly two weeks now. Last seen walking down the Mission Road trail."

"The Shiners take him?"

"We don't know what's happened to him."

"We can add that to the list, I guess."

Grund looked at Yakabuski contemptuously before adding, "If it wasn't the Shiners who took him, who the fuck would it be? Are you thinking it could be that lunatic Mexican who killed Gabriel Dumont? Or maybe he's sleeping somewhere. Is that a possible theory, Detective?" Grund flashed him another sneer.

People with money knew how to sneer, thought Yakabuski. The slap-in-your-face sneer, not the hide-behind-your-hand sneer most people have. The rich had a sneer perfectly suited for people who enjoy driving fast down city streets on rainy days, a sneer with a disregard and contempt for others that must take generations of pampering to perfect.

"No, we don't think he's sleeping somewhere, Mr. Grund. Although now that you've expressed an interest, when we find Jason McAllister we'll make sure to notify you."

"You think I give a fuck about your missing kid?" He crumpled up the cocktail napkin. "It's his map I'm worried about. I've seen it. It looks like your map. Did someone in your fuckin' department leak it?"

"No. It's not exactly our map. He did it himself."

"There will be people coming. You know that, right?"

"I know that."

"This is about to turn into a fuckin' scavenger hunt, with my fuckin' diamonds as the prize."

"We'll post as many cops as it takes to keep Mission Road secure and under control, Mr. Grund."

"Like your airport."

"Like your airplane."

Grund's sneer froze on his face. When it melted, it became a look of rage. Those were the only two facial expressions Yakabuski had ever seen on the man — contempt and anger. He wondered if he had found a way to combine the two, so he could flash someone a look of contemptuous rage, or glare in angry contempt.

"If you know what is good for you, Detective Yakabuski, I'd be careful talking about that plane."

"If I knew what was good for me, I probably wouldn't be living on the Northern Divide, Mr. Grund. Probably wouldn't be a cop. And I sure wouldn't be wasting a sunny winter afternoon sitting in the Baton Rouge bitching about the Manhattans."

Grund said something that Yakabuski didn't bother catching. He turned to look around the restaurant. The Baton Rouge was a Centretown steakhouse frequented by forestry and mining executives, senior government bureaucrats from the Department of Northern Affairs, and anyone else in Springfield lucky enough to have an expense account.

The bar had a wood-burning firepit in the middle of the room and low-hanging chandeliers about as bright as tea candles. Entering the Baton Rouge during the day was like turning your clock ahead ten hours. It was always the depths of a boozy, drunken night at Baton Rouge, no matter what time it might be in the rest of Springfield.

Grund had limited his threat to no more than hissing the words "be careful," which meant he was more worried about that plane than Yakabuski had thought. In the aftermath of the heist, all the stories were about the Shiners and the Travellers, the dead pilot, the missing diamonds, nothing about the plane. When he figured enough time had passed, he turned to look at Grund and said, "Why should I be careful?"

"Because this robbery is not only a criminal matter, Detective Yakabuski, it is also a business and political matter. The commodity price for northern diamonds, the share price of De Kirk and other mining companies, how many people we employ at Cape Diamond — much depends on the outcome of your investigation. I would be careful about casting aspersions."

"I'm not casting aspersions, Mr. Grund. I'm telling you straight up that your security protocols are what made this heist possible."

"Really? Not your unprotected airport? Not the gangster who can steal my diamonds and stash them in some fuckin' cubbyhole in your backyard and you can't fuckin' find 'em? None of that?"

"No. Your decision not to have a security detail on that plane."

Grund flashed Yakabuski a look of contemptuous rage and there it was. His answer.

"No security and a billion dollars in untraceable diamonds in a fully fuelled cargo plane?" continued Yakabuski. "It's a miracle you don't get ripped off every month, Mr. Grund."

The South African's eyes were now as red as the pimentos in the glass jar on the bar. "If I read anything about this in any fuckin' newspaper," he sputtered, "if I hear about this on any fuckin' television show, if I—"

"You'll sue my fuckin' ass. I know."

"You should take the warning seriously, Detective. Our damages would be real and very provable. Our shareholders would be . . . distressed . . . to hear such a wild story. The ripple effect, by the time it reached you," — and here Grund leaned over the table so he could hiss his final words — "would be a fuckin' tsunami."

Grund leaned back in his seat just as the second-kick-at-the-can Manhattan arrived. He took a sip and scowled, but before he could say anything the maître d' had already taken it out of his hands and was racing back toward the bar. The white soles of his shoes showed clearly in the darkened room. Yakabuski didn't like to see people run. In the woods, running was a shortcut to bad things happening. He stood up from his chair and grabbed his parka. Grund looked at him in surprise.

"What? Are you not fuckin' staying for lunch? I'm buying."

"I think I'll pass. And just so you know, I'm used to storms. Most people around here are. It's almost funny, that sort of threat. Next time you want to talk to me, pick up the telephone."

CHAPTER TEN

Yakabuski stood beside his Jeep for several minutes before getting in and driving away. The sun sat low in the sky, sending a glare so strong off the snow it hurt his eyes. But coming from the dungeon that was the Baton Rouge, it was a good hurt. Same for the cold, which didn't bother him right then.

Grund was right. People would be coming to Springfield to look for those diamonds. What he was wrong about was thinking anything could be done about it. There'd be a natural progression now, one thing leading to the next, no way of stopping it, just like Benjamin Chee taught him, back when Yakabuski was a teenager.

Chee was an Ojibwa trapper whose family owned rights to a trapline that ran for nearly a hundred miles down the Northern Divide. Yakabuski helped the old trapper with the line on weekends, and the year he was sixteen, for two weeks at the end of season. During that two-week trip,

Yakabuski awoke one morning to find Chee already outside their tent, staring at birds circling a distant bluff. Yakabuski stayed in his sleeping bag for several minutes before asking, "Is anything wrong, Ben?"

But the trapper didn't answer the question. Just said it was time for them to leave, so they broke camp early that day and spent the morning walking through a dark green forest with water falling from pine needles. There was the tart smell of spruce gum and hemlock. When they reached Lake Claire they found it already open, with only a thin skiff of ice hugging the shore. Spring had come early that year.

When Chee saw the open water, he stopped walking and took a pair of field glasses from his packsack. He began glassing the bluff, which was not so distant anymore. There were more birds. Yakabuski could see now that they were turkey vultures. As he stood there watching, the birds began to dive.

When this happened, Chee began to run. He was an old man, but Yakabuski had trouble following him. By the time Yakabuski reached the bluff, Chee was already on the trail leading to the top. Yakabuski heard animal sounds coming from above. Braying and howling. The beating of large wings.

When he reached the top, Yakabuski saw a whitetail doe. The animal was caught in one of Chee's traps and a pack of wolves was circling, taking turns lunging at her hind legs, her long, tawny neck, her belly, which was already ripped open; and that was what the turkey vultures were diving for, the blood and entrails that had fallen to the ground.

It was carnage like Yakabuski had never seen before, a cowardly and unnatural violence that did not seem right to him, did not seem to belong in these woods, was, in some way the boy could not articulate, a disgrace.

When the doe had finally fallen and the wolves had begun to move in for the kill, the trapper said, without looking at Yakabuski, "It only happens when Lake Claire is open. The deer can't get across the lake, so they cut over this bluff. The trap never kills them. Sometimes it is a fisher that finds them. Sometimes the birds are osprey. You never know."

"But it always ends like this?"

"Yes. One thing will lead to the next and the deer will die."

Yakabuski looked at the wolves ripping apart the doe's body. Her glassed eyes bounced on the snow.

"If you know it's coming, why not change it?"

"What would you suggest, Frank?"

"Maybe not run the line through here?"

"Lake Claire is not always open. We might have caught a fisher, had it been a different year."

Yakabuski thought about that. "Maybe you could use a different trap?"

"I have no trap that would have spared the life of that deer. Knowing how a story ends does not mean you can change it, Frank."

Yakabuski thought about that too. Thought about it until, in a frustrated rebuke that embarrassed him immediately, he screamed, "Damn it, Ben, you must be able to do *something*!"

"I can," said the trapper, looking at Yakabuski with a sad tenderness that confused him at the time. "When Lake Claire is open, I can watch out for wolves and circling birds."

❖ ❖ ❖

Pete Watkins sat at the bar in the Cornet Lounge and thought about Springfield for the first time in years. He had been watching the television set above the bar when a story came on about a $1.2-billion diamond heist. Happened two months ago, but Pete had been released from the Bolton State Penitentiary the day before, after serving five years of a ten-year manslaughter sentence for killing a Legion Hall waitress, and it was the first he'd heard of the robbery.

He was raised on a farm twenty miles outside Malone, New York. People around Malone called it the Watkins Farm, because that's what it had once been, though by the time Pete arrived, no cash crops had grown on Watkins land in three generations. Not even the family farmhouse was around when Pete was born, having burned down in a meth-lab explosion in the early '90s. Pete was raised in a double-wide his father parked over the toxic ashes of the original homestead.

Pete had nine brothers and sisters, although he never met the four oldest and was not close to the others. He was the youngest child and, by the time he was six, the only one still living in the double-wide with Cecelia Patrick and Tom Watkins, a former PepsiCo driver from Rochester living on a disability pension that paid him just enough to stay drunk every day. If he was careful with his money. Pete's father did most of his drinking at home, except on cheque day, when he drank in Malone. Sometimes the day after.

Cecelia Patrick, Pete's mother, was a disappearing and returning presence in his childhood, often doing time in the county jail for cheque fraud or solicitation, or disappearing on long road trips with men she had recently met, trips that always ended with Tom Watkins crying in the kitchen of the double-wide and sending her bus fare. She left for good when Pete was eight. After that it was just Pete and his dad.

Tom Watkins started drinking even more heavily when his wife left, something Pete didn't think possible, but there it was. His father started beating him without reason or cause, just whenever Pete was within grabbing range. He was beaten for something he had done. Or something he was sure to do. Tom Watkins didn't need time or place, or actual events, as reasons to beat his son. He beat his boy because he was sure the boy deserved it. And because, most times, it made Tom Watkins feel better.

When Pete was twelve, after one particularly savage beating, he went looking for his mother. He was going to run away and thought she might be able put him up for a night or two, until he could get everything figured. Not for long. A few days at most, and then he would be gone. She'd never gone far. Still lived in Malone.

He left the Watkins farm early in the morning, the sun just breaking behind the cedar break in back of the farm. It was late spring, and the walking wasn't bad. The blackflies had gone, as had most of the mud. The road to the farm turned to asphalt after three miles, and that made the walking easier. He didn't try to hitch a ride as he had never done that and wasn't sure what he'd say. He took off his blue windbreaker around noon, but it never got so hot that he needed to untuck his shirt.

He got to Malone around two in the afternoon and found his mother two hours later, leaving the Cornet Lounge. He'd heard his mother mention the nightclub, and Pete had stood on the sidewalk out front for more than an hour, waiting, telling himself he would find another bar when dusk came, if nothing happened here.

She came through the frosted-glass doors of the Cornet,

a man in a badly wrinkled brown suit following her, and when Pete approached, she stared at him a second and then kept walking.

She hadn't recognized him. It had been nearly four years, Pete told himself, so maybe that wasn't surprising. He chased after her, and she and the man turned to look at him. Pete stopped running and tried to remember the words he'd rehearsed during his walk.

"Hello . . . it's Peter. *I'm* Peter. I was wondering if . . . if I might be able . . . if it's all right with you . . . ."

"What's the matter with you, boy, are you a retard?" his mother said, laughing and bending down to take a closer look at him, losing her balance so the man needed to grab her by the waist before she fell. Pete's eyes locked on hers just before she was grabbed, and he thought there was recognition there. But it passed quickly, and maybe he was wrong.

"I'd like to . . . ." he started again, but his mother laughed this time, turned her back on him, and said, "Kid's a loon. Come on, sugar, let's get out of here."

Pete watched them walk down Hastings Street, his mother tittering and stumbling whenever the man squeezed her. He watched a long time, until he couldn't see them anymore. After that, he walked home.

The next summer, Pete was sent to Springfield, during that brief time when his father had a girlfriend, a waitress at the Legion Hall in Malone, who hated Pete. His father had a brother — one of eight — who lived on a farm outside Springfield and had boys around Pete's age. It would be good for him, his father told Pete, spending some time with his cousins, though Pete knew his father didn't care that much about things that were good for him. He knew his father wanted him out of the double-wide for the summer so the waitress could move in.

His father had told Pete he would need to help out with the chores, and when Pete arrived he learned that meant working on a nearby farm for six days a week, dawn to dusk. His uncle John had jobbed Pete out and was keeping the money. When Pete asked about pay — it would have been his second week — he got such a savage beating, he had two front teeth chipped and his left eardrum permanently busted, or at least that's what Pete figured since he never heard too well from that ear again.

"You think food is free, you fuckin' pup?" his uncle screamed while beating him. "Be glad you gets what you gets, and don't think 'bout complainin' to your papa 'cause he don't give two shits 'bout you neither."

Pete Watkins never asked for money again. Still, he had enjoyed that summer in Springfield. He liked his cousins. They all worked beside him in the hayfields, his uncle having jobbed his sons out as well. In the evening the boys drank home-still whisky, and on Saturday nights they went into Springfield to fight French boys at the Catholic Youth dances and talk girls into going into the woods with them. When one girl complained to her parents about it, the cops showed up the next Saturday to crash their bush party. But it was easy to outrun the cops; fun, almost. Of course the girl who'd complained needed to be taught a lesson, but even that had been fun, another nice summer memory Pete Watkins carried for years. Fishing. Drinking. That girl in the woods apologizing for what she had done.

Now there was a television news story about Springfield. *Damn.* The story wasn't about the robbery, exactly, but about some college kid who'd gone missing while searching for the diamonds. A yearbook photo was put onscreen, and the kid looked like the kind Pete would want to hit, with his punk-ass cardigan and slicked-back hair. The news then ran a video of a cargo plane sitting on an airport tarmac with its rear doors open, and another of some bulked-up Paddy being led away in handcuffs. It ended with footage of a blond-haired woman who didn't look half bad, crying for the cameras. The kid's mother probably.

It was a long story, and halfway through Pete leaned over the bar to turn up the volume on the television. When the bartender told him to sit down Pete said, without bothering to look at the man, "Fuck off and go pour something."

Pete Watkins stood six-two and weighed 220 pounds. Not an ounce of fat on him. His body covered with jailhouse tats and his hair shorn to the lowest setting on the Bolton State Pen barber's clippers. His eyes were cold and mean and didn't look like the eyes of a twenty-three-year-old. The bartender went away to pour something.

Springfield, thought Pete, as a screen-grab of a Facebook page appeared on the television. *That is fuckin' amazing.*

CHAPTER
ELEVEN

The Great Springfield Diamond Hunt, as the *Springfield Sun* was calling the influx of visitors come late spring, kicked off March fifth. That was Ground-Zero Day — six days after Jason McAllister's map was posted online, and the day the daily flight from North Bay landed in Springfield with no vacant seats, the first time anyone could recall that happening.

Within a week, there was not a vacant hotel or motel room anywhere in the city. After that people started pitching tents along Mission Road. Within two weeks of that no-empty-seat flight from North Bay there were tents stretching for more than a mile down the hiking trail, brightly coloured nylon tents that looked like a string of costume jewellery beads thrown into the forest.

That they had come in search of stolen diamonds didn't seem to faze any of the fortune hunters. Many were even under the mistaken belief there was a reward being offered. Rumours had the reward being as much as ten percent of the value of the diamonds. None of it was true.

There were as many kinds of fortune hunters as there were kinds of tents. There were the lone-wolf hunters, usually middle-aged men in grey beards, who mumbled to themselves and ate breakfast with one hand protecting their plates. There were out-of-work oil-patch kids and shanty-men from Fort Francis; laid-off mill workers from Buckham's Bay and college students from the States. There were retirees driving camper vans, and many families, including one from Concord, New Hampshire, with four teenage girls who rummaged through the snow and mud each day, then gathered around a campfire each night to give their parents a report on the search, as though they were giving seminar presentations.

Because Mission Road was on Crown land, none of the fortune hunters could be evicted. The city was in court trying to get an injunction, but potential third-party litigants had already come forward to say they would fight any such order. The Northern Divide Fish and Game Association was the largest and wealthiest of these, and the right to camp on Crown land was a hill they seemed prepared to die on.

It didn't look like anything would be settled soon.

If there were a few more third-party litigants and a few more lawyers, it might never be settled.

Yakabuski had taken to walking through the tent city each morning, as though he were back walking a beat. He walked by people huddled around campfires, their breath coming out in thick clouds that twirled around their heads, people wrapped in blankets and others stirring large black-soot pots. You could tell, by the tremors in people's bodies and the colouring in their faces, which of the fortune hunters had brought good sleeping bags and tents.

As he strode between the tents, there was the tine and ring of metal on metal. Shouted commands. The choruses to old pop songs, sung by one, then by several men. The sound moved down Mission Road until it faded away. Men setting off for a day's work. It was just like a bush camp, he thought. An absurd, searching-for-Sean-Morrissey's-stolen-diamonds bush camp.

❖ ❖ ❖

Twenty-two miles from Mission Road was Ladoucer Street, an eight-block, dog-legged street in the heart of the French Quarter of Springfield. Each weekday morning, shortly before ten, Henri Lepine could be found walking down Ladoucer. The Popeyes motorcycle gang had its clubhouse there, and Lepine was its acting president.

Henri Lepine had been in this role for five years, since Papa Paquette was sent to Dorset Penitentiary on racketeering convictions. While most full-patch, thunderbolt members of the Popeyes lived in their clubhouses, Lepine hadn't lived on Ladoucer Street since Paquette was sent to prison. He owned a Tudor in Mission Road Estates, where he lived with his wife and two young daughters.

He didn't look like a member of Popeyes motorcycle gang anymore either. Although Lepine had thunderbolt tattoos on the inside of both forearms, people rarely saw those now because he tended to wear French cuffs with jewelled cufflinks, and expensive suits, under more expensive winter jackets or trench coats. His hair no longer fanned out over his shoulders, running down his back, but had been cut fashionably to one inch below his collar.

He drove his BMW to the French Quarter every morning, parked in a long-term lot on St. Jerome Street, and made the ten-minute walk down Ladoucer to the clubhouse. The street was in the industrial area of the French Quarter. Although it was the geographic centre of the neighbourhood, it was more than two miles from the cafés, patios, and tourist shops that surrounded the statue of Champlain. Lepine enjoyed strolling past the one-bay garages and red brick warehouses, the french fry stands and four-stool diners. He'd been brought up in an industrial area not much different than this, in Verdun, just outside Montreal, and he enjoyed the smell of gasoline and fried potatoes, the look of black-metal fire escapes and chipped red brick. It reminded him of his childhood, and every morning he marvelled at how far he had come.

He stopped at the garage next to the clubhouse. Collected money from his chief mechanic, who had the proceeds from one shipping container of registration-altered Jeeps delivered to the Montreal rail yards two days earlier. From the garage, he cut through a side door in one of the bays and walked into the kitchen of the clubhouse. There was a fresh pot of coffee waiting for him. All he had to do was nod his head and a biker sitting at a kitchen table stood up and started making him a cup. As he poured in the sugar and cream, the biker gave an update on a shipment of meth that had taken off from an abandoned forestry airstrip fifty miles up the Divide, and a drug debt owed by a bartender at Le Baron that had gone into collection earlier in the week.

"He's waiting for you," said the biker.

"What have you gotten from him?"

"A little. Not what you want." Lepine nodded, took a sip of his coffee, and walked upstairs. The bartender was in the security room, sitting in a wooden chair with his hands tied behind his back. His eyes were swollen shut, and there was so much blood on his head his hair looked like strands of a wet mop. Lepine put his coffee on a nearby table and slapped the man on the top of the head.

"Patrick, it is time to pay your debts."

The bartender tried to talk, but couldn't. His teeth were smashed, and his lips were slabs of flesh ripped from their nerve circuitry. Talking would be several weeks away for him.

"I fraaaa, I fraaaa," he mumbled.

"Don't try to talk, asshole. You're spraying shit all over my jacket. I need you to write something down."

Lepine reached into the breast pocket of his jacket and pulled out a steno pad and pen. Then he reached into a pocket of his overcoat and pulled out a hunting knife. He put the steno pad and pen on the table, unsheathed the knife, and placed its blade against the bartender's crotch. He leaned down and whispered, twisting the knife as he spoke. Two minutes later Lepine walked out of the security room and handed the steno pad to the biker.

"His mother's address," he said, and the biker nodded. Lepine went down the hallway to his office, placed the coffee cup on a desk, and looked at a clock on the far wall. Five minutes past ten. A fairly typical day so far, but Lepine knew that was about to change. Papa Paquette had scheduled a phone call for 11:30 that morning.

It was not easy placing an illegal call from Dorset Penitentiary. It took subterfuge and burner phones, accomplices inside and outside the prison, money, and a bit more money. Rarely in the past five years had Patrice "Papa" Paquette felt it necessary to place a person-to-person call to Henri Lepine.

There had been plenty of communication between the two men. That's what lawyers were for. But only three times had there been matters so sensitive not even a lawyer could convey the message. Not a lawyer you wanted to keep around, anyway.

Lepine tried to keep his mind on his work. He put the money from the garage in the office safe. Went through the accounts and made arrangements to ship the proceeds from the last four shipping containers to a money launderer in Vancouver, a man who owned a string of travelling carnivals, the small ones you find in strip malls and back-county fairs. Shortly after eleven he phoned his girlfriend at her home, got her to talk dirty to him, knowing her husband was somewhere in the house.

But nothing worked. Time crawled. The clock on the wall seemed to taunt him. What did Papa need to talk to him about? Could it be a good thing? How could it be a good thing?

At 11:25 he put the burner phone on the desk and stared at it the way Hindu mystics stare at walls. The phone rang at precisely 11:30. After letting it ring twice, Lepine answered.

"Papa."

"Henri," a man answered, his words low and gruff, spoken with a thick French accent. "It is good to hear your voice."

"Yours as well, Papa."

"Are you sitting in my office?"

"Yes."

"You are alone?"

"As you requested."

"Good. We need to talk about those diamonds."

Lepine sat straighter in his chair. Papa sounded calm, but that could change in a heartbeat. He'd seen it often enough. "Would you like a sitrep?"

"*Ben oui.*"

He started with Jason McAllister, telling Paquette how the university student had gone missing on Mission Road, where most people thought the Shiners had hidden the diamonds. He told Paquette there was a — what would you call it — a gold-rush camp out on the road now, with more people arriving every day. Because of the map the kid had.

"There are probably more than a hundred tents out there, Papa," he said. "The kid posted a treasure map or something, showing where the diamonds might be buried."

"A treasure map?"

"It's even got a red *x* on it. Right at Mission Road."

There was silence. Lepine tried to picture the cell, if it was a cell that Papa was sitting in right then. Lepine didn't actually know what arrangements had been made at Papa's end — but he had never done time in max, so he was free to conjure what he wished. He imagined Papa hiding under bedsheets and sweating whenever he heard a sound coming down a cell-lined hallway. It helped steady his nerves, keeping this image in his head.

"I'm beginning to wonder if we have as much time as we thought," said Paquette. "I hear the Bristol brothers might be coming to Springfield."

"They're already here. They checked in to the Grainger two days ago. There are some people from Newark here as well. They have most of the fifth floor rented. We're trying to track down who the fuck they are."

"*Already here*," said Paquette quietly. "Well, that settles it, Henri. We can't wait for Morrissey to get out. We need to find those diamonds now."

"We've been looking, Papa. We haven't just been waiting around for the Shiner to come home. We've rousted a couple of them — on the six, like you said — but I don't think anybody knows where those diamonds are except Morrissey."

"What about the second thief?"

"It was nobody local. That's all we know for sure. The cops have been going *crazy* looking for him."

"What about the girl?"

"The girl?" Lepine faltered; not as quick as he should have been. "You mean Grace Dumont?"

"Of course I mean Grace Dumont. What has she told you?"

Lepine didn't answer. When a few seconds had passed Paquette said, "You dumb fuck. Go get the girl. Find out what she knows."

CHAPTER TWELVE

Yakabuski took a sip of coffee and pulled the stack of paper on his desk a little closer. Some of the new arrivals in Springfield, as photographed at the airport and the bus terminal, along with mug shots of people already identified. The photograph on the top of the stack was of a middle-aged man with hair so poorly shorn it looked like a geometric pattern, mismatched tufts sticking out from the crown of his head. His facial hair was just as interesting, short stubble and longish black strands that ran off his cheek. His neck was tattooed, a full circle of art that left no skin un-inked. If he were ever talking to you, his Adam's apple would look like some small animal scurrying beneath a sheet of coloured comics.

"What do we have here?" he asked Griffin, who sat on the other side of his desk.

"Walter Bristol. Flew into town from Buffalo two days ago with his three brothers. Somehow they managed to get rooms in the Grainger. Those are the brothers' mug shots you have underneath."

Yakabuski flipped through the next three photos in the stack on his desk. He saw three more men with bad haircuts and sleepy eyes, two more necks full of tattoos. They all seemed to be in their mid-to-late twenties, and you would have guessed a family connection if you hadn't known about it.

"The brothers' names are Patrick, Neil, and Shamus." Griffin continued. "All four work for Danny Biloxi and are known to every police agency in New York State and most of the seaboard, but only Shamus has a criminal record. Customs and Immigration is thinking you can get him deported. He probably shouldn't have cleared customs in Toronto."

"Shouldn't be here. That's comforting. Do I just snap my fingers and make him disappear?"

"If dreams came true . . ."

"The Buffalo mob? Is that what you're telling me these guys are, Donna?"

"That's what I'm telling you."

❖ ❖ ❖

Yakabuski sat at his desk after Griffin had left, looking at the stack of paper and wondering how many bandits you could squeeze into one northern mill town, even one as large and potentially crazy as Springfield. When those diamonds first went missing, he had done some research, trying to find out what the largest armed robbery in Springfield had been before the De Kirk plane. Near as he could tell, it was an armoured car heist in Buckham's Bay by the Ma Racine Gang, in 1934. Total take was $47,341.

It was the largest score for the Ma Racine gang by far, most of its other robberies being almost of the liquor-store variety, though there was another armoured car heist in La Toque that netted them close to twenty grand and a Bank of Montreal job in Springfield that was worth a little more than ten.

Considering how much attention Ma Racine and her three sons were given in the '30s and early '40s, the numbers surprised Yakabuski. He tallied up all the robberies he could attribute to the gang and ended up with $127,488. After that he came up with the number 0.011 — the percentage of what the Ma Racine Gang stole, in comparison to what was stolen from the De Kirk cargo plane in December.

It took less than twenty-four hours after the heist for reporters to start calling the diamond theft the largest armed robbery in history, larger than any mail-train robbery, or any theft of any Spanish galleon by a British privateer, even when adjusted for inflation. Larger than the fortunes that reportedly exchanged hands at the point of a gun in the dying days of the Second World War. Larger than any of it.

What the reporters never got into, though, or at least Yakabuski never saw it, was that the De Kirk robbery was far from the greatest theft in history. A billion dollars was what many white-collar criminals played for today when they set up their Ponzi schemes and their land flips, their rigged government bids and their initial public offerings on dot-com companies that would never produce a sellable product or service.

The tinniest of tin-pot dictators fled in the dark of night with a billion dollars waiting for them in Swiss bank accounts. The most junior of junior banks laundered billions of black-market dollars every year. The slush funds large energy companies kept off the books to secure and maintain government contracts in Russia and the Balkans and southeast Texas made the De Kirk diamond theft look like a dinner tip.

Yakabuski wasn't surprised that no one in the media had pointed this out yet. It was the difference between money and numbers. Those diamonds were money and those IPO schemes were numbers, and people nowadays tended to notice one but not the other.

He had an uncle once who used to buy his automobiles by showing up at a car dealership with a gym bag stuffed with twenty-dollar bills. The uncle would ask a salesman for the best price on a car he was considering buying, and once he had it, he would empty the gym bag and offer a thousand less. He said the trick always worked.

"People respect money when it's sitting on their lap," his uncle told him. "They don't respect it so much when it's a number on a piece of paper."

The uncle was in his nineties now and hadn't bought a car in a long time. Yakabuski wondered if the trick would still work and some days he doubted it. For most people now, there was no distinction between money and numbers. People worked their whole lives and never saw their money. Just numbers moving across a computer screen. He imagined his uncle emptying his gym bag today and a salesman sitting there wondering what it was that just got dumped on his desk.

Which made the heist of the De Kirk diamonds special in ways the media hadn't considered yet. What would matter most before the story was finished, Yakabuski suspected, was that $1.2 billion hadn't been stolen with the stroke of a computer key. It had been lifted off the back of a cargo plane.

The difference between numbers and money? It was going to come back to people.

CHAPTER THIRTEEN

Pete Watkins crossed the border at night in a cigar boat he stole from a marina in Ogdensburg, ditching it on the north shore of the St. Lawrence River and making his way to Kingston, where he caught a Greyhound bus and was in Springfield the following morning.

He hitched a ride to the farm, remembering roughly where it was, guessing he could figure out the rest once he was near enough. The driver that picked him up said, "The Watkins farm, that's where you're going?" and you could tell by the way he said it that he was amused.

"That's right. What's so funny?"

"Nothin', nothin'," said the man, flashing Pete a quick look of concern. "It's just . . . well . . . I guess not many people call it a farm anymore."

"Why not?"

"'Cause it ain't no farm. Not since John died."

"He's dead?"

"Going on ten years, I reckon."

"But there's Watkins still living there, ain't there?"

"I don't know who lives there now. But the place ain't been sold, or foreclosed on, so I reckon it belongs to John's boys."

Pete remembered there being six cousins. Or was it seven? The eldest was John Jr. and the boys closest to him in age were Arnott and Ken, Brent was a few years younger, but he always tagged along that summer. There was a Chris. Was that right? And the other brother's name?

"You look like you could be related," said the driver. "You a Watkins?"

"I am."

"Where you coming from?"

"Malone."

"Upper New York State. I'd heard there was some Watkins down there."

"Not that many anymore. Just my dad."

"Well, that can happen."

They drove for nearly an hour before coming to the intersection Pete remembered, where the gravel road to the Watkins farm met the asphalt highway. The driver made the turn and took Pete the last two miles, so he wouldn't have to walk. When they got there, Pete looked at the farmhouse and said, "You sure people live here?"

"See for yourself. There's smoke coming out the chimney."

Pete took another look at the house. It was clapboard in bad need of paint, a few of the windows boarded up, one on the main floor, near the kitchen. The front porch didn't look safe to stand on, and the stoop had collapsed. Scattered around the yard were rusted tractors, cars sitting on blocks, a piece of farm machinery so old and so bent Pete couldn't tell you what it was supposed to be.

But there was smoke coming from the chimney.

He turned to the man who had given him a ride and said, "Do you think you could help me out with a couple bucks? I'd hate to see my cousins with nothing in my pockets."

The driver looked startled, then he looked into Pete's eyes, which he hadn't noticed much until then, after that he reached for his wallet. He gave Pete every bill he had — $87 — figuring that was the way it was going to turn out anyway. Pete respected the man, for knowing that, for sparing him the extra effort of physically taking the money from him. He took the bills without saying anything and got out. The man did a quick three-point turn and drove away. Pete walked up to the farmhouse, turning once to look at the taillights of the truck, wondering if he could have played the old man for more.

❖ ❖ ❖

Pete threw his duffle bag on the front porch and jumped up after it. He banged on the front door, hard, figuring that was going to be needed as he had yet to see a light or hear sound from inside. He checked the knob, but the door was locked. He went back to banging, harder this time, sawdust and dead bugs falling from the doorframe. He was about to give up and look for some other way into the house when the door was yanked open.

"What the fuck do you want?"

The man standing in the doorframe was dressed in red long underwear, and his black hair was as tangled and wild as a briar patch. It was ten o'clock in the morning, but he stank of alcohol. From a bad binge the night before, or an early start to the day, Pete wasn't sure. Although he was angry enough to be hungover.

"You don't recognize me?" Pete said.

The man blinked his eyes a few times, scratched his belly, and said, "No. You some fuckin' celebrity?"

"Fuck, no. I'm better'n that."

The man stopped scratching and took a closer look at Pete. "You ain't from around here. Where you from?"

"Malone. I've been here before, John," — the man in the long underwear looked surprised to hear his name — "I spent a whole summer up here haying with you, partying with you, slept in that bedroom right up there."

"Pete?"

"'Bout time you recognized your own cousin, you dumb motherfucker."

"What the fuck?"

"Is that how you say hi to family when they come for a visit?"

"No one comes here for a visit, Pete. I don't know how you're supposed to fuckin' say hi. Fuck. How long has it been?"

"Ten years."

John Watkins Jr. nodded. That's right. Ten years. That had been a good summer. His father died the next year, so maybe that had been the last good summer.

"Well, shit, Pete, it's good to see you. Come on in, I'll mix us up some drinks. Everyone is out ice fishing. They'll be back soon."

"Wanna know why I'm here?"

"I already know."

CHAPTER FOURTEEN

The Grainger Hotel was built in 1892, when people thought the riches being made by selling wood to the British Royal Navy would last forever. It was built in a Gothic Revival style, with a gilded and multi-frescoed lobby, wrought iron balconies, and a white marble fountain out front that needed to be turned off every year no later than early October to ensure the water pipes below the hotel didn't freeze and burst.

The hotel nearly went bankrupt in the '30s, but it converted the restaurant into a speakeasy and rented discount rooms on the first three floors to enterprising merchants and survived. A major renovation was done in the '80s, when softwood lumber was having one of its periodic booms, and the restaurant was restored, along with much of the foyer. There were 148 rooms in the Grainger, spread out over eight floors. The suites on the top floor were built in the days when lumber barons ruled the earth, and they were the most expensive hotel rooms in the city, maybe anywhere on the Northern Divide or in the Springfield Valley.

The Bristol brothers had decamped in two corner-unit rooms on the sixth floor. It was a convenient layout for Yakabuski, as it allowed him to knock on both doors at once. The carpeting in the hallway behind him was a dried-mustard colour and the lighting was the same shade, light cast by a row of wall lamps that disappeared in shadows long before Yakabuski's gaze reached the end of the hallway.

Both doors were answered at the same time, and the light inside the suites seemed garish and startling in contrast with the gloom of the hallway. Yakabuski saw several young women in the suite on his left, and what looked like a several-hours-running poker game set up on a collapsible card table in the suite to his right.

"Gentlemen," he said, holding out his badge and moving it from one open door to the next, all four brothers crowding the doorframe. "My name is Frank Yakabuski, and I'm a senior detective with the Springfield Regional Police Service. I'm here as part of our Welcome Wagon committee. You boys familiar with the Welcome Wagon?"

"What the fuck do you want?" said Walter Bristol, the oldest brother and the one standing with his arms crossed in the right-side door.

"I want to know if you've ever heard of the Welcome Wagon. I thought that was pretty clear."

"Never fuckin' heard of it."

"That's what I was afraid of. All right, I'll start from scratch. Welcome Wagon is a civic group that welcomes newcomers to a city. We give out gifts and friendly advice, that sort of stuff."

"You know what you can do with your gifts?"

"I know what you're thinking, but we're not one of those chintzy Welcome Wagon groups that give out coupons or family gifts. We have something for everyone. Now which one of you is Shamus?"

Yakabuski smiled and shoved his jaw forward. Clasped his hands behind his back and rocked back and forth. Tried to think of other things he could do to make himself look like a small-town, bumpkin cop. The Bristol brothers were so close in appearance, he actually wasn't sure which one was Shamus, although he suspected one of the men standing in the left-side door. After a few seconds had passed one of those men said, "Why d'you care about Shamus?"

"Ah, there you are, Shamus. Pleased to meet you."

"I never said I was Shamus."

"I think you did. Here, let me get your official Welcome Wagon gift."

Yakabuski had his service revolver drawn and pushed against Shamus Bristol's right temple before he finished the sentence. At the same time, the exit door ten metres down the hallway crashed open and two full-kit tactical officers came running into view, AR-15 rifles aimed crotch level at the open doorways. The Bristol brothers stopped, reaching their hands behind their backs.

"On your knees, motherfuckers. Right the fuck now," one of the tactical officers yelled, and that's what they did. Two men wearing the grey and yellow uniform of Customs and Immigration came through the exit door, walked to where Shamus Bristol was kneeling, and brought him to his feet.

"These two gentlemen will escort you back to Buffalo," said Yakabuski. "I'm afraid Welcome Wagon rules state you can't get the fruit basket if you're deported the same week you arrive. It's in the fine print, and I didn't see it. Sorry about that, Shamus."

Yakabuski turned to address the three men still kneeling in the hallway. "As for you gentlemen, you're still eligible for all sorts of free gifts and friendly advice. Why don't we send the girls home, and I'll give you a proper Welcome Wagon greeting."

❖ ❖ ❖

The Bristol brothers didn't scare. Yakabuski never thought they would, but he'd been trained to not make assumptions.

The brothers and Yakabuski had taken seats around the card table. The riot police and the customs officers had left. It was just Donna Griffin and a beat cop in the room with them. Griffin was standing beside the card table, staring at the brothers with a bemused smile. The beat cop stood by the door.

Yakabuski took one last flip through the men's passports and threw them on the card table. "So, tell me again what brings you to Springfield?"

"A fishing trip," said Walter Bristol. He smiled at Yakabuski. It was the third time he'd said it, and each time his smile got a little bigger at the obvious absurdity of these four men in black-hose socks being in Springfield to fish.

"That's strange. We haven't found any fishing gear in your rooms. Isn't that right, Constable Griffin?"

"That's right, Detective Yakabuski."

"How were you boys planning on fishing?"

"We were going to buy the gear here."

"Because everything is so much cheaper in Springfield than it is in Buffalo?"

"Are you harassing us for not having the right fishing gear? What are you? The fuckin' fish police?"

"The fish police. That's good, Walter. Would it surprise you to learn there are indeed fish police up here? Same as there are fish police in the United States. And because trout season doesn't open for another month, and because you keep insisting you're here for the fishing, maybe you've just confessed to the crime of poaching. What do you think, Constable Griffin?"

"There's probable cause to think that," she answered. "Might explain why they don't have any gear. That's something a poacher might do. Not bring their equipment through customs."

"Good point."

"Of course, they might just be pan fishermen. Crappie and pumpkinseed are always in season. Don't need much gear for that. This one here looks loser enough to be a pan fisherman."

She was standing directly in front of Walter Bristol.

"He look that way to you?" said Yakabuski.

"He sure does."

"Damn, he looks that way to me too. Big, dumb, pan fisherman. So, we don't really know what we have here."

"We know what we have here. We just need the right word to describe it."

"Cunt," Bristol finally spat out.

"That won't work for you gentlemen. Any other suggestions?"

"Know what we do to cunts like you in Buffalo?"

"All right, Walter, ramp it down," said Yakabuski, getting up from his chair.

"I want to call my fuckin' lawyer," said Bristol, "so I can start suing your ass and the ass of that bitch-cunt dyke of . . ."

Griffin slapped him across the cheek. Not hard, but enough to get his attention. Yakabuski stepped forward and grabbed her arm.

"Whoa," he said and backed her toward the door of the hotel room where he said to the beat cop, "Please escort Constable Griffin outside." She glared at him but didn't say anything. The beat cop stepped forward, moving as though he were going to take over from Yakabuski and grab her by the arm to lead her outside. Then he seemed to think better of it and stood with his arms by his side, simply following her out of the room.

When she was gone, Yakabuski walked back to Walter Bristol, who was smiling and chuckling. Yakabuski pulled his service revolver and pointed it at his head. Walter stopped chuckling.

When Yakabuski motioned with his gun to stand up, that's what Walter did, and then Yakabuski waved him to the balcony ·and through the sliding doors. His brothers had drawn guns of their own and pointed them at Yakabuski when he stepped onto the balcony. He laughed at them and closed the sliding doors, then said. "Motion for them to put their guns down. You and I need to talk."

Walter Bristol gave him a quick look, then motioned for his brothers to lower their guns. When they had, Yakabuski turned Bristol around so he was facing the Springfield River, his back to the hotel room. Yakabuski stood beside him, staring out over the river, which was moving fast that evening and making sounds that ranged from murmurs to thunder-claps to every once in a while a sound that might have been the shriek of a mandrake, some fantastical, anguished sound. The sounds of the spring run-off.

"You're in Springfield because you work for Danny Biloxi," said Yakabuski, still staring at the river. "Your boss thinks he might have a play for those stolen diamonds. He knew Augustus Morrissey, but he doesn't know the son, and he thinks the son might not have the strength to keep what he's stolen. You are here to offer Sean Morrissey fencing services for those dia-monds, on behalf of Mr. Biloxi. If the play is there, you're to kidnap Morrissey when he is released from Wentworth, torture him, and steal the diamonds. Not a bad plan, really."

"You are so fucked when I contact my lawyer."

"Walter, it's important you start taking this seriously. We don't have time for bullshit. Do you know why you're standing on a balcony?"

Walter looked at Yakabuski but didn't speak.

"Balconies help people get serious. Get dangled off a bal-cony, and I tell you, Walter, it's 'Shine a Light' time. No more bullshit, no more lying. You're in an honest state of grace when you're hanging upside down from a balcony."

"You're fuckin' crazy."

"I'd prefer not to do any balcony-dangling tonight. I'm going to be honest with you about that. It's a lot of work, and your brothers seem a mite unstable to me, so I'd probably have to use my left arm to hold you, keep a gun drawn on them with my right, and that makes it a *lot more* work. But if threatening to throw you off this balcony is the only way to get you right thinking, well, it's not really my decision anymore, is it?"

Walter Bristol looked at him, and you could tell he wasn't sure what to make of Yakabuski. This hulking, long-haired cop standing next to him. Whether he was someone he needed to take seriously.

"You'll be dead before you get a chance to try it."

"I'll take that bet. Want to start?"

"All right . . . I'll play along. What do you want to know?"

"Christ, Walter, I want to know nothing, you dumb-ass fool. It's you that needs to know a few things. Like you'll be dead five minutes after I leave this room. That would be a good thing to know, don't you think?"

"What sort of hustle are you trying to run?"

"Not running anything, Walter. Three chords and the truth. See that van parked down there?"

Walter Bristol turned his gaze to where Yakabuski was pointing. A white cargo van was parked at the intersection of Water and O'Brien.

"There are four Shiners in that van," continued Yakabuski. "There's another four in a van parked two blocks from here. The van you're looking at has the main crew, the men who will kill you and your brothers as soon as I leave this hotel. Morrissey has men watching the airport. He spotted you the second you landed.

"The other van is the back-up crew. There are four sedans maintaining a rolling perimeter four blocks from here, two men per car, to hunt your ass down quick if you somehow manage to get out of this hotel alive. That's a sixteen-man crew. You have what, those two clowns the other side of the glass?"

Walter stared at his brothers through the sliding door: trying to look tough but looking more petulant than anything. He looked back at the white van. In the gathering darkness of the evening, it might as well have been parked under a spotlight.

"Why are you telling me this?"

"Because you need some help," Yakabuski said.

"Why would you want to help me?"

"Think."

Walter Bristol started to smile. "You want money."

"Who doesn't want money?"

"How much is the shakedown?"

"I want a cut of the diamonds." Yakabuski kept his gaze on Walter.

"In return for what?"

"In return for me bringing Sean Morrissey to you."

"I would need to get approval for something like that."

"How much are you cleared for?"

Walter Bristol considered it before speaking. "One hundred thousand. I can give you that right now."

"Onsite?"

"Sure."

"We missed it?"

"Course you did. You have rules to follow."

"Someone's carrying it. All right, I'll take that as advance against future royalties. My cut of the diamonds will be twenty-five percent. I keep the hundred no matter what."

"That'll never be approved. You're too greedy."

"Think so? I can deliver Sean Morrissey to a place of your choosing. You don't have any sort of play unless that happens. He's smarter than you think. And as a bonus, Walter, I'll chase those Shiners away from the hotel for you."

Walter was silent for a few seconds and then he said, "I can ask."

"You do that. I'll take the hundred now. Come on, let's go tell the kids we've made up."

✦ ✦ ✦

Walter Bristol told his brothers about the white van, and they nearly tripped over each other rushing to the balcony. When they came back into the room, one of them said to Yakabuski, "Sixteen men?"

"The full op," he said. "And Biloxi sent you four. Is it always amateur hour, working for him?"

"Watch your tongue. The fortunes of war change often."

"But not tonight. I'll take my money now."

Walter Bristol snapped his fingers and one of his brothers began unbuttoning his shirt. When he was halfway down, he reached inside the shirt and took out a money pouch. Threw it on the card table in front of Yakabuski.

"One hundred thousand U.S. right there," said Walter. "You can count it if you like."

"I trust you. But just so there's no dumb-gangster misunderstandings later, this money is only an advance. I get twenty-five percent of net recovery on the diamonds, and you're going to bring my demands to Danny Biloxi. Is this understood?"

"Yes, this is agreed."

"And the services you're expecting me to render, in return for this financial compensation?"

"You bring Sean Morrissey to a location of our choosing. And you get rid of the Shiners parked around this fuckin' hotel."

"Sean Morrissey will not be leaving your meeting?"

"What are you? Some sort of fuckin' comedian?"

94

"I don't want him coming after me. I need to hear it," Yakabuski said.

"He will not be leaving the meeting."

"Because you will . . ."

"You really want me to say it?"

"Please."

"Because I will kill the son of a bitch," Bristol said.

"Thank you."

Yakabuski stood up and made room for the police officers rushing into the room. Griffin came in near the end of the stampede, wiping away what looked like tears.

"My lord, that was one for the ages," she said. "It's a shame you never like to look at the videos, Yak. That one is a classic. Right up there with 'Who's on First?'"

"So the cameras worked all right. Wasn't sure if the tac boys had enough time in here to get them working. Aren't you a little young for Abbott and Costello?"

"We're all a little young for them. When did you come up with the Shiners-surrounding-the-hotel bit? I practically peed myself."

"There's a white van parked on the street. It just came to me."

"That was just flamboyant nonsense, you know that, right? We had them with trying to bribe a law-enforcement official. The paperwork is already with Judge Walters."

"A little insurance doesn't hurt. Did we make the deadline?"

"Time to spare. They'll be on the same plane as Shamus, back in Buffalo tomorrow night. The customs guys say you can come out and play with them anytime you want."

Yakabuski shook his head. It shouldn't have been that easy. Money had made them stupid.

CHAPTER FIFTEEN

Pete Watkins stayed drunk for two weeks. The first week, he drank with his cousins at the farm, ice-fishing and playing poker for the most part. The second week, the Watkins clan migrated to Springfield, where they hooked up with strippers who shared a house in the French Quarter. Most of that second week was a blur to Pete. He remembered a fight in the parking lot of a 7-Eleven with some mill workers. Going back to the farm once to change his clothes. Going to a bootlegger who lived in Cork's Town a few times. Going to a meth dealer a few more times. Going back to the French Quarter to track down the girls.

The week after St. Patrick's Day he awoke in the bed of one of the strippers, a girl whose name he couldn't remember. It was midafternoon and he lay in bed several minutes before giving her a rough shake and saying he needed coffee. When she was walking out the room he told her to find his cousins. He needed to talk to them.

❖ ❖ ❖

They gathered in the bedroom, passing around a forty of Crown Royal. It was John who asked, after they each had a few pulls, what Pete wanted to talk about.

"It's time we got serious about finding those diamonds."

"All right. What's your plan, Pete?"

Watkins took a buck knife from his jacket pocket. "The Shiners know where those diamonds are stashed. I say we pick one up and stick him till he tells us."

The cousins stopped drinking. They stared at Pete.

Again, it was John who spoke. "That's your plan, Pete?"

"Damn straight. And we gotta move quick, because that map has been out there weeks now. Somebody else is going to find those diamonds if we don't start looking. We should grab us someone tonight. Where can we find one?"

"A Shiner?"

"They're the ones who stole the diamonds, ain't they? Who else do you think I'd be talking about?"

"How much do you know about the Shiners, Pete?"

"I know they're a bunch of backwoods Micks that're sitting on my fuckin' diamonds." Pete began twirling the knife around in his hands, moving it from knuckle to knuckle, a trick that used to get him laid in Malone if he showed it to the right girl. Flash of metal. Jailhouse tattoos. Lithe muscles rippling. Pete thought it looked pretty good. "So, where can we find one?" he said.

"They hang out at the Silver Dollar."

"Let's go there and grab one."

"Fuck, Pete, do you think every Shiner knows where those diamonds are hidden?"

"Course not, John. That would make me stupid. We need to grab us an important, high-ranking Mick."

"And what if he doesn't know? Most people think the only one who knows where those diamonds are stashed is Sean Morrissey."

"Well, let's go fuckin' find out."

The cousins stared at Pete until John started laughing. Then they all started laughing. "You are one bad-ass coco motherfucker, Pete. I am proud to call you my cousin," said John.

The other cousins cheered and clinked their glasses. They stayed in the stripper's bedroom drinking rye whisky until her roommates came home from their afternoon shifts, then they went looking for the meth dealer, to continue celebrating Pete's plan.

CHAPTER SIXTEEN

The Popeyes made their move against Grace Dumont the following afternoon. Two bikers had watched the girl's apartment for more than a week. Watched her cut across Filion's Field every morning and afternoon on her way to and from school. They sat in a Cadillac suv and watched her cut across the soccer pitch, through the parking lot, then enter the alleyway running between Buildings C and D. They opened the doors of the suv and stepped out.

It was the driver who screamed first.

A shout of pain that broke the quiet and stillness of the afternoon, that made Grace Dumont stop walking and stare down the alleyway. She saw a man slamming the door of the cadillac against another man's body. She heard bones breaking and then she saw the beaten man fall to the ground. The other man started kicking him.

Another man ran around the car, something in his hands it looked like, but as soon as he made it to the driver's side of the Cadillac, the other man stopped kicking and threw something. The running man clutched his chest and fell. The other man looked at him a second, then walked over and started kicking him too.

It went on for quite a while. When it was finished the man walked to Grace Dumont, reached into his jacket pocket, and pulled out a package of cigarettes. He flipped one out, and lit it. After he'd taken a long, deep draw, he said, "Those men won't be bothering you anymore."

"Are they dead?"

"No."

She looked down the alleyway. The front doors of the Cadillac were still open, and the two men lay just beyond. She couldn't see their full bodies. Only their legs. One man's chest. Crows had begun to hop toward a pool of blood underneath the driver's door.

"I hear you haven't told the police anything about me," the man said. "Why is that?"

"My mother said it was up to me what I told the police."

"But your mother gave the police the diamond."

"She said it would've been wrong to keep it. They're different things."

The man kept smoking. He finished one cigarette and lit another.

"It would have been better if she'd kept that diamond and never told anyone."

"She did what she thought was right. Who are those men?"

"Bikers. They've heard about that diamond somehow. Figured you might know where to find the rest of them."

"Popeyes?"

"That's right. Popeyes. You know a thing or two, don't you, Grace?"

"I do. Just like I know you saved my life in that apartment, when those two men came to see us the night of the riots. They were going to kill me, weren't they?"

"Is that why you haven't spoken to the cops?"

"It doesn't feel right, getting someone in trouble after they've saved your life."

The girl looked him straight in the face. Rocked back and forth on her feet, her arms clasped around her parka. One of the bikers in the alley began to move, and the man looked over at him. Soon saw he was unconscious and only moving in pain, probably blood pushing against his kidneys.

"You need to tell you mother what happened here," he said, turning back to her. "There will be more people coming."

"Should I tell her about you?"

"Say whatever you'd like. I'd never tell you what to say."

"I'll tell her some passerby saw it happening and broke it up. He ran off. I don't know who he was."

"Tell her that. But make sure she knows the Popeyes just made a play for you."

"All right."

She kept staring at him. Tempted to address him by name. So he would know that she knew. Too scared to risk it. The Bangles family had never been people you messed with. She was still debating when she heard the siren of a police car crossing the North Shore Bridge.

"You should probably go."

Bobby Bangs looked at her, and she thought he was going to say something more. But when it didn't come to him right away, he turned and walked away.

CHAPTER SEVENTEEN

Yakabuski didn't spend much time sitting in young girls' bed-rooms. Last time would have been with his niece, Julie, the weekend Trish and Tyler took Jason to a hockey tournament in Toronto. Four years ago? Five? He looked around Grace Dumont's room, at the shelf of stuffed animals she probably didn't play with anymore, the desk with a computer printer and neatly stacked piles of paper, posters on the wall of sun-sets, horses, and a teenage boy who looked thin and useless enough to be the latest pop sensation. Not much difference, the bedrooms of young girls in the Mission Road Estates and those of young girls on the North Shore.

Grace Dumont sat on her bed. Her feet were almost touching the floor, but not quite. She swung them back and forth, waiting for Yakabuski to ask another question.

"Which direction did he go?"

"Across Filion's Field, toward the exit in the fence by Building G."

"You think that's where he lives?"

"I don't know."

"Because you've never seen him before?"

"That's right."

"This stranger who stomped two Popeyes, saved you from being kidnapped, and then ran away. You've never seen him before?"

"I think he ran because he heard the police sirens. He probably didn't want to talk to you, after what he'd done."

"You figure?"

"Uh huh."

She held Yakabuski's gaze longer than he expected, even though she was a smart girl and the sheer implausibility of what she was saying made her uncomfortable. After a while she looked away.

"Those bikers thought I knew where the rest of the diamonds were, didn't they?" she said.

Yakabuski looked at her mother before answering. He wondered if Rachel Dumont regretted phoning him, when Grace gave her the diamond. Regretted doing the right thing. He couldn't blame her if she did.

"They might have thought that," he said. "Though they're bikers, so they're not known for thinking too well, Grace. You're a living connection to those diamonds, to where they were after they were stolen. There aren't too many of those people around. None that can be easily found, anyway. That's why they came."

"That doesn't make any sense. Can't you tell them I don't

know anything? Put out a press release or something. Maybe I could do another TV interview?"

"You think that will take care of the problem? You telling people you don't have those diamonds?"

"Won't it?"

Yakabuski thought of the squatter's camp he had walked through that morning, the faces of people who looked at him as though he might know something, a hungry, unstable look that unnerved him more than he wanted to admit. He thought of Jason McAllister, missing six weeks now, and the possibility of finding that boy alive seemed beyond remote. He thought of the Bristol brothers, and Cambino Cortez, and Robert Bangles, circling like birds over a bluff. He thought of Sean Morrissey getting released from Wentworth in a month.

"Grace, I don't think anyone would even hear you right now," he said.

❖ ❖ ❖

Ten minutes later, with Grace in her bedroom, the adults in the kitchen, Yakabuski had his first argument with Rachel Dumont. Maybe argument was too strong. She certainly wasn't listening to him.

In the three months since the diamond robbery, Yakabuski had spent more time with Rachel Dumont than he had with his sister, his father, anyone in the Centretown detachment with the exception of Donna Griffin. He'd been in her apartment at least once a day for almost ten days, at the height of the gang war between the Shiners and the Travellers. Had been by many times since, after she'd phoned to tell him about the diamond. After he'd started questioning Grace about her captors.

Many of the recent visits had been short interviews with Grace and a cup of tea in Rachel Dumont's kitchen. The interviews were often conducted on Friday afternoons, and Yakabuski had begun to think of the kitchen as a calm and sensible place to end the week, a place that felt right, the perfect counterpoint to most of what had happened in the previous five days.

But she wasn't being calm and sensible right then.

"A safe house *is* the best way, Rachel," he repeated. "You can't deny it. Anything else is a poor second choice."

"I don't think there *are* any good choices, first, second, or dead last," Dumont retorted. "There haven't been any good choices in a very long time. I am not pulling Grace out of school. I am not leaving my home."

"It wouldn't be for long, Rachel. What's happening in Springfield, it can't last. Those diamonds are going to be found, or they'll be put into play as soon as Sean Morrissey walks out of jail. That's one month from now."

"I'm sorry, Frank, but it doesn't matter to me if it's one month, one day, or one hour. I won't be running from my home. Neither will Grace."

Yakabuski leaned back in his chair. Rachel Dumont was dressed in a dark blue skirt and white blouse, her work uniform, thought Yakabuski, what she must wear most days when she went to her PS4 clerk's job with the Ministry of Northern Affairs, because that's what she was usually wearing when he came to see her. More formal than she probably needed. She had her own opinions on certain things, Yakabuski knew. Even calling him by his first name was something she had deigned appropriate no more than two weeks ago.

"If you won't agree to the safe house, let's at least get you and Grace some police protection."

"I'm not going to have cops living in my apartment."

"What if I found you one that was toilet trained and passably clean?"

"Not funny."

"We can make something work, Rachel. What if I had a patrol car stationed here and a female officer in the hallway? The officer can walk Grace to school and home, and she'll check the apartment anytime it's left empty, before you come in."

She thought about it a few seconds before saying, "That might be okay . . ."

"Thank you. I can have someone here within the hour. The patrol officers will stay until she arrives. Did Linus Desjardins ever contact you?"

"It's not easy getting in touch with a Traveller. But he phoned just before you arrived. He'd heard about Grace. He's agreed to meet you. He's going to get back to me with a time and place."

"Is he in Springfield right now?"

"I'm not sure."

"How did he sound?"

"Not happy. But that's the way Linus always sounds."

❦ ❦ ❦

As Yakabuski drove home that night from the North Shore, he got a phone call from the hospital, a doctor telling him both bikers were going to make it. The one who took a knife to the chest was still on the operating table, the other one in intensive care, so forget about interviewing anyone tomorrow, but they would be there waiting for him. Hell of a beating to take, for trying to talk to a girl who knew nothing.

What people did for money, little of it surprised Yakabuski anymore. Years ago there was a financial planner who embezzled twenty million dollars from his clients, most of whom were old and most of whom had considered the financial planner a friend. This was before Yakabuski's time. Back in the '80s. He heard about the case from the lead investigator, Jim Patterson, a long-time fraud detective who ended his career in major crimes. He told Yakabuski it was the strangest case he'd ever worked.

The financial planner confessed to the crime, which wasn't that unusual for white-collar fraud cases, but he phoned Jim Patterson to tell him about the crime, and *then* he confessed. It all happened in one phone call.

In court the financial planner said he was so guilt-ridden he couldn't continue with the fraud. He was a gambler. Got in over his head. The money was long gone. When he testified he cried so long and so often Patterson said it became contagious, with everyone in the courtroom crying and dabbing away tears by the time he finished testifying. The guy was in his mid-thirties. Had a deep receding hairline. Testified in a rumpled brown suit while pushing up the bridge of his eyeglasses and fidgeting with a pencil. Looked like a financial planner you could maybe trust and feel sorry for at the same time.

The judge sentenced him to ten years. With good behaviour he was out in four. Right after he was released, he divorced his wife, who had stood by him through the trial, and he moved to the Bahamas. Four months after leaving Springfield, he phoned Patterson to tell him he'd been planning the fraud for nearly a decade. He'd worked out how much money he would need, the possible sentencing range in Ontario for a guilt-ridden schmuck finance guy who self-reported his crime and pled guilty at his first court appearance.

He also researched where he could go after that where civil restitution decrees from another country would be laughed at. The day all the numbers lined up right — that was the day he'd phoned Jim Patterson. He wanted the cop to know.

"Some people will tell you only murderers are pure evil," Patterson told Yakabuski after finishing his story. "Some mutt like a Manson, or a Bundy, some scum-killer like that. But I think that financial planner was pure evil. To do what he'd done, to work the scam the way he did, I don't think you can do that if you're a human being with a human soul."

Yakabuski drove over the North Shore Bridge, the ice starting to break now, floes moving downriver under the moonlight. He'd never had a case that made him disagree with Patterson. The desire some people have to kill, it's no different than the desire to rob. Smile at a friend and steal his money. Put a sawed-off shotgun in the face of a teenage girl working cash at the 7-Eleven. Try to kidnap a young girl from the back alley of her apartment building. Same sort of desire. Same sort of people doing the smiling, the robbing, the killing.

Early in his police career, Yakabuski had a case where a sixteen-year-old boy killed another sixteen-year-old boy. Happened in a bus shelter in Centretown. The kid who got killed was from the Mission Road Estates. The kid who did it was from the North Shore.

It happened after a Slayer concert at the Palace Auditorium, and it happened over an iPod. There was no dispute. No words exchanged between the two boys. The killer simply took out his hunting knife and stabbed the other boy until he was dead. Then he took the iPod, walked to the next shelter, and caught the 95 bus home. He was arrested later that night. When Yakabuski interviewed the boy in the holding cells, he asked if he knew his victim.

"Never seen him before," the boy said, a smirk on his face.

"So this was just because you wanted the iPod?"

"Yeah."

Yakabuski didn't know what to say to that. He looked at the boy's criminal file, which was already three pages, and then he looked at the murdered boy's student ID, sitting on his desk. He noticed their birthdays were six days apart. He looked up and told the boy.

"Yeah? Younger or older?"

"Younger."

"Uhhh."

He didn't say anything else, and after a while Yakabuski said, "That's it? That's all you're going to say?"

"What the fuck do you want me to say?"

"I don't know. Something."

"You think I should be wondering about him being me and me being him, that sort of shit?"

"Maybe."

The boy laughed. "How the fuck was I ever gonna own an iPod?"

Just two years ago, in Mission Road Estates, a woman killed her husband for the insurance money. The couple

110

lived in a large Cape Cod on a cul-de-sac, not far from where Yakabuski's sister lived. Both were in their mid-forties, healthy and attractive. The husband was a lawyer, the wife an interior designer, and the couple's finances were in excellent shape. They had no children, four automobiles, and owned holiday homes in the Thousand Islands and Aspen.

The wife was polite and helpful during Yakabuski's first interview, conducted in the living room of their home, a room with white shag rugs and lots of chrome furniture, a small dog dyed pink that kept racing from one end of the rug to the other. She accepted Yakabuski's condolences at the sudden death of her husband, drowned on the lake at their summer home. "Paul was never a good boater," she'd said, dabbing away tears. "He thought he was, but he truly wasn't." And she cried at the memory of that.

She treated Yakabuski's questions about her financial situation as though they were nothing more than expressions of concern for her well-being, patting him on the arm twice and telling him he was kind, but she would be all right. Yakabuski stayed longer than needed. Waiting to see if she would give some sign of worry, some indication she was aware a cop might wonder about the three life insurance policies taken out on her late husband in the past eighteen months.

But there was nothing.

Not so friendly the second interview. Surprised when Yakabuski appeared at her door. Thought they had covered everything. Now wasn't a good time. Could he come back? Or better yet, send her an email with his questions? That would probably work best.

Back in the white-and-chrome room with the pink dog tearing around and Yakabuski told her the insurance agent had confessed. Took less than two hours in the holding cells and he'd signed a full confession to his part in the crime. He was already at the regional detention centre and would be arraigned for first-degree murder the next morning.

As he was saying this, the wife got a sad, wistful look. When he was putting her in handcuffs, she told Yakabuski people had always let her down.

Mean greed. Stupid greed. Violent greed. Yakabuski figured he had probably seen every form there was, and he didn't think it mattered much what you coveted, or how much you had when you started coveting; as soon as you started wanting things you couldn't lawfully possess, bad things were on their way.

CHAPTER EIGHTEEN

Pete now knew his cousins were never going to help him. They would talk. They would dream. They would drink and pat Pete on the back, call him "one bad-ass coco motherfucker," but when it came time to lift a hand against the Shiners, to actually help Pete find those diamonds — that was never going to happen.

As Pete stared at the front door of the Silver Dollar he cursed his cousins one more time. They were dirt poor. They ran tabs with moonshiners that had to be settled by selling farm equipment. They should have been all over Pete trying to make this happen. Instead they were passed out back at the farm. Recovering from another three-day party. Leaving Pete to get this show on the road.

Being given land made you lazy, Pete supposed. Even bad land, like the Watkins farm, was enough to make you that way. Didn't have to worry about much once you owned land.

He watched the front door of the Silver Dollar for two hours. He was looking for someone who looked like he owned the joint, or someone who looked like he enjoyed bossing people around. Some arrogant shithead. That was the Shiner he wanted.

He saw plenty of tough men, but that wasn't what he needed. Same for the rich bastard who strode in with a hooker on each arm. And the dealer selling speedballs out of a tinted-window Dodge Charger in the parking lot. If that car wasn't a heat score, Pete didn't know what was.

Around midnight a giant of a man showed up at the nightclub, wearing a green tie and bowler cap, a jacket with the sleeves riding high on the arms. He stood at the front door smoking a cigarette while people bowed their heads and walked past him. Everyone seemed to know him. Everyone was deferential.

Watkins opened the door of the pickup, adjusted the buck knife in the waistband of his jeans, and started toward the Silver Dollar.

◆ ◆ ◆

Henri Lepine sat in the darkened office and stared at the clock. He blinked his eyes from time to time and wondered if the hands had moved. He would change it to a digital clock the next day. Who had clocks with hands anymore?

The girl would be under police protection now, and Lepine doubted they would get another chance at her. Also doubted she knew anything about those diamonds. It'd seemed like a long shot. A successful kidnapping might have created more problems than it solved. This struck Lepine as a good argument. He sat in the darkness of the office and tried to think of others. Papa would be phoning in ten minutes.

❖ ❖ ❖

The teenage boys stood on the Mission Road trail by the edge of a field of mud that stretched farther than they could see. Bubbles formed and popped before them, a wet, sticky sound that was indolent somehow, almost profane, in the quiet of the forest.

"Do you see it?" asked one boy.

"No."

"It has to be there. Right there," and the boy pointed to the popping bubbles.

"If you're so sure, Ralph, go get a chain and hook it up."

"How deep do you think it is?"

"That's the fuckin' question, isn't it, genius?"

It went back and forth like that, incredulity and anger at the condition of Mission Road in early spring. Two boys did all the talking. Two other boys stood back, tremors moving across their faces from time to time,. One of the boys had a boot-print on his cheek.

As they were debating what to do, the boys heard what sounded like whistling coming from atop the ridge. They stopped talking. In a few seconds they heard it again. Someone whistling a song. There was no mistaking it this time.

"What the fuck is that?" whispered one boy.

"Someone's out there."

"Did you hear a motor?"

"No."

"What the fuck? No one lives out here, do they?"

The sound became louder, a perfectly pitched whistle that blended with the chirps and trills of the night birds, the tune getting louder and louder until the boys knew that someone was coming down the ridge toward them.

"Who's out there?" one boy finally yelled, and the whistling stopped. For a moment there was only the sound of the night birds and a light wind rustling the upper branches of the surrounding pine. Then the boys heard a man's voice yell, "Having trouble?"

"Trouble . . . yeah, I guess you could say that. We've got . . . well . . . we've got an ATV trapped in the mud here."

A boy pointed to the bubbles popping in the mud field just as a man came into view. He approached the boys, then walked past them and stood on the shore of mud, staring at the bubbles.

"You think your vehicle is trapped?" he said, turning to look at the boys. "I would say it is gone. There is a difference between things that are trapped and things that are gone. To know the difference is a useful thing."

He was a middle-aged man, dressed in a tan-coloured windbreaker, a Texas A&M ball cap on his head. He spoke with a slight accent that the boys had trouble placing. Not French. Not Polish. Something sweeter and more melodic. Spanish?

"You need a fire," he said. "Stay here. I'll be right back." Without saying anything more, he went to gather wood.

II
MURDER

NINETEEN

Piers Grund didn't call the next time he wanted to talk to Yakabuski. Rather, the De Kirk executive demanded a meeting in the office of the chief of police.

Yakabuski walked in expecting to see lawyers sitting with Grund, men wearing suits that would never keep them warm in Springfield, ready to snarl and throw paper at him and O'Toole. But it was just Grund. Yakabuski took the seat waiting for him, beside O'Toole. Grund sat the opposite side of the desk. As soon as Yakabuski was seated O'Toole said, "All right, Mr. Grund, we're all here. Maybe you can tell us now why you wanted this meeting."

O'Toole didn't make any attempt to hide his annoyance. Not even the mayor demanded meetings with Bernard O'Toole, who had been with the force nearly forty years and whose family could trace their law enforcement roots on the Northern Divide back to the canoe brigade that paddled up the Springfield River in 1845 to form the first Springfield police force. But just like Yakabuski, O'Toole knew deference had to be given to the man representing the company that dumped more annual revenue into the provincial coffers than every forestry company on the Northern Divide combined.

"No coffee, Chief?" said Grund. "It's a cold day."

"There might be some in a pot down in the lunchroom. You've been in the station often enough, Mr. Grund. We'll wait for you."

Grund crossed his legs and gave O'Toole one of his sneers. Then he looked around the office, at the fishing trophies on top of the wooden bookshelf, the framed photos of O'Toole with his wife and four daughters, each photo a little out of focus. When he had taken it all in he said, "Very well, I'll get on with it. I have come to tell you that I will be checking out of the Grainger this evening and leaving Springfield. Everyone who works for De Kirk will be leaving in the next day or two."

Yakabuski looked at Grund and tried to hide his surprise. There were a few different ways he had expected him to start the meeting: Threaten legal action against Yakabuski. Threaten legal action against O'Toole. Threaten legal action against the cop he'd met on the elevator ride up. Packing up and leaving town had not been on his list of possibilities.

"And why will you be doing this?" said O'Toole.

"Because the recovery of those diamonds has entered a new phase, and my presence is no longer required in Springfield. Can't say I'm going to miss the shithole."

No one spoke for a minute. O'Toole leaned back in his chair and studied Grund. "It's a shame you won't make it to opening day," he said. "Good trout fishing around here.

I'll make sure you get a tourism brochure before you leave. What do you mean the recovery has entered a new phase?"

"Exactly that, Chief," said Grund. "In robbery situations like this, you hope for a quick recovery. That is the best-case scenario. The stolen property is returned, De Kirk endures a few days of unwanted publicity, and we continue on with our fuckin' business. Unfortunately, that hasn't happened. It's been more than three months, and our actuaries now tell us the best chance for De Kirk to be made whole is through compensation, not recovery."

"An insurance claim?" said Yakabuski. "Is that why we're here? So you can tell us you've filed an insurance claim?"

"Detective, we filed a claim with Great North Insurance the same week the diamonds were stolen."

"So what's changed?"

"Every fuckin' thing." Grund looked at each of them in turn. "You know the stats, Detective. If stolen property is not recovered in twenty-four hours, the odds of recovery are cut in half. And they keep dropping. Earlier this week, it became the opinion of our actuaries that we have a better chance of being made whole through an insurance claim than through salvage or recovery."

"Did they have the day marked on a calendar?"

"They *did*. They're actuaries. It's what they fuckin' do. The change happened this past Tuesday. On that day, all of our computer models had our best-case scenario shifting from recovery to compensation."

"So you're just walking away?" said O'Toole.

"Flight is already booked. Wings up at six."

With that, Grund rose and headed toward the door. He hadn't sworn all that much, for him, and he hadn't threatened anyone. Yakabuski knew what that meant. Grund was already gone. Springfield no more than a memory to him. Threats and profanity were what bullies used on people that mattered.

Before he reached the door, O'Toole said, "Who do we contact when we find those diamonds?"

"If it's before the insurance settlement you can contact me," said Grund. "If it's after the settlement, I don't give a fuck who you call."

And just like that, De Kirk was gone. Those missing diamonds had been converted to lines of code that had flown from one computer terminal to another, digital sub-particles that danced next to the old-school particles that formed the physical world; danced and spun until they changed shape and landed in the bank account of the De Kirk Mining Corporation as an insurance payout of $1.2 billion, plus accrued interest.

The modern world of high finance had done its digital alchemy and left behind an old-school fortune hidden somewhere in Springfield. A fortune De Kirk just threw away as casually as though those diamonds were litter thrown from a car; bright, shiny objects that caught the attention of people living in the hinterlands, far from the financial capitals of the world, the peasants and unsophisticates who still thought money was a tangible thing, who did ridiculous things like save it, who stood in valleys and fly-over fields and watched the taillights of fast-moving cars disappear over distant hills, walked slowly toward what had been thrown from the windows, quickening their pace when the objects began to twinkle and sparkle with the refracted light of a sinking sun.

CHAPTER TWENTY

When John Watkins and his brothers awoke they found Pete gone. Along with the pickup truck with the gas in it. They stared through the frosted windows of the farmhouse at where the truck should have been and shook their heads sadly. After that they moaned and, one by one, took turns throwing up in the bathroom. When the sun started to set and Pete had still not returned, John went to the barn and got a jerry can of gas, poured it into the tank of a Pontiac Sunbird he thought might start. Gave the car a boost off a tractor when it didn't. Then the brothers piled into the car and headed to Springfield.

They couldn't find Pete, but found a bootlegger in the French Quarter who agreed to sell them four bottles of rye whisky on credit. They searched for the girls after that but couldn't find them. They gave up searching and headed home.

Shadows fell across the dirt road when they turned off the highway. It was a waning moon and the sky had a blackish-yellow hue to it that seemed more autumnal than spring. There were no birds chirping. No insects calling out. No sounds at all, other than the crunch of the Pontiac's tires bouncing up and down the muddy ruts of the dirt road. When they cleared the last break of spruce, they saw the pickup truck in front of the farmhouse. Not parked where it should have been, but right next to the collapsed front stoop. Which was odd.

"Is he drunk?" said John.

"Don't care if he's drunk, sober, or passed out cold, that boy's gonna get a beat-down like he's never had a beat-down," said Brett. "Pete fuckin' knew that was the only truck with gas in it."

"Let's talk to him first. See why he left," said John. "Fuck, he's bought most of the booze since he showed up."

As the brothers exited the Sunbird, they adjusted the collars of their coats, stomped their feet to loosen the frozen denim of their jeans, blew air into their mitts. They were doing that, stomping and cradling their hands over their mouths, when a man screamed from inside the farmhouse.

They stared at each other in half-drunk confusion. Then they bumped into each other trying to jump up on the porch at the same time. It was Pete they saw first when they threw the door open. Standing in the living room, back to the door, arms bowed out to his side, left hand holding a claw hammer, his right a corkscrew. He was naked from the waist up, and the sweat and blood on his arms and back glistened in the weak light of the room.

He turned to his cousins and said, "'Bout time you got back."

"Fuck, Pete, what have you done?" yelled John.

"Moved this thing along. Did you bring back anything to drink?"

Pete turned and strode toward them. Only then did they see the rest of the living room. The blood splattered on the walls. The furniture overturned. And in the middle of the room, tied to one of the kitchen chairs, his blood-soaked head slumped over his chest, Eddie O'Malley.

The brothers stared at the doorman from the Silver Dollar in wonder. Didn't speak or move. It was the most marvellous, awesome, mystifying thing they had ever seen inside their farmhouse. Pete Watkins opened one of the bottles of rye and poured himself a drink. It was a long time before John Watkins found the words he thought were appropriate for the occasion.

"Fuck, Pete."

"Don't need to thank me, John. Wasn't as much work as you might think. He's a big bastard, but he's a fuckin' pussy."

"Is he alive?"

"He was a few minutes ago. Didn't you hear him scream?"

"Fuck, Pete . . . that's Eddie O'Malley. He's the doorman at the Silver Dollar."

"Makes sense. That's where I found him. Want to know where those diamonds are?"

"He told you where they are?" said Brett in astonishment.

"No. But he told me who could tell us. Ever hear of someone called Bobby Bangs?"

❖ ❖ ❖

The cousins left and returned in two hours. Pete Watkins watched a man with long blond hair follow them into the room. He wore a three-quarter-length leather jacket and was blowing warm air into his hands. He looked at Watkins, looked at O'Malley, and then he said with a laugh, "What the fuck did you think the bouncer knew?"

He was a couple inches shorter than Pete, but looked more muscular. His biceps pushed on the seams of his leather coat, and his shoulders were broad. There were marks on his face that could have been scars from an old knife fight, although there were so many of the marks, in such a criss-crossing pattern, it might have been something else. An industrial accident?

"What punk-ass shit is this?" yelled Pete, staring at his cousins in anger. "We don't need any more partners."

The cousins looked uncomfortable for a moment, but then the moment passed and John said, "Pete, you really fucked up. We were willing to play along with you, no harm no foul, you know, but you *really* fucked up, bro."

"Who is this guy? We're family, what the fuck have you done!"

"Pete, we don't know you that good."

John turned to look at his brothers and they nodded in agreement. Then they looked sad for a moment. Then they left the room.

Pete Watkins watched them walk away. The man with the long blond hair also watched. Pete could see now that there were tattoos on his neck, so many you couldn't see his Adam's apple unless he spoke. When they heard the engine of the pickup truck, he turned to Pete and said, "Family. It's a bitch sometimes, ain't it?"

"Those guys are my fuckin' cousins."

"John tells me you were here once, a decade ago. Be honest. You came back for the money. Got nothing to do with your family."

"How the fuck would you know?"

"How the fuck could you *not* know? Did you really think money was going to change your life? Money changes what you wear and where you sleep, doesn't change much more'n that."

"Bullshit."

"That's right. John tells me you grew up 'bout as dirt poor as dirt poor ever gets. Poor people never get it."

"Get what, motherfucker?"

"It ain't the thing you should die for."

Pete stared at him a second. "Who the *fuck* are you?"

"The man you were looking for." And with that, Bobby Bangs stood up and took a long Bowie knife from the pocket of his leather coat. He motioned for Pete to get on his knees.

As Pete lay on the living room floor of the farmhouse ten minutes later, he remembered the one and only time his father had visited him in prison. It was two months after he'd arrived at Bolton, and his father walked into the visiting room, sat the other side of the Plexiglas divider, took a photograph from his pocket and pushed it against the glass — the smiling face of that Legion Hall waitress.

"I loved her, and you took her from me," he said. "I hope you die in here you fuckin' bastard."

If Pete had found those diamonds, he was going to visit his father. See if the old man still felt that way. He was pretty sure things had changed. He was going to track down his mother too, see if she finally recognized him. After that they were going to spend time together, travel around, go places they never thought they'd ever see, just the two of them.

It annoyed Pete that this was not going to happen. He was just as annoyed his father was going to outlive him. Those were his last thoughts, his last emotions. When he'd run out of both, Bangs loaded his body into the bed of a Dakota pickup, covered it with tarps, and drove away.

CHAPTER TWENTY-ONE

The teenage boys sat around the campfire. The rings of shadow and light cast by the flames were brightest by the hearth, then darkened and fluttered away as they approached the mud fields of the La Vase Basin. Every object in the firelight had been subject to some degree of wavy distortion. The man in the tan windbreaker pushed the embers around in the fire and said, "We need to talk about those diamonds."

"What makes you think we're here because of the diamonds?"

"What makes you think you can lie to me?"

"Who the fuck *are* you? Do you live around here?"

"This would be a miserable place to live, don't you think? The ground swallows cars."

"If you think you can laugh at us and get away with it . . ."

"I think I can do whatever I wish to you and get away with it."

The boys sat in stunned silence. Cambino studied their faces. One by one. He had been taught the skill by his father a long time ago, what to look for in a man's face, the details that would tell you everything you needed to know. If you cleared your mind and did it right, in five seconds you could gather the essence of a man. It worked like Hemingway's one true sentence. If you had done the training, and were in the right place at the right time, you could catch it.

When he had finished studying the boys, he put another hardwood log on the fire. Began to whistle a tune that so perfectly mimicked the trilling of a night bird one flew onto a rock close to him, tilted its beaked head, then gave a startled flap of its wings and flew away. Cambino looked up at the four frightened faces and said, "I am curious. You are the children of rich families. This is obvious to me. If you can avoid addiction and bad women, bad friends and bad health, you will live pleasant lives. Why are you here?"

"You're kidding, right?"

"No."

"We're here because of one-point-two billion fuckin' dollars. Maybe you didn't know that's what those diamonds are worth."

"I'd heard something like that."

"That would set us up for life."

"But you are already set."

"Set, sure, but not jet-plane-rich set. Not buy-part-of-a-baseball-team set."

"The Marlins, man," said another of the boys, warming to the conversation. "You can buy them right now."

Cambino looked at the boy who had spoken, who wanted

to buy the Florida Marlins. He was the boy that had the boot-print on his cheek.

"How does it feel," he asked, "to know that one of your friends used you as a bridge to save his life?"

The boy didn't answer.

"That's what happened, right? You were in the lead vehicle, the one that sank, and you were slow to get out. The boy who climbed over you, the one who was on the ATV with you, it's that boy right there, right?"

Cambino pointed to the boy sitting closest to him. The boy with the boot-print on his cheek said, "It all happened so quickly."

"Yes it did. And he was quicker than you."

"Now hold on," said the boy Cambino had pointed at. "It *did* happen quick, like Robert said. I didn't even know what I was climbing over. There is no damn way I would ever—"

"Shut up," said Cambino. "That is a conversation you need to have another day. For what it is worth, I like your odds."

"My odds?"

"Yes, you may even be my favourite."

He smiled sweetly at the boys as he took a Buckmaster hunting knife from the belt-sheath under his windbreaker. He walked to the boy with the boot-print on his cheek and grabbed him by the hair. Then he lifted him up and slit his throat.

The other boys scrambled to their feet, but before they could run Cambino yelled "Stop!" and that's what they did. He hung onto the boy's hair, blood gushing down his chest and pooling on the ground, until there were no longer any tremors and then he let him fall.

He would have been the first to go, Cambino told himself, and he had no doubt of it. Although it did not matter to him, he also thought the boy would have preferred dying by his hand, instead of the hand of one of his friends.

He wiped his knife clean and threw it into the woods. The boys stared in surprise at the dark shadows where the knife would have landed.

"Forget 1.2 billion," he said. "The number that matters to you boys is one. That's the number of drivable ATVs you have left. And the number of witnesses I need to tell the story of what happened here tonight. I'll be waiting by the camp-fire. First to make it back gets the ATV."

He sat down. He wasn't sure if there would be any questions, but he thought not. They were smart boys and scared enough to figure it out. One of them already had the requisite intent. Cambino picked up a branch and started moving the embers in the fire around again. Without looking up, he said, "You can stand there staring at him as long as you want, but me, I would want to be the boy who finds that knife."

TWENTY-TWO

Yakabuski was walking through the rain. Spring was coming to the Northern Divide the way it did most years, with great hesitation, appearing and disappearing, tentative but holding promise, the seasonal equivalent of early love. Now the rains had come. He was walking Mission Road and there was more mud than snow now. The crime-scene tape that had been up more than a month had started to fade, no longer the same bright yellow as the slickers worn by the patrol officers walking grid formations in the rain. There was the smell of cedar and spruce gum, and somewhere a fire was burning.

The call came shortly after 8 a.m., as he was walking back to the trailhead. Yakabuski figured she didn't want Grace to hear, and didn't want to make the call from her desk at work. She was probably walking to the bus stop.

"Rachel," he said, bending his head to keep the phone out of the rain.

"I've heard from Linus," she said. "He's agreed to meet you. Tomorrow afternoon, on the portage trail under the North Shore Bridge. Do you know where Sleigh Bay is?"

"I do."

"That's where he'll meet you. Two o'clock. He asked that I come along. Is that all right?"

"It's fine with me. Do you *want* to be there?"

"Not really. But Linus wants it that way. And if it's going to help Grace, yes, I want to be there."

"Works for me. Do you need a drive?"

"Yes. I'm going to take the day off work."

"I'll pick you up at your apartment at one."

She didn't speak for a few seconds, and Yakabuski thought the call was about to end. But when the silence dragged on, he knew there was something more she wanted to say. He waited until she said, "I once thought my father could never be killed. *Gabriel Dumont.* King of the Travellers. It was unthinkable to me. The man who killed my father — in his own office, with nothing more than a knife — that would have to be a man of great skill and resolve, a dangerous man."

"I'd say you're right about that."

"It seems some days like Grace and I are surrounded by evil. I'm not sure why that's happened to us. I look for answers every day. Do you know where that man is today?"

"The man who killed your father?"

"Yes. When did you see him last?"

Yakabuski thought of the best way to answer the question. He knew Rachel Dumont was a hard woman to fool, and a woman impossible, likely, to placate with half-truths and kind acts of omission. She wanted the truth and would ferret it out soon enough. She also deserved the truth.

"Rachel," he said, looking out on the rain and the early-morning fortune seekers heading down the road in their slickers and boots, "we've *never* seen him."

❖ ❖ ❖

Yakabuski picked her up the following afternoon. The rain had subsided to a light drizzle, and a warm wind was blowing up the Northern Divide from the great lakes to the south. Earlier that morning, Yakabuski had heard the honking sounds of geese flying overhead, an anomaly, for it was still several weeks before they should be returning for the summer, but it was a sign of what was coming.

Dumont was dressed in jeans and a heavy wool sweater, Sorel boots on her feet and a bright red parka over her shoulders. It was the first time Yakabuski had seen her not in a dark skirt and blouse. She sat in the passenger seat of the Rubicon. Unlike most first-time passengers, she had not commented on the poor heating system, or the bucket seats that made not even a passing pretence of comfort.

Sleigh Bay was a quarter mile downriver from the North Shore Bridge. To get there, you needed to park in a lot then go down an old portage trail. They walked through a birch and spruce forest, the spruce green and lush looking from the rain, the gum already moving, a sweet scent you caught easily when the wind was blowing off the river. They had only been walking a couple minutes when Dumont said, "I googled you last week."

"Find anything interesting?"

"It was all interesting. Your war record. What happened at Ragged Lake. You've got a colourful background."

"Didn't set out with that as a goal."

"You remind me of men I used to know, the tough men from Fort Francis. Do you know what I mean by tough men?"

"I believe I do."

"Yes, you would. The tough men were the ones who worked in the bush camps and at the fishing lodges, men of great competence and skill that you never doubted, never wondered if they would find their way home in a bad storm, or disappear in the woods one day. Do you know what I remember best about those men?"

"I suspect you're going to tell me."

"It's what happened to them when they became old. They were men who had lived without family or companions, and so they were all sent to nursing homes, places they tried to run away from only to be brought back in their nightgowns and slippers by RCMP officers who rolled their eyes whenever they spoke."

"Why are you telling me this, Rachel?"

"Because you've been in my dreams recently. You were one of the tough men from Fort Francis. I wasn't sure if I was going to tell you about it. But then I thought maybe you should know."

"How many dreams have you had like this?"

"Three."

That was not a good omen. The worst possible. Yakabuski would need her to tell him if she had a fourth.

"You've taken these dreams as a warning I suppose?"

"I have. That's the other thing I remember about the tough men. They all had great situational awareness. That's the military term, right?"

"It is."

She pulled up her red parka hood to keep her hair from blowing. "They all had that. One of their great skills. They were never deceived about the world around them, always knew where they stood, and what was coming. Yet for some reason I've never understood, no tough man ever thought to use that skill on himself. Why do you think that is, Frank?"

It didn't sound to Yakabuski like a question that needed a fast answer. They made the rest of the hike in silence.

❖ ❖ ❖

Linus Desjardins was waiting for them at Sleigh Bay. He was a tall man, with long grey hair running halfway down his parka. He had good thick mitts but no toque. His boots were Sorels, and his pants were fleece-lined splash pants with the name of a fashionable outdoors store in Montreal embroidered on the right pocket. Yakabuski remembered Gabriel Dumont dressed in the hides and skins of animals — leather pants and breech-skin moccasins, beaver hat and the red sash of the voyageur dangling down his leg.

Linus Desjardins saw the world differently. Yakabuski could tell just by his clothes. He was staring at the North Shore Bridge, and they were standing on either side of him for several seconds before he said, "Boys used to swing off that bridge from a rope that hung beneath it. Do they still do that, Detective Yakabuski?"

"They do. The city cuts the rope down a couple times each summer, but a new one always shows up right after."

"It used to be a rite of passage for boys on the North Shore. You needed to jump out far enough that you wouldn't hit the bridge cable, but you had to get the angle just right, so when you hit the bottom the rope would swing out and not snap tight. There were a couple different ways that jump could kill you. The trick was knowing when to let go."

They stared at the bridge a little longer and Yakabuski said, "Are you suggesting I walk away from this mess? Is that the point of the story?"

"Not what I'm suggesting at all, Detective Yakabuski. In fact, the story has nothing to do with you. A common settler mistake." He smiled when he said it. Not a sneer. Not a gloat. An old man's bemused smile. "The story was meant to tell you what the Travellers will be doing. That's why you asked for this meeting, right?"

"You're letting go?"

"More or less. We are not looking for those missing diamonds, and we won't be."

Yakabuski took a closer look at him. The Travellers had been on the Northern Divide before there were permanent settlements, travelling with the French fur traders to protect their wares from marauding war parties of Mohawks and English privateers; mercenaries who practiced an arcane religion that pre-dated the birth of Christ. It was said Travellers never forgot a slight or an injustice and could wait generations to avenge a wrong.

"That surprises me," he said.

"Of course it does. You're a settler. One-point-two-billion dollars in riches from the land — how can you walk away from a thing like that? It would be impossible. That's the reason you're here. To take from the land. It's not the reason I'm here."

"Good speech, Mr. Desjardins. But the Travellers were trying to steal those diamonds, and they got played by Sean

Morrissey. Gabriel Dumont got killed. You're telling me you're just going to walk away from that?"

"Gabriel overreached. Many of us told him that was what he was doing, but he wouldn't listen. He saw that robbery as some sort of atonement for past wrongs. He used that word all the time. *Atonement.* I was worried about him long before he died."

He looked at Rachel Dumont after he said it. Bowed his head.

"I mean no disrespect, Rachel."

"You're telling the truth, Linus," she said. "There's no need to apologize."

"Maybe it *was* some attempt at atonement," said Yakabuski.

"No, it was just a jewellery heist," said Desjardins.

"Biggest one in history. You're underselling it a bit."

Desjardins looked at Yakabuski with a sad expression on his face. Then he said, "I think I could like you, Detective Yakabuski. I've heard good things about you, and Rachel speaks highly of you. But, my man, if you don't stop talking like some dumbass settler, I'm going to hit you."

The two men looked at each other. Yakabuski wondered what would happen if Desjardins went through with it. He had a good fifty pounds on the Traveller, but could tell he was quick and tough and the ensuing fight didn't seem like a gimme. A seventy-three-year-old man. It was inspiring in a way.

"You think money is here for a second," continued Desjardins. "If you don't grab it, you've lost it. Think if someone else grabs it, you need to grab it back. Do it today. Do it yesterday. Gabriel was beginning to think like that. His death cannot be forgotten, but that was how he was thinking at the end. Did you know it takes a billion years to make a diamond?"

Desjardins didn't come right out and say it, but the message was clear enough. The Travellers weren't going anywhere. The betrayal of Gabriel would be settled another day. And diamonds were nothing more than a passing glint. Even after a billion years.

"I agreed to this meeting so you can tell the Popeyes and the Shiners what I have just told you," said Desjardins. "We are not players in this. Tell them also that if they make another play for Grace Dumont, or her mother, it will be the last bad decision they ever make. They are Travellers, the children of Gabriel Dumont, and are under our protection."

It was strange to hear a Traveller use the word *Traveller*. The old man almost winked when he said it. Then he turned to take a last look at the North Shore Bridge. The steel was a slate grey that on a morning like this blended into the drizzling rain and the dull sky so it looked at times like the cars were suspended in air, toy cars floating across the river. Yakabuski looked at the bridge and waited for one to tip and fall.

"I'll make sure they know, Mr. Desjardins. So you're staying free and clear of this?"

"Oh yes. This rat fuck is all yours, Detective. Have fun."

He laughed, gave Rachel Dumont a hug, and then started down the old voyageur trail. After a hundred metres, he cut off into the bush and was gone.

CHAPTER
TWENTY-THREE

Yakabuski saw the video on YouTube the next day. Mid-morning, after returning from his daily inspection of Mission Road, and finding Donna Griffin waiting for him.

"There's something you have to see," she said, and she walked into his office, put her laptop on his desk. When she had the video called up, Yakabuski looked at the frozen image of a scared-looking young man in a University of Vermont sweatshirt. His hair was tousled, his eyes red-rimmed and bugging out. There was a thick sheen of sweat on his face although the ground around him was covered in snow and mud and you could see his breath.

"Before I play it, look at the ATV. Tell me if you see anything."

Yakabuski looked at the ATV in the top right corner of the screen. It was parked a few feet behind the boy. Was something showing in the side mirror? Yakabuski enlarged the frame until he could see a man's face. Not much of the face, really. Dark aviator glasses. Texas A&M ballcap.

"So we were right. He never left."

"You're going to want to sit down, Yak."

◆ ◆ ◆

"My name is Brady Dekker . . . I'm a sophomore at the University of Vermont. I came to Springfield to search for those missing diamonds. I came with Ryan Morrison, Josh Green, and Bobby Friedman."

The boy stopped talking. Looked around him. He had that look on his face people have when they're first pulled from a bad car crash.

"Tell us what you did to your friends, Brady," said the voice of a man you couldn't see on the video.

"I . . . I . . ." and he started to cry. "I was made to—"

"Leave that part out. It doesn't matter. Tell us what you did."

"I . . . I, fuck, I . . ."

"Going to be a short video, Brady."

"I killed them."

The boy looked straight into the camera after he said it, a surprised look on his face, as though the words were foreign or spoken by someone else. "I killed them," he said again. "Ryan Morrison and Josh Green — I killed them. Bobby Friedman got killed too."

◆ ◆ ◆

The rest of the video was hard to watch. Not only because of the story the boy told, but because Yakabuski knew how it was going to end. And only the most twisted and damaged among us enjoy movies like that.

Brady Dekker told how he and his three schoolmates came to Springfield after finding a treasure map online. They'd been on Mission Road, at the encampment, for four days when they rented ATVs, to help them in their search. One ATV sank in a field of mud. They were looking for a way to get it out when a man appeared.

"He said we shouldn't have come," said Dekker. "He said the diamonds didn't belong to us, and it was wrong to have come here looking for them. Then he killed Bobby."

Dekker stopped talking. Or stopped making sounds. His lips kept moving but the boy was mute. So shocked by the words he'd just spoken, his subconscious mind was trying to keep him from uttering any more.

"You need to keep talking, Brady."

The lips kept moving and in a few seconds the sound returned. The boy's subconscious had figured out the greater danger.

"The man said he would kill us all, or let one person live, to be a witness. He said there were no other choices. Just those two. I . . . I . . . ."

"Brady."

"I killed Josh after finding a knife in the woods. I stabbed him. I don't know how many times. I left his body in the mud. I found Ryan hiding under a bush. He wouldn't fight me. I told him he had to, but he wouldn't. I . . . the decision was his, not to fight."

"You're doing well, Brady. What else do you want to say?"

"Everyone that's here looking for those diamonds, you need to leave. If you stay, the man who made me do this will come looking for you. He's going to stay until everyone is gone. He's a serious man. He wants you to know this."

The boy stopped talking. Lips and sound this time. He stared at the camera. At a range of six feet, a bullet is instant death. The time to target, the thinnest shaving of an instant. So no eyes grew large. There was no startle. No fear. Dekker stared at the camera. Then his face exploded. Then he was gone.

CHAPTER TWENTY-FOUR

Wentworth was thirty miles from Springfield, built on an archipelago sticking out into Horsehead Bay. It was built in the late '30s, when the bandits and stickup gangs that roamed the Northern Divide during the Depression had been rounded up, fallen victim to an invasion of federal agents and better telephone communications. There wasn't a jail around that people felt comfortable putting them in, so they built Wentworth.

It was constructed with no thought to rehabilitation, comfort, or aesthetic. It was ugly and it meant it. Two cement-brick perimeter walls. Twelve turrets with gun slits. Barbed wire atop both the outer and inner walls. Whatever it took to make sure Ma Racine's four sons, the Cherry Hill Gang, Alvin Karpis, and any and all Shiners stayed locked up and out of view.

A young guard who knew Tyler Lawson met him at the front gate of the jail.

"Good morning, Mr. Lawson. You're here to see Mr. Morrissey?"

"That's right, Dan," and he passed over his driver's licence. The guard started writing down the information on a sheet of paper he had on a clipboard.

"The lot is pretty near full this morning, but if you give the keys to François, he'll squeeze you in."

"Thanks," said Lawson, taking back his driver's licence. As a defence lawyer, he could come to the jail to see a client any day of the week, but Morrissey had told him to come on visitors' day, Tuesday, so that's what he had done. It would make his visit longer, because of the other visitors the guards had to deal with, but he hadn't complained.

He gave his keys to the guard in a security booth by the second entrance, the one with a traffic bar that got raised for service vehicles and a tunnel running through the main wall of the jail for the pedestrians. He was wanded and patted and sent through three metal detectors before he reached the interview rooms in the west wing of the prison.

Lawson had scheduled a conference call, which meant he was taken to one of the private interview rooms, not one of the cubicles that lined the walls of the visiting room. He was still separated from his client by a sheet of Plexiglas, but there were desks on either side of the glass, where you could lay out legal papers, and speakers were suspended from the ceilings. The walls in the room were a dingy off-white, still nicotine-stained from when you could smoke inside, which would have been nearly two decades ago. Compared to the rest of Wentworth, it was cheery.

Lawson had to wait nearly twenty minutes for Sean Morrissey to be brought in. Another consequence of a Tuesday visit. Any other day of the week, it would have taken less than ten. A door on the far wall of the room the other side of the Plexiglas opened, and there was Morrissey.

He was in his mid-forties and there was grey showing in his hair, the first signs of a jowl appearing beneath his chin. But not much grey and not much jowl. He must have been lifting weights every day, thought Lawson, marvelling at the size of his arms, the thick muscle that had become his neck. He was dressed in an orange jumpsuit and white sneakers, the sleeves of the jumper rolled up so you could see the Celtic cross tattoos and the slithering snakes, the angels and gargoyles.

His hands were cuffed behind his back, and the guard that followed him into the room tossed a folder on a desk and pointed to a chair. When Morrissey was beside the chair, the guard unlocked the cuffs and he sat down, giving his wrists a quick rub. The guard, who was older than most of the staff at Wentworth, pushed a button on a speaker fastened to the wall and said, "Can you hear me, Mr. Lawson?"

"I can."

"We have your call booked for eleven, is that correct, Counsellor?"

"That's correct."

"You've done these conference calls before?"

"I have."

"You don't need to use the phone," the guard continued, as though Lawson had not answered. "The call will be piped through the speakers. The speakers are activated now, Mr. Lawson, so you can talk to your client while you're waiting. The person we are to be phoning is Alison Demers, a lawyer with the firm of Lawson and Associates. Phone number is 592-737-5549. Is this correct?"

"Yes it is."

"You have informed the warden of the Wentworth Correctional Facility that Ms. Demers represents Mr. Morrissey and this is a privileged call. Has this changed?"

"It has not."

"Then your conference call will not be monitored by the Department of Corrections, nor will the Department of Corrections allow any other government agency to monitor this call. When your associate ends the call, the privilege for outside calls to Mr. Morrissey will cease. Is this understood?"

"It is."

"When we have Ms. Demers on the line, the call will be routed to this room. Speak as though on a regular conference call. Again, there is no need to touch the phone."

Lawson nodded and the guard left the room. Morrissey watched him leave. Then he turned away from the door, smiled, and said, "Tyler, nice of you to drop by."

"Nice of you to invite me."

The two men chuckled, and Lawson opened his briefcase, took out some file folders, and spread them over the desk. Morrissey did likewise, with the file folder the guard had placed on his desk. They looked at their papers and didn't speak. A few minutes later, they heard a woman's voice: "Tyler, are you there?"

"Hi, Alison. I'm here. Mr. Morrissey is here with me as well."

"Hello, Sean."

"Hello, Alison."

"If you have the files in front of you, Alison, we can begin."

"I have them right here, Tyler. Would you like to start with the release conditions Corrections wants to place on Sean? It's absolutely draconian, what they are suggesting."

"Yes, let's start there."

Alison Demers started reading from emails the law firm had received from Correctional Service. Lawson looked at his watch while she spoke. He had gone through the case law, and there was one case in British Columbia where the government had tried to get a privileged jail-house phone call submitted as evidence in a criminal trial, arguing the cops mistakenly recorded the first four minutes of the conversation — no intent, in other words — and what they recorded clearly showed the lawyer was as much of a crook as his client, so no privilege should apply.

They almost got away with it. What saved the lawyer was an appeals judge ruling that four minutes was too long a time to be an honest mistake. That set the benchmark. Lawson gave it five minutes, just to be safe, then he said, "I think that should do it, Alison. Is Mr. Bangles there with you?"

"He is."

"Can you confirm he knows not to talk until you have left the room?"

"We've discussed it, Tyler. He knows."

"Let's do it then."

Lawson walked to the speaker on the wall of the interview room and turned the volume to zero. He went back to the table, pulled more papers from his briefcase, and started to read.

Let's do it? When had he started talking like that?

"Sean, are you there?"

"Bobby, it's good to hear your voice."

"Yours, too, Sean."

Morrissey leaned back in his chair. He put his hands behind his back, knotted his fingers, the muscles in his biceps rippling whenever he tightened the grip or moved his head.

"You said it was urgent, Bobby. What's happening?"

"The Popeyes have made a move against us. They went after the girl."

"Because of that diamond you gave her."

"Yes."

"That was a mistake."

"No. The mistake was going after the girl."

"You made her a target, Bobby. It was a complication we didn't need."

"I don't see the complication. They come after you. We'll slap them down."

Morrissey laughed. Took his hands from behind his head and put them on the desk. He gave his arms a quick squeeze, like a mini push-up, then started moving papers around. "Might as well give me the full sitrep," he said.

Bangles started with the attack on Grace Dumont, then told Morrissey about the Grainger Hotel being full and some sort of gold rush camp out on Mission Road, more people coming every day. He said a map had been posted online and there was no stopping people now, things were getting out of control, probably why the Popeyes made a move for the girl, thinking this whole thing could go south in a hurry. Then he told him about the YouTube video.

"So he's here."

"He's always been here, Sean. It's all those people on Mission Road. They forced his hand. He's been waiting for you."

Sean Morrissey thought back to the last call he'd had with Cambino Cortez, the morning after the robbery, when he had phoned to make arrangements to get him his share of the diamonds and Cambino had said, as casually as though he were ordering a coffee, that he would need to have all of the diamonds. It was bounty of the land, and Morrissey didn't have the right to claim it. That's what he'd said. Some crazy talk Morrissey couldn't follow.

"He's trying to clear the field before I'm released," he said.

"Looks that way. He won't get anywhere fuckin' near you, Sean. I can promise you that."

"There are people we do business with who think he's a demon, Bobby. Some sort of fuckin' spirit that can never be caught."

"You got to be on the other side to meet demons, Sean. On this side, *we're* the demons. I have an idea what we can do about him. The Popeyes too."

Morrissey looked around the room, at Tyler Lawson the other side of the Plexiglas, the dirty white brick walls, the speaker protected by a wire cage thicker than a baseball catcher's, the bolted-to-the-ground desk he sat behind. Eventually he said, "Go ahead, I'm listening."

❖ ❖ ❖

Tyler Lawson sat in a silent room with a door he couldn't open, a familiar face the other side of separated space he couldn't touch, terrified he might hear a human voice, for any overheard word right then would probably end badly for him. It reminded him of a scene from a bad dream, although much of his life now resembled a scene from a bad dream and maybe that wasn't saying much. The absurdity of this particular day was hard to ignore though — a mute lawyer in a silent room.

He picked up some papers from the desk and smiled for the camera.

❖ ❖ ❖

"It's a good plan," said Morrissey. "Use our enemies against each other. Yes, a good plan. I'm going to need you though, Bobby, when I get out of here. I'm wondering if we should wait."

"I don't think we can. The Popeyes can't be the only ones who know about Grace Dumont. There must be more than a hundred tents out on Mission Road, with more people coming every day. Linus Desjardins has been in Springfield too. He met with that bohunk cop that arrested you. We don't know why."

"Yakabuski?"

"Yeah, that's the guy."

"When did this happen?"

"Two days ago. Real private meeting. Underneath the North Shore Bridge. The girl's mother was there as well."

"What the fuck are they doin'?"

"Who the fuck knows? That's what I'm telling you, Sean. This thing could blow any day, in any fuckin' direction."

"The cops are still on Mission Road? They're not searching anyplace else?"

"Not that we've seen. But Sean — so fuckin' what? I'm getting tired of putting out fires and checking out what other people are doing. I think it's time we reminded people whose show this is."

"What you're suggesting is crazy, Bobby. And you're telling me you don't want a crew, don't want anyone helping you. That's beyond crazy."

"It'll seem crazy to them too. That's why it'll work. But we gotta move now, Sean, before things get any more complicated."

After thinking about it a few minutes, Morrissey said, "That's exactly what your uncle would have said."

"Tommy? Fuck, he'd've already done it."

CHAPTER
TWENTY-FIVE

People were leaving the squatters' camp. When Yakabuski arrived that morning, he could hear the snap of fly-poles being taken apart, see brightly coloured sheets of nylon and Gore-Tex spread out in the mud, waiting to be rolled up and put into a bag. The YouTube video had made the rounds before it was taken down.

In the parking lot, cars were pulling out and people were hugging. Families for the most part, and that made sense. It was time to get the children out of here. Rain was falling, and Yakabuski knew what that was like, breaking camp in the rain. You tried as best you could to stay dry, keep the gear dry, the sleeping bags dry, but it was an impossible task. Some people accepted that. Most didn't. Breaking camp in the rain was a miserable experience for all sorts of reasons, futility being one of the most obvious.

By noon the families were gone. Most of the retirees went at the same time, and that didn't surprise Yakabuski either. People became cautious as they got older. It's not that you slow down, the way he once thought; he was getting old enough to see that. Most old-timers were capable enough. It's more that they'd done the math and weren't sure they had the years left to recover from one more bad decision. So they stayed between the lines. Walked away when trouble arrived, knowing they probably didn't have the time anymore to play with it.

In a sane world, that video should have scared everyone away. But Yakabuski knew some people would stick around. The covetous ones, whose world had shrunk to nothing more than dreams of finding diamonds, they would be staying. So would the young ones, who knew the fate of the four students from the University of Vermont would never be their fate. The desperate ones would be staying, and they would be in the majority, those who had convinced themselves those diamonds were their last good shot at a better life. A strange conviction to hold when you're lying in a wet tent pitched in a parking lot on the Northern Divide, but he knew desperate people never saw world the way it was.

Yakabuski had his morning debrief with the Ident sergeant. They were two miles down the road now, another mile to go before they reached the outer limit of the search area. The La Vase Basin lay two miles past that, where other police officers were now searching, and when the sergeant asked Yakabuski if the bodies of the four students had been located he said no. The sergeant gave his head a sad shake.

"Those boys were never going to find any diamonds," he said. "They weren't anywhere close to the right area. Two miles past it."

He spoke as though this made their deaths sadder somehow, the pointlessness of it. Yakabuski wasn't sure if it made much difference. If you shed more tears for the soldiers who died in pointless battles, you'd never stop crying.

"We located their ATV," said Yakabuski. "No sign of the boys."

"They can't be that far."

"Hard to say. The man who killed them knows how to make bodies disappear."

"And he's got an ocean of mud to work with."

"That he does."

He hiked down the trail after that to where the teams were working. Patrol officers were trying to walk a grid formation through a forest of mud and glacier-deposited boulders, the lines impossible to keep, the cops even bumping into each other from time to time. Two Ident cops walked behind them, sweeping the ground with hand-held sonar machines. Some conservation officers were working the other side of the trail, looking for signs of recent digging, scanning the trees for ropes or pulleys.

There had been full departmental meetings to debate the best way to search for the missing diamonds, and this is what Newton and his team had come up with. Yakabuski couldn't think of a better way either. Only reason he didn't scream, or want to hit something, every time he saw how easy it would be to miss those diamonds. But you had to do something. No cop out here was getting paid to throw his hands up and quit. So you searched, and maybe you'd get lucky, but Yakabuski was becoming more convinced by the day that those rocks would never be found by a patrol cop walking a grid. It would be different than that, the next time anyone saw the diamonds.

When he was back at the parking lot, he spoke again with the duty sergeant. Took a last look around the trailhead parking lot. Most of the fortune hunters that were staying were already in the forest, but one man sat by his cook-fire. He was drinking a coffee. Looking at Yakabuski.

He got up and walked over, raised his coffee cup, and said, "You're Yakabuski, ain't ya?"

"I am. Frank Yakabuski. What's your name, sir?"

"Tom Flanagan."

"You're not joining the search today, Mr. Flanagan?"

"Ahh, I'm in no hurry. How long is this rain going to last, you figure?"

"Weather reports say two days. That looks about right."

"But you never know."

"You never know."

The man laughed and took a sip of his coffee. Yakabuski figured he was middle-aged, somewhere in his early forties, but he looked older. Deep lines in his face. A nose that had been broken a few times.

"Have you seen that YouTube video, Mr. Flanagan?"

"I have."

"Lots of people leaving because of it. Might be a smart idea to join them."

"You know the guy who did that to those boys?"

"I do. He's not a man you'd ever want to meet."

"And he's out there. Down that road."

"He was. Less than six miles from here."

"How many boys got killed?"

"Four."

The man thought about that. Then he finished his coffee, threw the grounds in the bottom of the cup into his cook-fire, stomped out the embers, and hoisted his backpack.

"You're going out?"

"I guess so. Four don't seem enough to stop."

CHAPTER
TWENTY-SIX

Bangles cased the Popeyes clubhouse for six days. The first two were long-range reconnaissance, some drive-bys of the clubhouse in a taxi, one lunch at a diner on Lacasse, a street one over from Ladoucer, with a view into the backyard of the clubhouse. He walked down the street twice, stopping once right out front to tie his boots.

On the third morning, he moved to the roof of an abandoned warehouse two doors down the street from the clubhouse. He brought with him provisions for four days, along with a pair of Bushnell 200x field glasses, a plastic pail, and sleeping bag. He did not bring a notebook or computer, as his memory was excellent and he had never needed such tools.

There was what looked like a security hut on the roof of the clubhouse, but he knew by the end of his first day atop the warehouse that it was a decoy. He never saw a man positioned inside. The garage affixed to the clubhouse was a sort of decoy as well, staffed only with two old mechanics and a female receptionist during business hours, but many different mechanics at night, starting around midnight, and for the next six hours it was a busy garage.

Four men lived permanently inside the clubhouse, and by the third day atop the roof, Bangles had located the bedrooms and the common living areas. Just like the garage, most of the visitors to the clubhouse came after the sun went down, strippers each night, and lots of men driving BMWs and Italian sports cars, some full-patch members who normally showed up after the strippers. Traffic during the day was lighter, and the visitors were different: no women; most driving American sedans and looking like the prosperous, middle-aged men you see entering law offices and corporate boardrooms in downtown Springfield.

As for Henri Lepine, he arrived at the clubhouse every morning shortly after ten and stayed till midafternoon. Then he came back near midnight and stayed for another two hours. Which meant Bangles had a choice. A daytime attack would be easier. Fewer people, and the men who lived there permanently did not seem to be operating with any sort of security protocols. They left the clubhouse during both day and night. The times were random and uncoordinated. If he timed it right, there might be fewer than a half-dozen people inside the clubhouse when he came for Lepine.

Evening at the clubhouse was a different matter. A carnival run by meth-heads. Lots of people and lots of moving pieces. On two of the nights he was atop the roof, there had even been a marked police car that made a regular patrol down the street.

Daytime or nighttime? Bangles considered it. If he had

seen any sign of professionalism from the bikers, he might have made a different decision, but knowing the risk was slight either way, he decided there was something to be said for making a statement. His whole plan, in fact, was rather premised around making a statement, so why be shy?

He waited until the sun was down. Waited until the mechanics and hookers had returned, along with the expensive sports cars and the full-patch bikers, and twenty minutes after Henri Lepine arrived, Bangles climbed down from the roof of the warehouse.

He took what he needed from his kit bag, and hid it behind a dumpster. Then he walked to the front door. He needed to be buzzed in, and Bangles held his finger on the button for several seconds before letting go. A red light on a security camera above the door started to blink. Bangles looked up at the camera and smiled. Pushed the button again.

"All right, all right, are we not fuckin' fast enough for you? Who the fuck are you?"

A man's voice. Coming from a small Bose speaker above the camera.

"Robert Bangles. I'm here to see Lepine."

Several seconds passed. The red light kept blinking.

"Robert Bangles? That's Bobby Bangs, right? Did I hear that right?"

"I didn't write the song. Go tell Lepine I'm here."

The voice from the speaker was angry when Bangles heard it next. "I don't know what the fuck you're doing, buddy, but you are wasting my time. 'Cause if you're really Bobby Bangs, you are a dead man. I tell Lepine you're here, he's going to tell me to shoot you. I should probably be shooting you already, just for saying shit like that."

"That would be a mistake. I think what I have to say to Lepine would be of great interest to him. Go tell him I'm here."

"You're fuckin' whacked. Some whacked, drunken Shiner."

"A Shiner, yes, but a poor one. I hope one day to change that."

Several more seconds passed, and when the voice came back it was different; smug, the way Bangles knew it would be. The sentry now thought of him as a man willing to betray his boss, and men without loyalty could always be treated with disrespect, especially by those who shared the trait.

"My, my, Bobby Bangs, ain't you something? Stay right there, and I'll get Lepine."

"I'd rather wait inside."

"Yeah, I guess you would."

There was a loud click, and Bangles put his hand on the old-fashioned brass doorknob. He turned it and saw it gave way easily. He turned until the deadbolt was free of the trap and then he nudged the door until it was almost free of the frame. After that he stepped back.

He had debated whether to wait in the lobby until someone came to bring him upstairs to see Lepine. He would get a good sense of the floor plan that way.

But he already had a good sense of the floor plan.

He unbuttoned his coat, adjusted the full-harness shoulder strap he was wearing, pulled two Glock 17 pistols from the front pockets of his coat, and kicked open the door.

❖ ❖ ❖

The man who should have been stationed inside the door wasn't there. Bangles looked around in a panic and then saw him sitting on the stoop of a spiral staircase. Bangles fired two bullets into the biker's face, just as he was beginning to rise. The two girls he had been sitting with jumped up, and Bangles dropped them right to left, a short blonde with spiky hair going down first, then a tall brunette.

With his left hand, he fired the other Glock blindly at sounds coming from the parlour, and when the two women were down, he pivoted. Another tall brunette slid down a wall, leaving behind blood splatter that looked the Tree of Life in a bad storm. A man who'd been sitting in the parlour was jumping up from a couch. A stupid man. Trying to pull up his jeans. Bangles fired two rounds into his head and he fell back on the couch, his pants dropping back around his ankles.

When the parlour and landing were clear, he threw off his coat and took the Uzi smg from its shoulder holster. He fired two quick rounds into the air, to freeze anyone upstairs that might have been thinking about coming down. Then he heard a noise in the kitchen and ran toward the back of the house. The kitchen had the only other exit from the clubhouse, and if anyone got outside this was going to end badly for him.

When he got there, he saw two bikers trying to get out the back door, one giant of a man in front, blocking the way, the other man trying to crawl up his back. Bangles dropped them both with a single burst from the Uzi. It was the dumb-biker equivalent of swimming in a barrel. He smiled and left the kitchen, walked back to the foyer.

He counted the stairs and estimated the height from stoop to upper floor landing of the spiral staircase at twelve feet. Probably exactly twelve feet. Only take a few seconds to reach the second floor. More than enough.

He went to the coat he had thrown off and turned out an inner pocket. Two stun grenades rolled into his hand and he went back to the staircase. He was about to throw the first when a thought came to him. A crazy thought. One that would never work and made no sense at all, but the more he thought about it the more he started to think it would be crazier not to try. You never know.

He did some quick math and yelled: "Seven dead down here. No one got out. No cavalry coming. I'm here for Lepine. What happened down here couldn't be helped, but nobody else has to die." Anyone wants to bug out, they can do it now. It's only Lepine that needs to stay.

Crazy. That anyone would give up a defensible position on high ground to surrender to a sole attacker. He was wasting his time. He tossed one of the stun grenades up and down in his hand, judging the height one more time, and just then he heard a door on the second floor open. He saw a man and woman come running from a bedroom. They ran with their hands above their heads, screaming, the man in the lead.

They came down the stairs and then ran behind Bangles and stopped, their hands on their knees, gasping for breath. The man was middle-aged and had a toupée. Bangles could see it easily, hunched over as he was. The woman was a stripper he had seen a few times at the Silver Dollar.

"Thank you. We're just here to buy drugs," said the man. "We know nothing about nothing, and we are so fuckin' out of here, I am not even looking at your face, bro."

Bangles took one of the Glocks from the waistband of his jeans and shot the man through his toupée. He put a bullet in the woman before she had a chance to scream, her face raised to him just before he shot her, a physical reaction from the propulsion waves of the first shot, no real awareness of what was about to happen.

Bangles looked at their bodies and shook his head in amazement. It's true. *You never know.*

He pushed his earplugs in a little deeper, pulled the stun grenade pins, and threw both flashbangs onto the second-floor landing, toward the back office, fairly confident there was no one left in the front bedroom. The noise was still painful, but tolerable, and he was up the stairs in under three seconds. By his count, there could be no more than four men left, including Lepine. If they were complete fools — a strong possibility — they'd all be clustered in the back office, though it was likely Lepine had someone in the back office and another man or two in the security room. The *second-floor* security room. It was hard for Bangles to believe parts of what he was seeing.

In a few seconds, when the bikers had recovered from the stun grenades and figured out he was standing alone in the hallway, they would come barrelling out of that security room. Bangles didn't plan on waiting. He lowered his Uzi SMG and fired into the exterior wall of the room. Chest high. The bullets ripped through the lath and plaster as easily as if the walls were corrugated cardboard. He heard men screaming and heavy objects falling to the floor, what might have been a landline telephone getting shot up, bells tinkling like crazy, paper whirling and making the sound a large bird might make if it flew too close to your head.

He fired another burst, knee height now, and heard more screaming, then the door at the end of the hallway opened and he fired at that, too, everything moving fast now, objects blurring, floating away, no gravity anymore it seemed. Was that a man who went flying back from the open door of the office, a fluttering red streamer arcing behind his head, body splayed in the shape of an X? The smoke was so thick in the narrow hallway Bangles couldn't tell.

He moved through the smoke, in a defensive crouch for the first time since entering the clubhouse. Turning his body from side to side, his gun rock-steady at twelve o'clock, heading toward the back office. When he reached the door, he fired a burst into the room, then tucked and rolled the rest of the way in. He jumped up, but didn't fire. Henri Lepine was standing at the other end of the room, also holding an assault rifle, also not firing.

The two men stared at each other a second. Then Bangles put the safety on, sat on an undamaged chair, and said, "Lepine, I need you to phone Papa for me."

TWENTY-SEVEN

The voice was incredulous. "Someone did what?"

"Killed them all, Papa. I don't know how many," Henri Lepine answered.

"He's there with you now? You're looking at him *right now*? Why aren't you trying to kill the fuckin' son of a bitch?"

"Papa, please . . ."

"Please! You're standing in *my* fuckin' shoes, you speak for fuckin' *me*, you just let an attacker into my fuckin' clubhouse and you're sayin' *fuckin' please*? If I were there right now, Lepine, I would fuckin' . . ."

Henri Lepine closed his eyes and pretended not to hear what Papa Paquette would do if he were standing there right now. He was just glad Papa had answered his phone. Lepine figured he would be dead right now, if Papa had not taken the risk.

He waited until there was a pause in the death threats, and then speaking quickly, he said, "It was Bobby Bangs."

There was silence for a few seconds. "What did you just say?"

"I said it was Bobby Bangs. The man who did this."

"He's the one in the office with you right now?"

"Yes. He wants to talk to you."

Lepine handed the phone to Bangles. Then he stood there wondering what to do next. He didn't want to sit. Didn't think he could leave. Bangles put the phone to his ear and said, "Papa."

"Is this really Bobby fuckin' Bangs?"

"I didn't write the song. My name is Robert Bangles."

"Well, whatever the fuck you're called, you are a dead man. Do you hear me?"

"Twelve."

"What?"

"Twelve. That's the number Lepine couldn't come up with. Twelve people dead in your clubhouse. You're threatening to kill me? I find that fuckin' funny."

"You whacked-out son of a bitch. The day I get my *fuckin'* hands on you—"

"Is the day I have to kill you, Papa. I've gone to a lot of trouble to get your attention. Maybe you should hear what I have to say."

"Your last words? Go ahead. Give them to me."

"I came here tonight to offer you a deal. You can't take those diamonds from Sean. I've just shown you that. But you can still get a taste of them. You can get that by providing a service. If you are able to provide this service, Sean will pay you fifteen percent of the net value of those diamonds. We're estimating a sixty percent brokerage fee."

"Sixty percent? You think that's what you're going to get? On diamonds as hot as yours?"

"The diamonds are untraceable, as you know. Soon as they're out of Springfield, it's no longer a problem. Yes, we expect to get sixty percent."

There was silence on the phone, and Bangles knew what Paquette was doing. He waited a few seconds and said, "One hundred and eight million dollars. We'll round it up to a hundred and ten. That's what you'll get."

"Long fuckin' way from $1.2 billion, pal. Sean should have done that score with us. We've been doing business for years. It was disrespectful, leaving us out of it."

"It was his score, Papa. And the disrespect was yours, when you went after the girl. Don't do that again. The deal I'm offering is one you should take. One hundred and ten million is also a long fuckin' way from twelve dead and fuck-all to show for it."

"You come and pull a full fuckin' op in *my* clubhouse, in my *fuckin' clubhouse*, and now you want to become business partners?"

"I do. And for $110 million, you can hold your fuckin' nose. This can end tonight. You have Sean's word on that. It doesn't have to be a war. You were aiming to do him harm, and you just got slapped down. Doesn't have to be anything more than that. I'm offering you an opportunity to turn a rat-fuck embarrassment into a payday."

"And just who would we have to fuckin' kill for this payday? That's what we're talkin' 'bout, right?"

"Someone who is difficult to kill, unfortunately."

"That whack-job Mexican."

"Yes."

"Sean is that worried about the guy?"

"He's not worried. He's prudent. If you can get rid of this man, it is worth $110 million to him. Of course, if you don't think you can provide this service, I'll shoot Lepine and be on my way."

Papa laughed. Lepine glared at Bangles but didn't say anything. "You are one crazy motherfucker," Papa said. "I thought your uncle was crazy, but you might be more coco than Tommy."

"Wasn't ever anyone more coco than Tommy. Do we have a deal?"

"Do you even know where the bastard is?"

"Last we heard, he was somewhere on Mission Road."

❖ ❖ ❖

The next day, the bodies were rolled into sleeping bags and moved to the garage. It took a full week to get rid of them. They were taken out in minivans, weights tied to their ankles, the bodies dumped downriver from the Kettle Falls after being removed from the sleeping bags because the Popeyes knew down filling had surprising buoyancy. Something you learned over the years.

The minivans were junked at a yard near Buckham's Bay, and the clubhouse was repaired by a general contractor who was also a two-patch member. No one came looking for any of the dead bikers. Nor the women. The man who had been there to buy drugs was reported missing by his ex-wife

three days later, and there were news stories for a while —
including a television feature a month after he disappeared,
with yearbook photos and an interview with his two young
daughters, who looked sad and slightly embarrassed their
father was missing. There was nothing after that.

And so, it passed. The Popeyes began searching for
Cambino the first week of April.

CHAPTER
TWENTY-EIGHT

Jason McAllister's body was found one week later. Yakabuski was on Mission Road, walking through the squatters' camp, when he got the call. An Ident officer told him what had happened, and that Inspector Newton wanted to see him as soon as possible.

"Where is it again?" asked Yakabuski, and then he shook his head, put the phone back in his pocket, and started walking. A light rain started falling, but he kept going. The spruce was so thick on this part of the trail the rain barely made it to the ground. He picked his way from rock to rock, trying to avoid the mud, and a half mile down the trail he turned off on a loop that went to McGregor Lake. He found Fraser Newton kneeling by the shoreline of the lake, next to a large, glacier-era boulder.

"This is for real?" said Yakabuski when he strode up to him.

"This is for real," answered Newton, getting to his feet.

"Half a mile off Mission Road? Not more than a mile from where we've been searching for diamonds the past month?"

"I'm afraid so."

Yakabuski knelt and looked at the body. It was wrapped in a sleeping bag, but the head was showing. McAllister looked peaceful and relaxed, as though he had lain down only moments ago, just picked an odd place to do it. His eyes held no terror, no ugly premonition, eyes that had not milked over in the cold but were clear and still able to refract the sun. It was possible to stare at Jason McAllister a long time before noticing the axe stroke cleaved in the back of his head.

Newton stood behind Yakabuski while he inspected the body. The sky was a faded-denim blue, and white geese flew overhead. The few clouds in the sky were the high cumulus ones you see in cartoons. It was not the sort of day you wanted to find a body.

"How long?"

"Probably since he was reported missing. A couple of fishermen found him earlier this morning. They were coming in to check out the lake, getting ready for opening day."

"How did we miss it?"

"Good spot to hide a body. Any snow around that boulder would have been the last to melt. He was also drenched in gasoline. Can't smell it much now, but he would have been covered in it when he was left here."

"Dogs were useless."

"Just a lot of barking."

Yakabuski looked again at the tranquil face of Jason McAllister. He had spoken to his mother earlier in the week. She phoned every week, was a tenured professor at the University of Pennsylvania, in the mathematics department.

She had helped her son do the calculations for the map he'd posted one week after he went missing. The guilt for that mother, as soon as he phoned with the news, would be eternal. The only story that would matter, from now until the day she died. The full life she once had would soon be a memory too painful to ever want to recall. No sentence ever passed by a judge would equal what he was about to give that woman when he placed his call. He looked out on the lake. It was open in the middle, but still ringed by several feet of ice along the shore. Not a lake, probably, that you could fish on opening day. He didn't know if the story needed any more unlikely absurdities, but there was one more. After a while he turned and said, "What can you tell me about the second body?"

"Come, I'll show you."

They walked around the boulder to the other side. The face on the second body had none of the tranquil disconnect of Jason McAllister. Another young man, about the same age, but there the similarities ended. This body was covered with poorly inked tattoos, right up to the cheekbones. The hair was shorn so short it was sharp bristles you wouldn't want rubbing against your skin. And the face was mutilated. Beaten and pummelled yet, judging by the bloodstains on the parka, not even the reason he died.

"He's been stabbed?"

"More than a dozen times, I'd say."

"Ever seen two bodies look more different, Newt?"

"Not at the same crime scene I haven't."

"One man gets beaten and tortured, the other one dies neat as you'd ever want. Any ID on the second body?"

"Nothing. But I figure those tattoos are going to help.

Want to make a bet Griffin has a mug shot by the end of the day?"

"Don't think I'll take that bet."

Newton joined Yakabuski in looking out on McGregor Lake. Grey jays were buzzing around a clump of tall white pine on the far shore, busy building their spring nests. It was the first day of the year that had the tangible promise of spring, instead of the imaginary promise people carried around in their heads most of the winter. Yeah, not the sort of day you would want to find a body, although a second later Yakabuski had trouble thinking of the day that *would* be good. Some thoughts weren't worth the time they took to fly through your head. Most thoughts of regret fell in that category, he supposed.

"You've got an odd one here, Yak," Newton said finally. "I agree with you about the victims. They couldn't look more different. But it can't be a coincidence, both bodies being found in the same location. They're connected."

"I agree. Maybe the connection isn't the killer."

"How can it not be? Why come back here, if you're not the person who did the first murder?"

"Come back here? What are you talking about?"

"That's the other difference, Yak. This man was not killed on the Mission Road. He was dumped here."

"You're sure about that?"

"Until I get exact cause of death for these two, it's maybe the only thing I am sure about."

❖ ❖ ❖

The bodies were brought out on gurneys carried by patrol cops because there was no way you could wheel anything down Mission Road right then. Yakabuski waited until the bodies were loaded into ambulances and the vehicles had left the parking lot, swirling red lights fading in the rain and then disappearing past a stand of spruce. On the way to his Jeep, Yakabuski saw Tom Flanagan, on his knees, rolling up his red nylon tent. His travelling pack was leaned against a cedar, a green garbage bag and ropes laid beside it. Flanagan worked without a hat, and his hair was drenched, wet pelts that fell across his face.

"You're leaving, Mr. Flanagan?"

"I reckon I am."

"That surprises me. I had you pegged for last man out."

"I might be damn near it. Seen many people on the trail today?"

Yakabuski thought back to the hike down the Mission Road, following the two bodies, his head turned down for most of it because of the rain, but he didn't miss much in the woods, and now that he stopped to think about it, he hadn't seen anyone.

"What made you change your mind?"

"Don't know if I have changed it. I was always willing to go so far. Don't want to go any further."

"There's a line you won't cross."

"Don't know if it's all that grand. Things seem different now. I figure it's time to go."

Flanagan put the tent in a compression sack and placed it on top of his travelling pack. He got the garbage bag and rope and began to tarp everything up. Without looking at Yakabuski, he said, "I counted two bodies you brought out. Is that right?"

"That's right."

"Yeah, it's time to go."

"Because of those bodies? You kept searching when we had four bodies."

"Four ain't six, is it, Detective Yakabuski?"

Yakabuski watched him walk out of the parking lot, following the road the ambulance had taken. He thought of offering him a ride into Springfield, but knew he wouldn't take it. Flanagan was taking care of himself the only way he knew how, and Yakabuski supposed he would stay clear of people for the next few days, because it was better that way.

Four ain't six, thought Yakabuski. That's a true thought.

CHAPTER
TWENTY-NINE

Cambino looked at his phone. It hadn't rung in four months, and he wondered who had broken the silence. He tapped the number flashing on the screen. After a moment he heard a man say, "Are you there, my old friend?"

"Papa."

"Ahhh, it is so good to hear your voice. It brings back pleasant memories. I was not sure if you would answer."

"Why have you called?"

"Right to the point. That was always your way, eh. Myself, I enjoy talking when I am on the phone. Do you know where I am phoning you from?"

"Dorset Penitentiary."

"That's right. And a big risk it is to me, my friend, to be talking to you right now. What they do to a man like me, when he is found with contraband . . . I am risking years of my freedom by reaching out to you."

"I understand, Papa. Please, speak freely."

"I think we have a mutual enemy."

"The Shiner."

"Yes, the Shiner. He has betrayed us both, I would say."

"My business with the Shiner is my business. Yours is yours, Papa."

"I disagree. I think we can help each other."

"How?"

"You're never going to get him, my friend. You're never going to get anywhere fuckin' *near* him. He's brought in Bobby Bangs, and he'll go right from Wentworth to the Silver Dollar, and you will never see him after that. He'll outwait you. How many years you got?"

"Bobby Bangs? From Boston?"

"That's right. His uncle was the Shiner's best friend. And my friend, you are good, you are *very* fuckin' good, but Bobby Bangs and a fortified Silver Dollar are going to be problems for you."

Cambino smirked. "You underestimate me."

"*You* underestimate how helpful I can be. I can make your problem disappear. The Shiner is expecting you to come after him. From what I hear, he's damn worried about you. But we're not on his radar. We weren't part of the heist. We don't have a back-end play. He's not expecting any trouble from the Popeyes."

"How can you say that? You made a play for the girl."

Papa Paquette placed his hand over the phone's microphone, fearful that Cambino might hear his intake of breath. *So he knows.* That was the flaw in the plan. It was important Papa didn't hesitate right now, give Cambino something to ponder later. He had rehearsed his story a few times.

"You're talking about Grace Dumont. That was a couple of two-patch guys who went rogue," said Paquette. "I phoned Morrissey myself to tell him that. Told him he'd never be seeing those two again. I ordered a hit on my own men. Told Morrissey it was done as a sign of respect, for what he'd done at the airport."

"*Was* it two guys freelancing?"

"Who gives a fuck? It's what Morrissey believes, and I know he believed it because we would have had a visit from Bobby Bangs by now if he didn't."

Cambino was silent a minute. Paquette was silent. Holding his breath silent. He exhaled when Cambino said, "How can you help me?"

"Ahh, you're starting to see the sense in this. You've always been a smart man, my friend. I can help by bringing Morrissey to you. You pick the place. You'll probably have Bobby Bangs to deal with, but you'll have the jump on him. You can make that work."

"Papa, I fear you have been behind bars too long. It does something to a man's brain, the air in there. If the Shiner's plan is to hunker down in his nightclub, it won't be a Popeye that brings him out."

"No. It will be you."

Paquette started laughing. It built and built until it sounded like the crack of approaching thunder. He was wheezing and gasping for air when he managed to say, "I'm going to offer the Shiner the same deal I'm offering you. Your head on a silver platter. Think he'll come out for that, my friend?"

❖ ❖ ❖

Cambino clicked off his phone and wondered if it could be true. He lay on his belly in the woods on the north shore of the Springfield River, not far from the French Line, near the place on the escarpment where the Racine River tumbled over the cliffs to the river ninety metres below. The forest he crouched in was cedar and poplar, with maple and oak farther from the precipice, the leaves just starting to bud. Although it was almost an open field, he had good cover behind a red-granite boulder.

He was holding a pair of field glasses and had sightlines on Mission Road. There were fewer hardwood trees on the south shore, a canopy of tall white pine for the most part, but you could follow the trail, the line of it, as it made its way around the ridge. He could see the Le Vase Basin. The trailhead. The two police sedans in the parking lot of the trailhead. A large cop with long hair standing beside a Jeep.

The yellow crime-scene tape still ringed the trees, but there was no smoke showing through the pine. Or colour anywhere on the trail. The fortune hunters had gone. The YouTube video had done its job.

Could it be true? The Popeyes hated the Shiners with a loathing that went back decades, had been looking for an advantage over the gang for years. Maybe the time had come. Their long-awaited opportunity.

Cambino lowered his field glasses, closed his eyes, and tried to match his breathing to the soaring exhales and inhales of the wind above the Springfield River, a wind that howled and shrieked because of the tumbling water from the Racine River, the sound twirling and eddying in the many crevices and ridges on this escarpment. When he opened his eyes, he rose and started making his way back to the French Line.

He would keep the meeting he had arranged with Paquette. There was too much to gain if the Popeyes were telling the truth. He only needed to make sure they had too much to lose, if they were lying.

CHAPTER
THIRTY

As Yakabuski drove away from Mission Road, he started thinking it through. The facts of the case as it stood right then. The uncontested facts, which were not as easy to find as you might think, because you needed to strip away all assumptions, all biases, all logical conclusions and preponderance-of-evidence beliefs. Everyone had those. Everyone carried around what they thought were uncontested facts, but weren't. The worst examples of the phenomenon are found in news stories published during the run-up to any war.

Jason McAllister was dead. That was uncontested fact. His body was found by the shore of McGregor Lake on a loop trail that ran off Mission Road. He had been a postgraduate mathematics student at Syracuse University. He had been looking for those stolen diamonds. Had posted a map, showing where they might be found.

Good so far. What could he add?

McAllister was taken to the Mission Road trailhead by cabbie Calvin Jayne, who then went on to tell the Shiners about it, the same day he took the fare. The cabbie told his story twice, first to Billy O'Donnell, then to Bobby Bangs.

Was that part true? As far as Yakabuski knew, Bangs had yet to be spotted in Springfield. Boston police confirmed he hadn't been seen there in nearly six months. His physical description was a perfect match for the second thief.

But none of that added up to an uncontested fact. He put Bobby Bangs aside.

McAllister was found next to another body, as yet unidentified. The second body was covered in tattoos that were either of the jailhouse variety or done by a tattoo "artist" someone had probably killed a long time ago. This homicide victim wasn't from Springfield. He was here looking for the diamonds.

No. That wasn't right. It made sense that the tattooed man was looking for the diamonds. Why else would he be in Springfield, and why else would his body be found next to McAllister, who *was* looking for those diamonds? But that still wasn't an uncontested fact.

It wasn't an easy game to play. Yakabuski remembered trying it many years ago, maybe for the first time, when a Christian revival show arrived in High River. The show was called Jimmy Cochrane's Christian Jamboree, even though Jimmy Cochrane died in the '50s. The name was kept because Cochrane had been a fire-and-brimstone preacher with a radio show in North Bay after the Second World War, and people remembered that radio show for a long time. Not to mention the new owners of the Christian Jamboree didn't want to pay for new signage.

When Yakabuski saw the show, the preacher was a man from Kansas who had once been a meth chemist married to an exotic dancer who cheated on him continuously. He spoke about it openly. Just when the chemist was thinking about killing his wife, she got cancer and died. He took it as a sign from God and bought the revival show when the insurance payout arrived. He still looked like a meth chemist. Long greasy black hair. Tallowed skin. Manic eyes sunk deep in the sockets. He quoted most often from the book of Revelation.

It was the Saturday night show that Yakabuski attended; brought by an aunt who thought it would do him some good. He was seventeen and in his last year of high school. The revival-show set-up was in the parking lot of the High River arena. There was a large, circus-style tent where the meth-head preacher gave the Saturday night sermon. In the smaller tents surrounding it were faith healers and women who spoke in tongues; old men selling Russian icons; children that had memorized entire books of the Bible; defrocked priests, warning about the evils of the Papacy; former circus carnies selling leatherette-bound Bibles, bottled sand from Jerusalem and splinters from Jesus's cross.

After the main service was finished, a bonfire was lit, and camp chairs came out. There was a small stage in front of the bonfire, from which apprenticing preachers sermonized. It was common for "miracles" to occur during the bonfire sermons, and most people hung around after the main service for that.

It was a boy no more than twelve or thirteen who conjured the miracle the night Yakabuski attended. He was the last of the apprenticing preachers to speak and didn't take the stage until nearly midnight. People suspected the boy

— with his long blond hair and flowing white robe — might have been something special and had stayed late to hear him.

But he gave a sermon that surprised people by its blandness, its predictability. Near its end, two women came out and laid hot coals on the ground nearby. A few people actually groaned. They had seen this many times before.

Still, when the boy started to walk across the red coals, they were polite and feigned interest. The boy took mincing steps, his eyes closed, his arms spread wide to maintain his balance, and when he reached the end of the coals, where people were expecting him to stop and turn around, he kept walking. Straight toward the bonfire.

The response in the crowd was instantaneous. People jumped from their chairs and put hands over their mouths. Some people screamed. Some fell to their knees and began to chant.

The boy kept walking. Just as he reached the fire a couple of men from the audience rushed toward him, but it was too late. He walked into the fire and his white robe burst into flames. His hair burst into flames. He raised his arms toward the heavens, so flames leaped from his fingers, and he gave a loud, anguished scream that seemed to go on and on, long after the boy had been engulfed, everyone staring at the bonfire as it surged and grew, as though someone had just thrown a good-sized cedar log upon it.

Everyone was screaming by then. Some were writhing on the ground, talking in tongues. The meth-chemist preacher rushed to the bonfire, as though he were going to jump in to try to save the boy, only to be held back by the heat, standing inches from the flames with his crooked arm shielding his face.

And just then, the boy reappeared. Floating high above them. Still dressed in his white robes. His arms still spread wide. A smile upon his face that looked either beatific or stoned. He floated right down to the stage where he had been preaching, and when his feet touched the wooden planks he knelt, lowered his head, and gave the sign of the cross. The crowd went crazy. The preacher cradled the boy in his arms. The donation plates came out.

Early the next morning, before anyone had arrived for the Sunday service, a teenage Yakabuski returned to the site of the bonfire. He rooted through the ashes and embers, looking for signs of burned cloth or hair. When he couldn't find any, he examined the nearby trees, confirming within a few minutes what he had suspected the previous night. None of them was close enough to have suspended that boy above the fire.

He looked through every sideshow tent, beneath every wooden stage, every flatbed cart, searching for wooden beams or metal rails or rope that could have been assembled and used as a winch, but he never found anything.

He never figured out how it was done. A month later he was finished school and had enlisted in the army, on his way to the Edmonton Garrison. He forgot about the boy, although the memory of what happened that night had come back to him recently, left Yakabuski once again thinking about faith gone bad and good people believing in all the wrong things, in deaths that couldn't be, and resurrections that didn't seem quite right, left thinking again about desperate people gathered in the night, staring at the wonders of the world and wondering if they were staring at miracles or trickery.

Someone moved that second body to Mission Road. Why would anyone do that?

CHAPTER
THIRTY-ONE

Yakabuski stood with Donna Griffin before the map showing the route of the Econoline van on the night of the robbery. After staring at it for several minutes, neither of them talking, Yakabuski said, "One more time for the world, run the time sequence for me."

Griffin started the narrative. The Econoline left the airport at 12:46 a.m. It was under steady surveillance for the next eight minutes and thirty-seven seconds, until it drove into a parking garage on Doucet Street. It was in the garage for eleven minutes, thirteen seconds. It came out as a new-looking van and took the Highway 7 on-ramp in the French Quarter. At 1:23 a.m. it was seen passing the Irving station not far from the trailhead for Mission Road, and that was the last the van was seen until a waitress from O'Toole's found it burning in the alley off of Belfast Street at 2:10 a.m.

"Why are you asking me these questions?" she said when she was finished. "Have I missed something?"

"We've all missed something, Donna. It's an unsolved case."

"Something has changed though. What is it?"

"The second body on the Mission Road, the one we haven't identified yet, it was moved there. That boy was killed somewhere else."

"Are you saying our victim wasn't out there looking for the diamonds?"

"There it is. The problem. Donna, we've been looking for those diamonds in the same place for so long it's become a fact to us: that's where they are. When we get any new fact, we try to make it fit the old facts. What we need right now are a few good, clean, uncontested facts."

"Why do I feel like something has just blown up on us?" She turned away from the map to look at him.

"Because I suspect it has. The truth is we don't know what that tattooed man was doing in Springfield. Probably looking for the diamonds, but we can't be certain. What we do know, according to Newt, is that his body was moved to Mission Road after he was killed. I've been thinking about that all day, and I only get two possible answers for why someone would want to do a thing like that. Either they didn't want people to know where the killing took place, or they wanted people thinking it happened on Mission Road, to keep police away from another place."

"What exactly are you saying, Yak?"

"I'm saying we need to take another look at that parking garage."

❖ ❖ ❖

Yakabuski stood in the middle of the main floor of the parking garage, two floors above him, one below. It was mid-afternoon and the lot was full. Donna Griffin and Fraser Newton stood beside him, along with the parking lot attendant, a boy of about nineteen, who had asked Newton if he had a search warrant when he first arrived, then stopped asking when Yakabuski arrived. Explained his boss told him to ask about stuff like search warrants, but he didn't mind helping the police.

About two minutes after that the attendant let slip that he was a police studies student at Springfield College. And that he'd read *The Battle of Ragged Lake*. And what model of service pistol did Yakabuski use? The attendant bet it was old-school. Some sort of .45-calibre Colt.

"Standard-issue nine-millimetre Glock," said Yakabuski, sounding friendly but not overly, not wanting to shut the boy down, because his boss was right about the search warrant, but not wanting to spend the rest of the afternoon talking about Ragged Lake either.

"We appreciate your help," he continued. "How about I come see you before we leave. Tell you what we found."

"That would be great!"

"I'll look for you in the booth," and Yakabuski shook the boy's hand, the attendant looking surprised at first, then blushing as he took Yakabuski's massive hand, not even noticing when he was gently turned around and pointed in the direction of his booth before the handshake was finished.

When the boy was gone, Newton said, "Fuck, should I be getting your autograph? Is that going to be worth something one day?"

"Not more than the paper it's written on, I suspect. Show me where they worked on the van."

They walked to the northeast corner. There were cars parked there but the aerosol paint marks on the pavement gave them a rough idea where the Econoline would have been parked. Yakabuski bent down and looked at the paint marks. Stood up and said, "There's just the one camera?"

"By the entrance, angle on the street outside. Owner cares about cars skipping out. Doesn't care much what happens inside. Are you thinking you might find them here? Is that what we're doing?"

"I don't know what I'm looking for, Newt." Yakabuski turned and glanced all around.

"Because the diamonds aren't here. We shut this garage down four hours after the heist," Newton reminded him. "No car left the garage after the Econoline. We've been through here with X-ray, sonar, dogs, you name it. No way those diamonds are here."

Yakabuski didn't answer. Kept walking around the garage. Once or twice he pushed against the walls.

"No secret entrance, Yak. We've checked every inch of all four walls."

"What about the walls upstairs?"

"Every brick."

Yakabuski nodded and kept walking. He made his way to the second floor, Griffin and Newton following. There was a bad mould smell in the air. Oil stains on the floor that had aged so they looked like ancient, mottled skin. Not many cars, so the pattern ran end-to-end.

He walked the circumference of the second floor. Examined the two stairwells. The ramp going up. The ramp going down. The wooden booth with the sign saying *Dan's Auto Wash*, a sign as weathered as the oil stains. The booth was against the far wall, the window boarded with a sheet of plywood that had been screened in. Hadn't been a car wash there in a long time. Yakabuski walked over to the booth and examined the mudding pails and rotting plastic hoses that lay beside it.

"Owner isn't big on maintenance," said Griffin, as Yakabuski examined the booth. It sat on wooden pallets that had been strung together, so the booth sat a couple inches above the floor. He got on his knees and shone a flashlight under. He pulled out more rotten hoses, and two metal rails about ten feet long and a foot wide. He stared at them a few seconds. Then he got up and walked around the booth. Walked back. Gave the booth a shove.

"Newt, Donna, come over here and give me a hand."

The three of them shoved against the booth until the wooden pallets began to move. They pushed and shoved until they had moved the booth about twelve feet. Then they stood back and looked at the sheet of plywood in front of them.

"This used to be an old warehouse, Yak," explained Newton. "They bricked up the windows when they turned it into a garage. We noticed this from the outside. Brickwork probably fell apart on the owner, and he was too cheap to do a full repair, so he boarded it up."

Yakabuski looked at the plywood. Ran his fingers along the edges. Newton saw what he was doing and reached into his coat pocket for his multi-tool. Eight screws popped it, and then the plywood was down on the floor and they were staring out an open window. Yakabuski got one of the metal rails and started pulling it toward the window. Newton went and got the second one.

"No way," he said, as he helped Yakabuski place the ends of the metal rails on the lip of the window. "No fuckin' way."

When they were finished, they stood back and Griffin said, "Are you serious?"

Newton laughed so hard he was gasping for air when he said, "Fuck. She's right, Yak. There's no way. Look at the drop."

Yakabuski leaned out the window. He was staring at Doucet Street, a short street, little more than an alley, which ran behind the parking garage. He was two storeys up, about dead centre of the block. He closed his eyes and moved his lips silently for a few seconds. Then he reopened his eyes and walked toward the stairwell. Halfway there he looked over his shoulder and called, "Those rails need to be lined up dead centre, Newt. I'll phone you in a minute with the measurement."

◈ ◈ ◈

Thirty-seven inches. Newton measured it out with the tape on his multi-tool, and then he and Griffin stood the other side of a cement pillar, as Yakabuski had instructed. They looked at the ramp coming up from the main floor. Looked at each other.

"He's not doing this, right?"

"It's a short list, Donna, the things that guy won't do."

"This would have to be on it."

"Are you sure?"

"Newt! It's suicide."

"People used to say that about going up against Tommy Bangles. Or going undercover and arresting Papa Paquette."

"Those were battles, Newt. Combat. This is a suicidal jump. It's not the same thing."

"Maybe not to you and me. What about to him?"

"Has everyone gone stark raving *bonkers* around here? You can see the opening isn't big enough!"

Newt gave her an impassive stare, and then he broke into laughter.

"My God, I couldn't keep that going any longer. Of course he's not driving through that window, Donna. He's bringing the Jeep up for measurements. That's all he's doing. Figuring out if it might be possible. Which it isn't."

Griffin thought about that. *Of course that's what he's doing. Taking pictures. Lining it all up. Seeing if it could be done.*

So why phone with the measurements?

Donna Griffin was just starting to think that one through when she heard the Rubicon coming up the ramp. The headlights were on, the top removed, the roll bar winched down, the deep throttle of the engine amplified inside the cement walls. The Jeep made air when it reached the second floor, already moving at a good speed. It bounced and then bounced again, like a bad airplane landing; after that it straightened and you could hear the engine shift to a higher gear.

The Jeep was heading directly toward the window. At one hundred and fifty feet away Griffin started screaming. At one hundred feet Fraser Newton started screaming. Fifty. Twenty-five.

Yakabuski lowered his head just as the Jeep hit the metal rails. The Rubicon made it halfway up before the weight shifted and the bottom end of the rails come flying up, like a teeter-totter. The nose of the Jeep went down but the front wheels were already over the ledge. The Jeep bounced once and then it was airborne and through the window. The metal rails tumbled to the ground with a bang that reverberated through the garage like rolling thunder.

Griffin stopped screaming and stared at the window. Newton was already gaping. Neither moved until they heard the parking lot attendant hollering from the street below.

"Holy fuck!"

When they looked out the window, they saw Yakabuski's Jeep thirty feet down Doucet Street. The attendant was dancing around the vehicle with his hands in his hair, pulling at the strands like a lunatic on ecstasy. He kept high-fiving Yakabuski. Pulling at his hair. For several minutes he said nothing more than "Holy fuck."

Yakabuski looked up at Griffin and Newton and yelled, "Check the security cameras again. You're looking for a ragtop, two-door Jeep. Probably would have taken the turn at Deschamps Street."

CHAPTER
THIRTY-TWO

When Yakabuski got back to the detachment, Tyler Lawson was in his office waiting for him. His brother-in-law had scheduled an appointment earlier in the week. Yakabuski was nearly thirty minutes late, and he was surprised to see Lawson still there. He sat in one of the Henderson chairs across from Yakabuski's desk, lawyer's satchel at his feet, crossing and recrossing his legs as he tried to get comfortable.

Official meetings between Yakabuski and his brother-in-law were always awkward, and more or less followed the same script. Pleasantries at the beginning about family, maybe a mention of some event they would both need to attend soon, and, after that, never seeming to find the right segue, Lawson would get around to mentioning the reason for his visit.

"Sorry I'm late, Tyler. I should have called."

"Where are you coming from?"

"Ongoing investigation, I'm afraid."

"You're spending a lot of time out on Mission Road."

"I suppose that's no secret. Maybe you could ask your client where he buried those diamonds. That would speed things up a bit for us."

Lawson uncrossed his legs and arched his back. Recrossed them and leaned toward the desk. Yakabuski was waiting for the pleasantries, but instead Lawson said, "I'm hoping we can discuss Sean's release next week."

"What would you like to discuss?"

"Whether it's going to happen. Maybe we can start with that."

Lawson gave him a sour look. No chit-chat, no attempt to ingratiate himself. This wasn't the brother-in-law Yakabuski had grown to loathe a little more each year that Sean Morrissey stayed out of prison.

"There's no problem on our end, Tyler."

"So he's walking out of Wentworth next Tuesday morning?"

"I don't know of any reason why he wouldn't. Do you?"

"Are you coordinating his release with the Mounties and the provincial police?"

"Hard to coordinate much with the Feds, Tyler. You know that. They prefer if you sit quiet and listen."

"So you haven't spoken to them?"

"I didn't say that. Just said I'm not coordinating anything with them. What would I be coordinating anyway?" He flashed his brother-in-law a goofy what-me-worry? smile.

"Oh, I don't know, Yak. What about the further detainment of my client? Come on, there's no need to go through the charade of a release if you're just going to arrest him again in front of the prison."

"That's what you're worried about?"

"It is something my client has concerns about. I would say he has valid reason for the concern. You've done that sort of thing before."

It was true. Releasing a criminal and rearresting them on the front steps of the jail was a good way to break them. Give them a glimpse of the Promised Land, then snatch it away. Some cops thought it was a better interrogation technique than bright lights and angry voices. Best of all, perfectly legal.

It was also a bait-and-switch hustle no one thought would work on Sean Morrissey. Nor could the police decide, and there had been several meetings with the Mounties and the provincial police to discuss it, whether they wanted Morrissey detained any longer. Eventually, they decided they didn't.

"What do you think we could charge him with, Tyler?"

"You expect an answer to that?"

"Too much to choose from? Yeah, I see your problem."

"You don't need to parade him, Yak. It won't work. You know that. I'm just here to try to make everyone's job next Tuesday a little easier."

"I can do my own job, Tyler. What about you? Need any help with those diamonds?"

Lawson sighed and ran the fingers of one hand through his hair. He looked around the office a second before saying, "Yak, if I can't get a straight answer from you, I'll leave and tell Sean not to bother packing his bags."

"You think they have bags at Wentworth? Bellhops, that sort of thing?"

"Why are you being such an asshole?"

Yakabuski gave his head a quick snap backwards. That might have been the most shocking thing he'd ever heard come out of Tyler Lawson's mouth. His brother-in-law prided himself on politeness — his decorum, his ability to act civil and patrician even when arguing for the release of stone-cold killers. He was more than tired, thought Yakabuski. Before Tyler could apologize for what he'd said, and Yakabuski knew that was coming, he said, "Tyler, have you given serious thought to what you're doing here?"

"I know exactly what I'm doing, Yak. I'm here to find out if my client is being released from Wentworth next Tuesday, or if I'm going to be dragged up there for some dog-and-pony show. What are you doing?"

"Wondering why you're still legal counsel for the Shiners."

"So I'm wasting my time."

"Tyler, do you fully understand the trouble your client has brought to this city? It's not going to end well for Sean. Might not end well for you, if you're standing too close to him. If you've ever given any real thought to getting clear of these guys, now might be the time."

Lawson opened his mouth and started to speak, made a sound that might have been the start to the word *listen*, or *like*, Yakabuski wasn't sure. But then he closed his mouth. Looked down at his Florsheims. Lawson still had a thick head of golden blond hair, a schoolboy's demeanour, and right then he looked like a student sitting outside the principal's office, waiting to be punished.

When Yakabuski knew one syllable was all he was going to get, he said, "We don't want him in Wentworth any longer. Sean Morrissey will be released next Tuesday morning, in time to catch the eleven o'clock corrections bus to the Springfield courthouse."

Lawson looked up from his shoes. No sign of relief on his face. "My client will be arranging his own transportation. I'll let him know. Thank you."

He stood up, positioned his body as straight as a parade marshal's, then leaned over the desk to shake Yakabuski's hand. He said thank you once more, and then Yakabuski watched him walk down the corridor to the elevators, his lawyer's satchel looking heavier than Yakabuski suspected it actually was.

He had never felt good about his sister being married to a mob lawyer. Could never summon the tricks of situational ethics that would let him say that's all right, we can still be friends. Different strokes. Worthy adversaries. All those clichés.

But as he watched Lawson walk away that afternoon, for the first time he worried about his sister's safety. Wondered just how many people were about to get caught up in the storm Sean Morrissey would unleash when he walked through the front gates of Wentworth prison in ten days.

❖ ❖ ❖

Tyler Lawson drove home thinking about culpability. A legal term, so he was familiar with its many parsings and shadings, the larger idea behind it, the many concepts, theorems, and well-reasoned arguments that had crawled up the word's back through the years so that culpability was now one of the clumsiest of English words.

Complicit. Now there was a leaner word. And a better one to start with, for there could be no doubt about it. He was complicit. Nearly twenty years working for the Shiners

200

and if in the beginning he thought he could build a wall between the gang and the legal work he did for them, it was a short-lived deception. By his own calculation, he was behaving like the caricature of a mob lawyer by his third year in Springfield. Privy to the secret location of smuggling routes and shipment dates; working like a zealot to get murderers acquitted on what he had convinced himself were legal hills to die on, but in truth were technicalities and loopholes.

Until recently, he'd believed being a mob lawyer never took him completely to the dark side. Yes, he represented murderers, guilty people he knew to be guilty, just like a million other lawyers. And yes, killing a competitor was an accepted business practice for the Shiners, as it was for a lot of political and military leaders, and bootleggers who now had sons living in penthouses on the Upper East Side in Manhattan.

What was the difference? It was a clever argument he had often used, back when no one was getting killed and strung up on fences on the North Shore, or getting gutted in their offices in Cape Diamond, or blown away in gun battles at a fishing lodge in Ragged Lake.

Complicit gets chipped away at and debated in court, but Lawson had begun to think it was legal fiction. Complicit was an absolute. Nothing that mitigates. Nothing that aggravates. If you're complicit, you're in for the whole ride, from the self-deception at the beginning to the moment when you can't turn away any longer from how guilty you are, the moment the legal framework of the clever argument comes tumbling down and you're exposed for what you truly are, as surprised as anyone by how grotesque it looks.

Tyler Lawson's stomach kept churning as he made the drive from the Centretown detachment to his home in Mission Road Estates. He parked his car in his garage, threw up in the half-bath off the mudroom, and walked into the kitchen, where Trish had his supper waiting on the table.

CHAPTER
THIRTY-THREE

A statue of Samuel de Champlain stood in the central square of the French Quarter. Forty feet tall and backlit every night with blue floodlights. You could see the light from just about any place in Springfield. Out on the river, the light was so bright it was used as a navigation aid by boats, the first beacon you saw when you were travelling downriver to Springfield and rounded Hog's Back Bend, three nautical miles from the harbour at Cork's Town.

There was no floodlight right then. Early afternoon, and Cambino leaned against the wall of a low-rise apartment building on Governeur Street, staring at the statue. He would have looked nothing like that, the French explorer who made twenty-seven trips across the North Atlantic in the days when making two would have made him a famous adventurer. Nothing like the bewigged and waxed-moustached dandy that stood every night in the French Quarter bathed in blue light, as though a cabaret star.

There was no known portrait of Champlain, and that was the problem. Everyone was free to make him up as they wished. But Cambino knew Champlain would have had his hair shorn to protect him from the flying bugs that infested this land, and his clothes would have been leather breeches and plainsong jackets, not the pompous frills and palace attire of the man in the statue. It was an embarrassment, what history did to people sometimes.

It was a warm day, one of the first of the season, and the patios had opened. He watched a black Cadillac Escalade enter the square, circle the statue, and then park on Lafontaine Street. The driver got out and lit a cigarette. He wore black jeans and a rope-patterned cowboy shirt. Another man stayed in the passenger seat, staring straight ahead and talking on a cellphone.

Thirty minutes later, a second Escalade entered the square, circled the statue, and stopped less than twenty metres from where Cambino stood. Two men sat in the front seat. One was talking on a cellphone. Within a few minutes the man put away his phone and got out of the Escalade, began walking through the square.

He stopped at a few of the market stalls. Bought a newspaper at the stand on Baude. Sat on a bench by the statue and began to read. After he had been on the bench for about twenty minutes, he stood up, threw the newspaper in a garbage bin, and walked back to the Cadillac.

He hadn't seen him. Cambino was so skilled at disappearing, at blending in anywhere, that he could only be spotted when he wished it. Almost that. In the next hour, he saw two more Escalades circling the square, although neither one parked. A hydro van came and parked beside the Baude Café, although no one got out to work. A Nissan 380ZX circled the square a few times, but then drove away. He wasn't sure about the Nissan.

Henri Lepine arrived at a quarter to three, strolling down Baude Street and entering the café, appearing a few minutes later on the patio, following a waiter who seated him at a table by the railing. He was fifteen minutes early. About what Cambino had expected.

Just as he had expected everything else that he had seen. Several vehicle sweeps of the square, one sweep on foot, positions taken on three of the four spoke streets that dead-ended at the hub of Champlain's statue, leaving only one line of egress, a line that was bottlenecked, he had no doubt, two blocks down Governeurs. Three at the most.

This was a good crew. The trap had been well laid. The only mistake they had made was showing up two hours before the meeting. When Cambino had shown up four.

♦ ♦ ♦

The boy had never seen a hundred-dollar bill. He held it in his hand and turned it from side to side, nodding at the man who had given it to him; not bothering to look at him, saying again it would not be a problem. For a hundred bucks he would drive his bicycle into a patrol cop.

The kid made it look good. Better than he needed. Faked going over a pothole when he was abreast of the Escalade, swerved and pedalled right into the driver's door. He flew over the handles, landed on the hood, and rolled off. The bike fell to the ground.

For one hundred dollars, it was way better than it needed to be. The kid had talent. The driver opened the door and got out. Still smoking a cigarette.

"What the fuck are you doin' kid . . ."

Cambino walked up behind him and shot him in the head. Right temple, so he would fall to the left, away from the open door. Without breaking stride he fired four more shots at the man in the passenger seat, who didn't even have time to raise the snub-nosed automatic rifle sitting in his lap.

Cambino reached in and grabbed the gun. Then he stood up and fired several rounds into the air. He quartered the weapon and looked around the square. People ran screaming, bumping into each other, trampling each other. There were flags flapping in the wind you couldn't hear for the screaming, and cars in the distance you couldn't hear either. A strange, silent world, just the other side of the chaos surrounding him.

Cambino walked toward the second Escalade. He saw the boy who had run his bicycle into the first SUV running with everyone else, which surprised him. He thought the boy would have been quicker.

He lowered his rifle and fired a short burst into the boy's back. He hadn't planned it, but when you're given the chance to eliminate a future witness, a person the cops may one day find and interview, you take it. General principle. Didn't need to think about it more than that. Cambino killed the boy without breaking stride, nor looking over his shoulder to see how the child fell.

❖ ❖ ❖

As Cambino expected, the two men in the second Escalade had exited their vehicle but not taken up positions. Unsure what was happening. Where the battle lines might be. They were standing on the street, Uzis in their hands, looking at the upper floor windows of the office buildings on Governeur. Pushing people away whenever they bumped into them.

The men thought the shots were coming from above, from snipers maintaining a high-ground position. It made sense. What trained men would do if they had the time and a fixed target. Cambino had neither. So the bikers never saw him coming.

It was almost too easy. A short burst through the chest of the first man, Cambino catching him deftly and lowering him to the pavement. Same for the second man, when he came running over to help his friend, thinking he had just been knocked to the ground. The man fell atop the first body so neatly Cambino didn't have to move a thing. He walked away just as people began to run into them and fall. In a minute or two it would be an incomprehensible scrum.

The two men from the hydro van were on the street now, and they had seen Cambino, but they were the surveillance crew and there was a reason he had left them to the end. Both men had handguns. Both looked scared. Cambino walked toward them while their bullets missed, and then he raised the assault rifle and took them out in two short bursts.

He looked around for Lepine and saw him still seated at his patio table. The furniture around him was overturned. The fence that once surrounded the patio was knocked down. There was broken glass and upturned umbrellas. People ran by Lepine, but he seemed not to notice. Kept drinking his espresso.

Cambino came toward him. As he approached, a lazy, sardonic smile spread across the biker's face. Lepine took another sip of his coffee, placed it carefully on the table, and said, "I think there are easier ways to—"

Cambino shot him in the head and kept walking.

CHAPTER
THIRTY-FOUR

Champlain Square was cordoned off with crime-scene tape, dozens of parked patrol cars and ambulances the other side of the tape, the twirling lights getting brighter as dusk fell. Yakabuski was waved through the throng gathered outside the yellow tape, but his Rubicon was recognized by some reporters and he could hear the questions being shouted as he drove through.

"We're hearing eight dead. Is that right? Eight—"

"—the Shiners? Did they—"

"Was this about the diamonds? Have you found—"

He kept his windows up, parked next to the Baude Café, got out, and looked around. It was easy to spot the victims. They each had their own crime-scene tape, their own cluster of police officers and first responders kneeling over them.

He walked to the Cadillac parked on Governeur. A man lay on the pavement next to the car, a single head-wound to his right temple. The man inside the vehicle had his head shot off. He was almost unrecognizable as having once been human, just a mass of pulped flesh that you couldn't figure out the proportion or the position of, because you needed a head to do that right.

Yakabuski walked to the second Cadillac, saw the two men lying on top of each other, not more than five feet from the vehicle. He bent down and rolled up their sleeves. He didn't need to. He'd already recognized the man lying outside the first Cadillac as Yves Vachon, a Popeyes enforcer who was one of Papa Paquette's oldest friends. Eighteen confirmed kills, including seven rival bikers at the Lennoxville Purge. That was the story, anyway. Vachon was never convicted of a capital crime and only served two years in prison, for a manslaughter conviction, when he was eighteen. A long, lucky run, although no one would remember that now.

Both men from the second vehicle had thunderbolt tattoos. He looked across the square, to where two more bodies lay next to a hydro van that was all shot up. One more body lay in the middle of the square, already covered with a blanket.

"Who's under there?" he asked an Ident officer standing near him.

"A boy, Yak. Innocent bystander. Got caught in the crossfire."

Yakabuski knew that boy would be the lead on every news story about the shootout. He had seen it happen during the Biker Wars, when for two years the Popeyes and the Hells Angels were killing each other on the streets of Quebec, no one caring about it that much, until one day an eleven-year-old boy was killed during a botched drive-by in Laval. Two days later, the army was marching into Montreal.

He let his gaze sweep across the square and then he said, "Only the boy?"

"Yeah. We probably caught a lucky break there."

Yakabuski saw nothing in the square that resembled a lucky break. He walked to where the boy lay. He looked around the square. Walked it one more time. When he was done he went to the Baude Café, where Bernard O'Toole was standing on the patio. Next to O'Toole was the body of Henri Lepine, laid out nice and crisp the way he would have liked. Just an overturned chair and a pen-sized hole in his forehead letting you know something was different about him today.

"One fuckin' man did all this?" said O'Toole.

"Looks that way," answered Yakabuski.

"And a young boy gets killed in the crossfire. It's out of control, Yak."

"The boy was part of it."

"*What?*"

"Probably a local kid that got used as some sort of distraction. Check his pockets. I'm betting you'll find money."

"How can you say that, Yak? He's a dead boy."

"And I'm telling you how he died. A lone attacker kills seven bikers without a single shot going astray, but he accidentally kills that boy? No way."

"Fuck, Yak, you can't be serious. He was an innocent bystander."

"I'll go along with that. You'll never hear any different from me. He probably was innocent enough. Just wasn't a bystander."

Yakabuski knelt and started going through Lepine's pockets. He doubted he would find anything interesting. Cambino Cortez may have been lured here with the promise of getting something, but it didn't look like the Popeyes had any plans on delivering. A ruse and an ambush right from the start.

He doubted the motorcycle gang would regroup anytime soon. Lepine dead. Paquette in Dorset for two more years. Judging by the thunderbolt tattoos he had already seen, most of the motorcycle gang's enforcers lay dead in Champlain Square. It would be a while.

It was getting down to last-man-standing time. Everyone else had fled, or been killed, or had the sense to stay away in the first place. Like Linus Desjardins and the Travellers. The people who were left looking for those diamonds, or protecting those diamonds, they were here for the duration. That's what you used to call it in the army, when you were on a mission and turning back was not an option, failure a thing you had convinced yourself would be a worse fate than death.

You needed to make that absurdist break in logic to be any good in battle. Yakabuski knew that. When he was a boy, he would sometimes read newspaper stories about Japanese soldiers found in the jungles of some Pacific Island, still thinking World War Two was underway and still refusing to surrender. He looked it up once, and the one who made it the longest was Teruo Nakamura. *Twenty-nine years.*

When he read those stories, Yakabuski didn't know what to think about the Japanese soldiers. It seemed heroic to him to have that sort of devotion to mission, that sort of fealty to purpose. But stupid too.

Stories about people who stayed with a mission long past the point of common sense, or basic self-preservation, were not uncommon on the Northern Divide. Almost origin tales. Around the same time Yakabuski was reading newspaper stories about long-lost Japanese soldiers, the *Springfield Sun* ran a story about the last Mormon from the ill-fated Mission Road colony. His name was Clifford Dulmage and he was ninety-two years old. Lived in an assisted care home on Albert Street. He had worked at the O'Hearn sawmill on Entrance Bay for thirty-seven years and once had a wife and two daughters, although they had died many years before.

When asked why he stayed in Springfield after the disastrous collapse of the Mission Road colony, Dulmage said it was because of the tabernacle. He explained that the families evicted from Mission Road had consecrated a tabernacle in an old workman's cottage by the shores of the Springfield River. It was still there, unknown now to anyone but Dulmage.

At one point in the interview the old man was asked, and Yakabuski thought it a brave question from the journalist, how it felt to be ninety-two years old with little more than failed dreams and aspirations to look back upon. The old man's answer was short but did not seem curt or ill tempered.

"I still have hope," he said, "that maybe one day a devout person will come to me, and I can pass along the taber-nacle." Dulmage died six months later. A follow-up story in the *Sun* didn't mention whether he had been able to pass along his secret.

Yakabuski felt about Clifford Dulmage the way he felt about Teruo Nakamura. The Mormon had been both heroic and stupid. Which confused the young Yakabuski, left him wondering how such a thing could be possible — a stupid hero — eventually coming up with no better answer to his riddle than people saw some things in life as the sorts of things you needed to play out to the end, without ever giving it much thought, or thinking they had a choice about it.

As for why people felt that way about some things but not other things, well, Yakabuski had been wondering about that a lot of years and there didn't seem to be any good way of ever knowing.

III
MISSION

CHAPTER THIRTY-FIVE

The wind had shifted to the northwest overnight, bringing cold air down the Upper Divide that built and built, and by morning it was gale strength — a wind that shredded trees and sent ripped-away branches flying through the woods like debris spinning from an automobile crash. The river churned into a white froth. Waves crashed on the public beach with a booming echo, and the tallest waves were more than a storey high. When the sun came, the sky was a dank grey that never darkened or lightened, never showed cloud or strata, a seamless shroud thrown over a world that screamed and lurched beneath it.

The freezing rain came when the sun rose. The wind brought it in at a sharp angle, like birdshot, ice shards so brittle they could cut exposed skin. By midmorning the rain had encased every pane of glass in Springfield so you couldn't see outside. Those who didn't have to work sat huddled around their fireplaces or gas-burning stoves, trying to identify the sounds coming from outside, the moans and shrieks, the whistles and bangs, wondering if they were human or animal, wind or forest, the physical world becoming less distinct as the storm worsened through the day.

Yakabuski and Griffin sat in the Rubicon, staring at the front gates of Wentworth Correctional Facility.

"I feel like I'm on the foredeck of the *Titanic*," she said.

"*Titanic* didn't go down in a storm. It was bad piloting."

"Think there was much of a difference at the end?"

Yakabuski turned to look at her. That was a smart question. She was dressed in her patrol officer's uniform, dark blue with yellow piping, pretty much a steal from a Mounties uniform, and he knew now she would never wear anything different unless her secondment to Major Crimes became permanent.

It was the last day of April, trout season had begun two days ago, but the Sports had stayed away. Maybe it was the heavy rains during the spring. Maybe it was the diamonds. No way of telling for sure, although nothing seemed quite right in Springfield just then, including Wentworth, which, with its gun turrets and barbed wire encased in ice, looked like some sugar-frosted castle, a child's birthday cake, left beside the road.

Despite the rain and gloom of the morning, the visitors' parking lot was nearly full. Television vans and idling minivans. Quite a few taxis. There was a police surveillance van as well, what looked like a tactical APC, and two patrol cars parked right next to the security hut. The red-and-blue roof lights of the police cars were the only bright colours to be seen that morning.

Parked ten feet from the patrol cars, the other side of the security hut, was Tyler Lawson's BMW. Its sleek black finish and rounded contours made it look like a large egg, thought Yakabuski, a well-built, seamless, metal egg. Maybe the perfect thing to crawl into on a morning like this.

"You've spoken to your brother-in-law today?" asked Griffin, looking at Tyler's car.

"Twice."

"He's that worried about what might happen?"

"I think the second call was just Tyler hoping we'd changed our mind. He doesn't care for this kind of weather."

"I'm shocked to hear that. The rest of us love it so much. So there's no chance of Morrissey being picked up by another agency?"

"That's what I'm told. He'll be walking out this morning."

Suddenly, light appeared on Wentworth Road. At first it was just a flash of white light seen through the driving rain, faraway light that disappeared a few times because of the dips in the road, then drew closer and turned into headlights that slowly passed Yakabuski's Jeep, then turned and stopped next to Lawson's BMW.

The car was a Cadillac sedan, although you couldn't tell much more than that because of the rain and the flickering lights. A car door opened and the driver stepped out. His form was hard to make out, little more than a shadow that wavered and fluttered just beyond the obscured wet light of Wentworth's main parking lot.

"He's standing *outside*?" said Griffin. "Who the hell is that guy? That's Morrissey's car, right?"

"It is," said Yakabuski.

His eyes were becoming accustomed to the distance and the optical illusions caused by the swirling lights, and he could now make out the driver's long hair, the upturned collar of a leather coat, the right hand that ran its fingers through the hair from time to time, the left hand that never left a coat pocket. The man turned his head toward the sky once and held it for a moment, as though wanting to experience the lash of the ice pellets, the punch of the wind.

Yakabuski had seen a man do that once before, on the front porch of a squatter's cabin in Ragged Lake, a gun muzzle pushed against an old man's head, and the man holding the gun had his face turned toward a raging snowstorm.

So he could take it all in. Experience everything.

"That's Bobby Bangs," he said quietly. "He's standing outside because it's what his uncle would have done."

❖ ❖ ❖

At quarter to eleven, a severely battered and dented lime-green corrections bus showed up at the front gate of Wentworth Correctional Facility to take away the prisoners being released that day. Although it was left idling, the bus's engine misfired several times. Yakabuski kept waiting for the motor to die, and everyone being released that day being told they had to try again tomorrow. He wondered if that had ever happened. He guessed the driver kept the engine revving wildly after every misfire because it would be a nightmare starting it.

"Looks like the bus Buddy Holly didn't want to ride in," he said.

"Too old for me, Yak. You gotta stop with the dead-musician references. Love the colour, though."

At 11 a.m. the interior gates of the jail were opened and two rifle-toting guards marched outside. They were followed by thirteen inmates walking a single line. Two more armed guards were in the rear. The guards wore yellow slickers and knee-high Wellies. The inmates had on cotton sneakers and nylon windbreakers. Sean Morrissey was the thirteenth man.

Several of the news vans had aerial arms, and Morrissey was spotted long before he reached the front gate. Doors opened and slammed and people ran from their cars. Photographers shielded long lenses from the rain and pulled up the hoods on their slickers. Television cameramen lined up next to the photographers. The people under the umbrellas looked to be reporters.

They were all bumping into each other when Morrissey walked through the front gate. He stood a little over six feet, and while in his youth many people thought he looked like Jim Morrison in his Lizard King days, back when he and Tommy Bangles were knocking over jewellery stores and banks up and down the Northern Divide, there was little sign of that now. He weighed more than two hundred pounds, his hair cut short and curls gone. You could see the tips of his tattoo sleeves sticking out from the cuffs of the windbreaker. He stood in the rain, Lawson now standing beside him, waiting for a guard to remove his handcuffs.

They made him wait. Uncuffed the twelve men in front of him, had them board the bus, the duty sergeant explaining the rules of transport, then explaining a second time to make sure they understood. After that they came for him. The guard with the key had a big, dumb-man-who-was-just-clever grin on his face as he approached. Morrissey extended his hands. When the guard bent his head to unlock the cuffs, Morrissey leaned in as if to say something. The guard's body twitched a little, it seemed to Yakabuski, and when he stood again the smile was gone. Morrissey rubbed his wrists and walked away.

Bangles and Lawson cleared a path through the cameras and the reporters, Morrissey ignoring the questions that were shouted at him — "Where are the diamonds, Sean?" "Are the Shiners still at war with the Travellers? The city has a right to know . . ." "Sean, over here, over here a minute."

When the scrum stopped moving, two patrol officers got out of their cars and helped them make it the rest of the way. Morrissey got into the passenger seat of his Cadillac and Bangles followed Lawson's BMW out of the parking lot. There was the slamming of doors, the starting of engines, and the television vans and the taxis followed.

❖ ❖ ❖

They sat in the Jeep for a moment. The bright lights and loud noises had moved on, and there was only the rhythmic swish of the wiper blades, the hum of the ineffective heater. The stone walls of the jail had retreated into the grey gloom of the morning, hard to pick out the lines of them through the rain.

"You're on your way to the Silver Dollar?" said Griffin.

"Guess I am."

"Want me to come?"

"Thanks, but I might have more luck on my own."

"Good luck or bad?" She moved her hands across the vent for the heater, a gesture she knew was borderline useless, but the motion alone would help keep her hands warm. "You arrested Morrissey last December. Not all that long after you killed his best friend. There's a bit of history there. Sure you don't want me to tag along?"

"There's always a bit of history around here, Donna. I think it's the rocks or something. Don't worry, I'll be all right."

Griffin nodded, did up the zipper on her slicker, and opened the door. Holding tight to the hood of her slicker, she ran across the parking lot toward her patrol car. She had a good stride and it didn't take long. When he saw the head-lights of the patrol car come on, he put the Rubicon in drive and headed out of the parking lot.

CHAPTER THIRTY-SIX

The television vans and taxis followed Morrissey for a while, then took the exit for Centretown and were gone. Clips of Morrissey walking out of Wentworth were all the journalists needed. They had little interest in where he might be going after that. And no interest at all in meeting him any place other than the parking lot of the prison, where there were armed guards staring down at him from fortified turrets.

The police vehicles took the same exit; they had been there to ensure there wasn't an incident during his release. Yakabuski kept following the Cadillac and the BMW down Highway 7.

The freezing rain was keeping people off the roads, and the highway was almost deserted. Two sets of red tail-lights and a slippery stretch of road was all that lay in front of Yakabuski. The storm had stripped away his peripheral vision, and most reference points were gone. The sky was a flat leaden grey. It was the sort of driving that could put you to sleep.

He knew where the cars were going, and knew he had ten or fifteen minutes to get there. He punched a button on the Rubicon's dashboard. His sister had already phoned him twice that morning, leaving messages both times. She picked up on the first ring.

"Frankie, there you are. I haven't been able to reach Tyler all day. Are you still at Wentworth? My lord, the weather today."

"I'm on my way back."

"Did everything go all right? Did you speak to Tyler?"

"No, just saw him."

"He was absolutely thrilled when he left the house this morning. My husband has never really acclimatized to Springfield. Maybe you already know that. Did you see Sean?"

"I did."

"Look any different?"

"'Bout the same. Might have bulked up a bit when he was in. Bobby Bangs was there too."

His sister didn't say anything. Yakabuski wondered if the news surprised her.

"Bobby Bangs? You're talking from the song?" she said.

"The one and only."

"My lord, Frank, I didn't think he was real, just some character from a song. No, hold it, I didn't think that. I must have known. He's related to Tommy Bangles somehow, isn't he?"

"Nephew. You should see the guy, Trish. It's like he's trying to out-Tommy Tommy. Any sane person on the planet would cross the street if they saw the guy walking toward them."

His sister went silent again and after a few seconds Yakabuski said, "I watched him for twenty minutes, Trish, standing in the rain, talking to your husband."

Yakabuski watched the two sets of taillights ahead of him. When his sister didn't say anything, he said, "Trish, I'm worried about you."

"Ah Frank, that's sweet, but don't be. Tyler knows what he's doing."

"I know you've thought that for a long time, Trish. Some years I may have thought it too. I'm not thinking it much anymore."

"What are you trying to tell me?"

"That this is going to end badly. The people who are looking for those diamonds, or want to protect those diamonds, they're not the kind of people used to walking away empty-handed. Your husband might as well be standing on a battlefield right now. Tyler ever struck you as much of a soldier?"

"If you're trying to scare me, Frank, it's working."

"That's exactly what I'm trying to do, Trish. Scare you. Scare you so much you start thinking about taking Julie and Jason, jumping on a plane, and getting out of here for a little while."

"They're still in school . . . Midterms are coming up."

"You're not listening, Trish. Swear to God, you're not listening."

❖ ❖ ❖

The Silver Dollar was one of the oldest bars in Cork's Town. It had been built by the Shiners in the 1840s, burned to the ground during the reform riots of 1856, burned again during the conscription riots of 1915, operated for many years as the Shamrock Tavern, and had been called the Silver Dollar since the '50s, a Springfield institution many people put in the same category as the Grainger Hotel and the Edwardian-era city hall. It was easily the largest night-club in Cork's Town, with separate rooms for a dance-club and a traditional tavern, with the pool tables, the quart bottles of beer, and the round tables.

Yakabuski wasn't sure what to expect when he arrived. He half thought there might be some sort of homecoming party for Morrissey, every Shiner in Springfield coming down to the nightclub for what they hoped would be an open bar.

But the parking lot was as empty as the highway. Four cars parked near the entrance — two of them being the ones he had followed down Highway 7. The neon lights had been turned off. The front vestibule of the club sat in darkness.

Yakabuski pulled his Jeep to the other side of the front entrance and waited. He'd give them ten minutes. He wanted everyone sitting down and settled.

When he walked in most of the interior lights were off as well, except for one track over the bar, which cast a weak, indifferent yellow light. Chairs had been upturned and set atop tables. The bartender glanced at Yakabuski when he walked in, then turned back to drying a rock glass. Yakabuski approached the bar and looked around.

"Thought there might be a party here tonight."

"Sean didn't want one."

"Doesn't sound like Sean to throw away a good excuse for a party."

"He wants to get right down to business."

"Yeah, I guess that's it. How come you're closed, though, Bernie?"

"Sean wanted to check the security arrangements. That's what I heard, anyway. We're supposed to reopen later in the week."

"What security arrangements?"

"Come on, Yak."

"Where's your doorman?"

"Haven't seen him in a little while."

"Eddie O'Malley? He's always here. I thought he *was* your security."

The bartender shrugged. He kept running a towel over the rock glass he was holding. After a while he said, "If you're looking for Sean, he's in his office." He placed the glass at the end of a line of perfectly dried rock glasses. Then he picked up another glass from the line and started rubbing a towel over it.

CHAPTER
THIRTY-SEVEN

There was an armed guard in front of Morrissey's office. At least, what Yakabuski assumed was an armed guard due to the bulge around the left armpit of his jacket, and a smaller bulge on the opposite hip. Snub-nosed pistol and some sort of baton, thought Yakabuski. The man wasn't tall, but he was built like a fire hydrant, right down to his peaked head. Yakabuski had a feeling the baton was his favourite weapon.

"I'm here to see Sean," he said, but the man just looked at him.

"I'm Detective Frank Yakabuski. Tell Sean I'm here."

"I know who you are. Do you have a warrant?"

"Don't need a warrant to have a friendly chat with someone."

"He doesn't want any visitors. That includes cops. Come back when you have a warrant."

Yakabuski stepped back and took another look at the man. He'd be tough enough. Body punches wouldn't matter much to him. He'd be hard to grip. If he rolled around on the floor with that baton, some variation on Brazilian Jiu-Jitsu, he could probably clear out a nightclub.

He might be a tough man to beat in a fight. But that wasn't why Yakabuski was there. And he had more than enough height and weight on the man to do what was needed.

"You got a name?" he said.

"Come back with a warrant."

"Right. Well, this is what's going to happen next, Mr. Come-back-with-a-warrant. You're going to knock on that door and tell Sean I'm here. Or I'll knock on the door myself, using your head."

Yakabuski stretched out his back after he said it, raising his arms just slightly above his shoulders, so the man could get a good sense of the size and weight he was about to go up against, just to make some point about a warrant. Without taking his eyes off Yakabuski, he backed up and knocked on the door.

"Billy," someone yelled from inside the room, sounding frustrated. But before he could say anything else, the guard said, "Yakabuski is out here, Mr. Morrissey. Says he needs to talk to you. He ain't got a warrant."

There were a few seconds of silence before Morrissey said, "That bohunk bastard wrecked half my club last time we made him wait. Send him in, Billy."

◆ ◆ ◆

Sean Morrissey sat behind a glass and chrome desk. He wore a black shirt with the cuffs rolled up, and his forearms were impressive. No question about it anymore. He had spent

230

some time doing curls in the weight room at Wentworth. Tyler Lawson sat on a chair across from the desk. A third man sat on a couch along the far wall, his face half in shadows. A table lamp and a lamp on Morrissey's desk were the only light in the room.

"Come to welcome me home, Yak?"

"Something like that. Wentworth treat you all right?"

"No complaints."

"Nice spring day we're having. Funny, but yesterday was beautiful."

"That supposed to mean something?"

"Not sure. Been thinking about it. What do you think?"

The two men stared at each other. Yakabuski pulled out a chair next to Lawson and sat down. Morrissey opened a drawer of his desk and, without taking his eyes off of Yakabuski, pulled out a large chrome object. Lawson took a quick breath, and the man sitting on the couch leaned forward. Yakabuski's body tensed, ready to move as soon as the gun was raised.

But then Morrissey opened another drawer and took out a bag of chestnuts. He placed one between the tongs of the nutcracker, one of the largest Yakabuski had seen, not much smaller than a pipe wrench.

"You know Tyler, of course," said Morrissey. "Have you met Bobby?"

At the mention of his name, Bobby Bangs leaned forward a bit more, his face now completely out of the shadows. Yakabuski found himself wondering if people gasped when first seeing that face, when it came out of the shadows at them the way it just had at him, then he wondered what happened to people like that a minute or two later. There were scars on Bangles's face, so profuse they looked like the bluish-red veins you'd see on the face of a bad alcoholic, so many little lines the face looked etched, or fossilized. His hair was long and blond. He had a strong jaw, a strong nose, eyes the blue of deep-cut ice — a handsome face, except for the scars, and the tattoos that ran across his neck, and the tobacco-stained teeth. He pushed away strands of hair and looked at Yakabuski as though the cop were a painting hanging on Morrissey's office wall. That sort of dispassion. That sort of disconnect. Nothing in that look to suggest one man regarding another man.

"We've never met," said Yakabuski. "I've heard a story or two."

Bangles kept staring. Didn't say anything.

"Tommy was his uncle," said Morrissey. "I guess you know that."

"I know that."

"So why are you here, Yak?"

"Thought we should have a little chat."

"Last time we chatted you arrested me."

"I picked you up for questioning. You got yourself arrested. Why'd you do that, by the way?"

"The cops you have in the holding cells — real drop in quality there, Yak. Don't know where you find the mutts."

"That cop you hit has worked the cells twenty-seven years. Never been a complaint against him. Volunteers at the John Howard Society. A real monster, that guy."

Morrissey laughed. He'd begun cracking chestnuts. He looked at Bangles, who finally took his eyes off Yakabuski and shrugged his shoulders. Morrissey said, "Tyler, I think we're done here."

Lawson looked surprised. Morrissey had just dismissed

him as though he were a waiter hovering too long at a table for a tip.

"I haven't gone through the parole conditions with you, Sean. There are some papers you need to sign."

"Tomorrow."

That's all Morrissey said. All he needed to say. Lawson gathered the paperwork from the desk, stuck it in his brief-case, and headed toward the door. As he passed Yakabuski, he gave a slight nod of his head. He was embarrassed. It was easy to tell.

When Lawson left the room, Yakabuski looked at Bangles. Who looked back at him. They held the stare a few seconds. Nope, still nothing.

❖ ❖ ❖

"So what have you come here to tell me, Yak? There *is* something you've come here to tell me, right?" Morrissey cracked another chestnut, threw his head back, and flipped the nut pieces into his mouth. Then he examined the next chestnut, looking for the best place to pinch it.

"I thought we'd finish our conversation about those missing diamonds. The one we were having the day I picked you up."

"As I remember, we were finished that conversation."

"Back then, sure, maybe you could think that. Not now, Sean. Not with two people dead on the Mission Road, Popeyes getting shot up in the French Quarter, four American college boys slaughtered out on the La Vase Basin. Not finished now."

"You don't think those murders had anything to do with me, do you, Yak?" Another squeeze of the metal tongs, and a loud crack. A bemused look on his face when he threw his head back.

"Why would I think that?"

"You know we didn't have anything to do with what happened in the French Quarter." It was Bangles, speaking for the first time. Yakabuski turned to look at him. If it was anger or passion that had made him speak, there was no sign of it anymore. His face was the impassive wood etching it had been a moment ago.

"Not denying your role in the murders of the men we found out on Mission Road, Mr. Bangles? That's probably a smart move."

"The reason you're here, Yak," interrupted Morrissey. "We're waiting."

Yakabuski looked around the office. The guard from the front door was now positioned inside the office. Hadn't moved or even twitched near as Yakabuski had seen. The man had standing still down to a fine art.

"Are you never alone anymore, Sean? Leading the cartel life these days? Might be better if it was just you and me for the next part."

"We're among friends, Yak. I think it's best if it stays the way it is."

"Right, well I came here to suggest something to you. Off the record, and nothing that's going to trip you up later. Why don't you tell me where those diamonds are, and I'll let you walk away from this."

Morrissey looked at Bangles, who looked at Yakabuski again. After a while, Morrissey said, "Speaking hypothetically, and only because you have just assured me you are not wearing a wire and nothing I say can be used against me in a court of law — that's what you've just said, right?"

"That's what I've just said."

"Well — why the *fuck* would I do that?"

Bangles laughed and finally turned away from Yakabuski.

"Because you've made your point," said Yakabuski. "The largest armed robbery in history. Nobody will ever be able to take that away from you, Sean. Best damn jewel thief history ever saw. That'll be you."

"I'm not that interested in history," said Morrissey. "I think the point of stealing something is to keep it."

"Not always. Not for you, certainly."

"What's that supposed to mean?" His grip tightened on the nutcracker.

"I mean you're a player, Sean. You're more of a thief than a gangster, and there was no way you could have stayed away from this one. I figure it was Gabriel Dumont who approached you with the scheme, and you saw what he had right away. You even worked in a back-end, so that Dumont walked away with nothing. Let that be enough, Sean. Why get killed trying to cash in?"

"You think that's what's going to happen to me?"

Yakabuski noticed he hadn't denied anything he'd just said. "I don't know how bad it will get for you, but I think that's possible. Sure I do. Don't you?"

"You don't think I can play with the big boys?"

"I don't think you even know what game the big boys are playing. Did you know De Kirk is gone? They couldn't care less what happens to those diamonds. They've already settled with the insurance company. Numbers on a piece of paper. That's the way you should look at those diamonds, Sean."

"Interesting argument, Yak. So tell me, if I go along with this, you'll be offering me complete immunity?"

"For the theft, yes, I can swing that. I don't know who to give those stones back to right now anyway."

"The rest of it?"

Yakabuski figured he was going to ask, but he still would have preferred if he hadn't. "I don't think I'll be able to swing immunity beyond the theft. You are the subject of several criminal investigations at the moment, some outside our jurisdiction or mandate. I would expect those to continue."

"So I give up the prize, but stick around for the consequences. That's quite an offer you're making me, Yak."

"There is no prize. I'm not sure if there ever was. That's what I'm trying to tell you, Sean."

Yakabuski sat quietly while Bangles sank back into the shadows. The guard by the door stood motionless. Morrissey examined another chestnut. Eventually, Yakabuski got up and left.

CHAPTER
THIRTY-EIGHT

When he left the Silver Dollar, Yakabuski was again surprised by the empty parking lot. Something he had now seen only twice in his life. Same for the neon sign out on Belfast Street, normally triggered by the sun going down, standing dark and useless that night. He'd never been on Belfast at night without the words *Silver Dollar* flashing in his face. He drove past the sign and wondered if there was anything in the world that screamed "left town" more convincingly than unlit neon signs. Boarded-up windows? Badly rusted cars sitting on blocks? Maybe something like that.

There was a sense of abandonment to the Silver Dollar that night so heavy it felt like swimming upriver. Strange that when he was sitting with Morrissey and Bangles they didn't strike him as men about to walk off the battlefield. The rest of the nightclub felt that way, but not the men in that office. They had that here-for-the-duration look in their eyes.

As he drove down Derry Street, he remembered a fishing guide he once knew in High River, one of the best guides to ever work out of the Highland Inn. The guide caught cancer in his mid-forties — not that you catch a thing like that, but that's probably how it felt to him. It spread quickly and within a few weeks of his diagnosis, the guide was going to Springfield regularly to get treatment. Not long after that, the federal government put him on long-term disability, which was the worst of signs and everyone in High River knew it. The government didn't do things like that for fishing guides unless it knew it was making a short-term commitment.

In autumn of that year, the guide went missing during a bad windstorm on Dore Lake. Because of his government pension the guide didn't work anymore and he was alone in the boat. He told his brother he was going to check his minnow traps.

Search parties were quickly organized and when he was found three days later — three days being the length of time it often took a drowned man to bloat and oxygenize and come to the surface — the guide's body was taken to his brother's farm. Yakabuski was only a teenager at the time, but he was with the group that found the body, and so he was one of the four men who carried the guide's body up the stone path leading to the farm.

In a dirt yard, they lay the guide down. The brother came out from the cabin with a sleeping bag he had unzipped and placed it over the body. The men stood in a semi-circle, looking at the sleeping bag and not saying anything. Eventually, William Dore, the oldest man there and the one who had known the guide the longest, said, "It's a shame

Edmund went out on a day like that, Tom. He didn't need to work anymore. It's a real shame."

The guide's brother, who seemed to Yakabuski to be older than Methuselah, stared at the sleeping bag a few more seconds, then turned to Dore and said in a polite tone, "What the fuck else was he going to do, Bill?"

They shook hands after that, and the men in the search party walked back down the stone path. The brother already had a shovel in his hands when Yakabuski took a quick look over his shoulder. Fealty to mission. You saw it in all sorts of ways.

Now, driving through Cork's Town, he kept searching the shadows around the buildings, looking for men holding shovels. When he reached the on-ramp for Highway 7 he was surprised he hadn't seen any.

❖ ❖ ❖

Morrissey dismissed the guard and sat in the office with Bangles, thinking about what Yakabuski had just said. One of these days he was going to ask that cop what really happened in Ragged Lake, what happened to Tommy and to Lucy Whiteduck, because that story didn't make any sense. In Wentworth, he had found himself missing Lucy. Other than Tommy, and his mother, it was the first time he'd ever missed someone. It surprised him, when the emotion came to him. Missing someone was a sad, dangerous business that Sean Morrissey had avoided most of his life.

"What do you think, Bobby?"

"I think he's whacked."

Morrissey laughed. "Why?"

"Because he thinks we've already lost. The battle hasn't even started. He's a soldier. He should know better."

"You don't think it's started?"

"So Cambino is in Springfield. We always thought he was. Now we know for sure. That video of those boys at the La Vase Basin — we should thank him for the heads-up."

"That's what you take away from that video?"

"Sure. What did you take away?"

Morrissey stared at him a moment. Bobby was so much like his uncle it was spooky at times. "Your plan didn't work," he said quietly, and shoved the nutcracker off to the side of the desk.

"The Popeyes fucked up. I should have known they would, after I saw their clubhouse. They're fuckin' idiots."

"No argument from me," Morrissey said. "It wasn't a complete failure though. The Popeyes are out of the picture now. Everyone who came to town has left. Except for Cambino. You've met him before, haven't you?"

"Twice. Once at his home in Heroica. Once at that summit in the Queen Elizabeth hotel, the one you and Tommy were at, along with Papa and Lepine, some of the cartel boys. I was there with Billy Adams."

"I remember. What did you think of him?"

"I didn't think anything of him. Less flashy than most of the cartel guys. What did you think?"

"I thought he was deadly. From the moment I met him. Quiet and sure of himself, set in his ways like an old man, although he was not that old. He didn't take advantage of the girls Papa brought. I remember that."

"You didn't either, Sean."

"I would never trust Papa's girls. Only an idiot would."

"So he is a cautious man. We will need to be more cautious. That's all it means. You should ask me, Sean."

Morrissey leaned back in his chair and looked at Bangles, surprised to see, for the first time, that if you took away the neck tattoos, the scars, made the hair grey instead of blond, he looked a lot like his uncle.

"Right to the point, eh, Bobby? Tommy was like that. You know that of course. It's one of the things I always loved about your uncle. You never wasted time with Tommy Bangles. You always knew where you stood."

"So ask me, Sean. You have my loyalty. The way you had Tommy's. Now is the time you need to ask me."

"Can you take him?"

"Yes," Bangles said with conviction.

"How will you do it?"

"I won't tell you."

"How much time will you need?"

"He's not far. Give me a week."

"All right. Take care of this problem for me, Bobby."

"Thank you."

"But tell me, before you start, a man who leaves no impression, that is a hard man to hunt, yes? Nothing? Are you sure?"

Bangles pondered the question one more time. Closed his eyes and remembered the house in Heroica, with the terracotta floor tiles and the warm breeze coming in from the Gulf of Mexico, a maid with long black hair who always wore a white uniform, a man in unfashionable shorts and wraparound sandals, smiling and scratching his chin, staring at him as though he were a bird that had just landed on the railing of his terrace.

"I think he lives in his head," said Bangles, when he opened his eyes. "That makes him dangerous, because he's invented his own rules, his own world. He struck me as a man of principle, although I don't have a clue what the principles might be. He struck me as a sick fuck, Sean."

CHAPTER
THIRTY-NINE

Donna Griffin was waiting for Yakabuski when he got back to the detachment. Sitting on the couch in his office, working on her laptop. He wasn't surprised to see her. Yakabuski had an open-door policy, and his meant more than most open-door policies. Many mornings he had to shake a major crimes detective awake and get him off his couch.

"You were right," said Griffin, when Yakabuski walked into the office. "You were so freakin' right."

"You found a Jeep leaving that garage."

"Found it on Deschamps Street, just like you said. Here, look."

Griffin put the laptop on his desk and hit a key. Yakabuski was looking at the intersection of Deschamps and Doucet, a block from the parking garage. The video was black and white, with the nauseous-green shading you always have with nighttime cameras, the linear lines diffused, a haze over the street that resembled a heat mirage. The intersection sat empty for five seconds and then the Jeep appeared. Heading north on Deschamps. A rag-top. Two doors. The time stamp read 1:23 a.m.

The Jeep stayed onscreen for six seconds, coming to a stop at the intersection, then continuing down Deschamps and disappearing in the shadows and pea-soup distortion at the outer limit of the camera's range.

"That's a Wrangler Sport," said Yakabuski.

"Yes it is. Pretty common vehicle around here. We've got nearly three thousand of them registered."

"Any belong to Sean Morrissey?"

"Ahh, wouldn't that be sweet. No."

"Any interesting names pop up?"

"No."

"All right then," and Yakabuski handed the laptop back to Griffin. "Go do your magic."

❦ ❦ ❦

The last of the snow lay in furrows deep in the forest and on north-facing slopes, but the trail was clear of it. Mission Road was now mud, pooled water, and mouldy leaves from last season, clumped together and starting to turn to peat. It was hard land to move across without leaving tracks. Bangles searched it for two days.

The land reminded him of Burk's Falls, without the hum of rushing water coming through the trees and the coolness to the air that was always there, but the hill country wasn't much different. Mixed forests of tamarack and spruce, maple and white pine, set atop a rock shield that dipped and rose like waves upon a choppy sea. Not ten feet of the land was level. Not ten acres of it was cleared.

He hiked the Mission Road trail and the logging roads that intersected, the deer paths and creek beds that ran beside it. He made camp the first night on a high ridge overlooking the Springfield Valley, not bothering to make a fire, and he spent the night looking down at the Valley through a night-vision scope, identifying every movement, every linearity, every man-made thing. He searched for signs of fire, searched until the stars had faded from the sky, and then he hoisted his pack and continued walking.

He thought about his problem as he searched. The man he was hunting was a skilled woodsman. His escape from Chicago showed that: cops from nearly a dozen different agencies looking for him, an international border to cross, and he made it through as easily as if he'd bought a bus ticket. Going overland from Cook County to the Northern Divide, in the eye of one of the most intensive manhunts ever undertaken in Illinois or Michigan, not so much as a verified sighting. That was beyond impressive. That was the stuff of folklore.

If you went north from the Mission Road, you had nothing but bush for hundreds of miles, practically all the way to James Bay. It made sense that Cambino would take advantage of the skills that brought him here. A man possessed of such impressive skills would use them again. Keep moving through the forest like some night wind.

Or did that make sense? To use that skill set once again? Cambino had wanted to get away from Chicago. He didn't want to get away from Springfield.

Bangles thought about that.

Cambino wasn't on a journey this time. He wasn't trying to get away from anything, or get somewhere. He wanted to stay hidden and out of sight until it was time to strike. That was a different mission objective that needed a different set of skills.

Near noon Bangles stopped walking and sat on a large boulder, left on the northern slope of the hill it had gouged out when it had come down with the ice ten thousand years ago. There was moss on the ground, and the air was cold enough to show his breath. The tall pine let in only a little light, and he could hear the sound of wings through the trees but couldn't see the birds.

Cambino must be holed up somewhere. In a city where he didn't know anyone except the man he wanted to rob. So, where would he go? Bangles sat on the rock for more than an hour, his eyes closed, thinking the problem through. Then he jumped off the rock and started walking again.

An hour later he was at the La Vase Basin. He stared around a minute, then went off the trail and tacked southeast, bushwhacking his way through the forest as there was no trail. He marched through mud and pools of cold water, the sun already on his back, his breath coming out in large, billowy clouds, marching until he cleared a stand of spruce two hours later and found himself standing on the French Line. He could see smoke rising from spruce stands up and down the road, showing him where the old settler cabins would be.

He had a cabin he liked by dawn of the following day.

◈ ◈ ◈

The old man sat at his kitchen table and watched the sun rise. It started as a red glow, just past the treeline of his cleared land, as though the sun were some sort of backstage light. It would be different, he supposed, if you were watching a sunrise on flat land, like the Great Plains, or out on the ocean maybe. The sun would announce itself if you lived somewhere flat. On the Northern Divide, the sun more or less crept up on you.

He stared at the distant glow as it transformed into a thin red line hovering above the trees, a line that shimmered and radiated as though electric. The upper ring of a bright orb appeared above the trees, and the shadows fell away. Forty-five minutes later, the sun was in the sky.

It was a process. Shadow and light. Form and illusion. The old man would find it hard to live on flat land, did not think the things that mattered in this world should ever announce themselves, an impertinence he found distasteful, a boldness that seemed reckless. He would be sad and worried if he ever needed to look upon the sun that way.

He turned away from the window and stared at the man seated at the table with him. Perhaps the old man should have been more surprised when the stranger arrived, but when you have spent your life, all seventy-two years of it, living in a place where the sun creeps up on you, where your first waking hours are always uncertain, it takes a lot to surprise you.

He came just as the sun was clearing the treeline, a little after six in the morning. He knocked on the door, which was an odd thing to have done, in hindsight, for there was no need. The old man never answered. He was still sitting at his table when the stranger walked through the cabin door.

Closed it behind him, looked around, and said, "I will need to stay here awhile, my friend."

"Why? Are the police after you?"

"Yes."

"There are better places to hide. My uncle hid from the cops for more'n two years, in a cave not far from here. It's still provisioned up. I can take you there."

"I am not worried about the police."

The old man didn't know what to say to that. The stranger was middle-aged, wearing a tan windbreaker and white running shoes with Velcro straps. He looked like an RV driver you'd find at an Interstate restaurant in Florida. It didn't sound like a boast, when he said he wasn't worried about the police. And it didn't sound like the sort of thing he was saying to make himself feel better. There was no emotion in his voice. No doubt. The words seemed a simple statement of fact. He wasn't worried.

"Why do you want to stay here?"

"I need a place to work."

"What sort of work do you do?"

"Consultant."

"What if I don't want any guests?"

"That would be a mistake, my friend. Hospitality would serve you well right now."

The old man went to make coffee.

That had been thirteen days ago.

CHAPTER FORTY

Bangles put down his field glasses. The small windows in the cabin had curtains drawn, and the snow around it was freshly fallen, with only animal tracks showing. Smoke was coming from the chimney. He had checked six cabins while making his way here. Two were abandoned, three had families living in them, and one had a bad drunk. He surveyed the inhabited cabins until he was satisfied no one had moved in. No signs of anyone being held captive, no signs of anyone under duress, other than the signs you would expect to see on the faces of people living on the French Line.

This cabin was different. He had approached it from downwind, walking the shoreline of a fast-moving creek. He had taken positions at three different lines of sight, done a thirty-metre perimeter sweep and a fifteen, but had yet to see anyone inside. Yet smoke had never stopped rising from the tin-pipe chimney in the roof.

He went back to his three positions, checked the sight-lines again, then crawled on his belly back to the second. It was on a small rise thirty yards from the front door, almost a direct line. He watched for another thirty minutes, but saw nothing through the leaden glass of the two front windows. Maybe someone was asleep. Maybe someone was reading a book by the airtight stove.

Maybe someone was avoiding the windows.

It didn't matter, from an operational point of view, and Bangles knew he was wasting time even wondering about it. To defeat the man he hunted, there could be no warning, no second-guessing: he needed to strike first, and he needed to strike without mercy.

Whoever was in that cabin was dead. If it had been someone sleeping, or someone reading a book, that was just their bad fortune. To beat a man like Cambino Cortez, this was what you needed to do. The unexpected. The merciless. It was how you kept the advantage.

And Bangles had the advantage. If Cambino was in that cabin, the game was as good as won. He put down his field glasses. Rubbed his eyes. Reached for the backpack that lay by his feet and took out the sniper's rifle. Had it assembled in thirty-seven seconds, scope activated and tripod levelled in the mud. Another thirty seconds, and he had wind and distance calculated, to a target point three feet in front of the cabin door.

He opened an outside pouch of his duffle bag and took out two incendiary grenades. A thatched-roof cabin. One door. Windows too small for a man to get through. It was too early to call it a gift from God, but it felt that way to Bangles when he pulled the first pin.

The old man had been wondering for thirteen days how it would end for him, and in all that time he'd never been able to get beyond moderately pessimistic. He had spent his life being proud of his honesty, the best trait of any bushman, but wished now he was more skilled at lying to himself.

It did not surprise him when the stranger looked up suddenly from the book he was reading, his face filled with an alertness that made you think of a predator animal that had just caught a scent. He had expected a gesture like that. Something like that.

"Someone outside?" he asked.

"Yes."

"They'll be on the rise to the north of the front door."

The stranger got up from his seat. Finished his coffee in two large gulps and put the cup down. Then he walked to the back wall of the cabin and started to inspect it. Ran his fingers along the mortar between the logs. Rubbed the chalk off his fingers when he was finished and then walked to the airtight stove and got the hatchet from the wood box. He was on his way back to the wall when the first grenade exploded on the roof. The old man jumped from his chair, covering his ears, casting his eyes to the ground. When he looked up, the stranger was standing in front of him, gently pushing him back into his chair.

"I am sorry, my friend," he said. "I wish it had gone differently for you. You have been a good host, and you deserved a better fate."

Cambino tied the old man's hands to the arms of the chair, using nylon rope that always hung on a hook by the front door. He did the job quickly, and then he started working on the back wall, swinging the hatchet and chopping out chunks of mortar. When the second grenade landed, he began to chop a little faster. He had not been expecting two, so that would cut down on the time he had to work. Thirteen minutes? Somewhere around that. Less than fifteen and more than ten. He was counting on the old man's screams to buy him time.

Without the screams, the man outside might become suspicious, might move in too quickly. The screams would keep him in position until the cabin burned to the ground. Thirteen minutes.

❖ ❖ ❖

Bangles saw the tracks as soon as the flames had subsided enough for him to approach. Soon as the smoke had cleared and the wind picked up and he had taken apart his rifle and walked from his position on the rise to the smouldering pile of wood that had once been the cabin.

The tracks led from what had been the back wall to the creek Bangles had followed to get there. The sun was starting to set, and shadows had already fallen across the water, so you couldn't see more than twenty feet in either direction. Bangles stood by the creek and tried to keep his anger in check.

He almost had him. He had the cabin dead right. He didn't know what Cambino would have been able to bring with him when he fled, but probably not much. He had no more than a ten-minute head start. Every twitch of every muscle in his body was telling him to pursue.

But it would be a mistake. He no longer had the sure advantage. It would be anger and vengeance that drove him down the creek, not clear-headed resolve, which is what you needed to finish a mission. He backed away from the dying flames. As he made his way down the French Line, Bangles didn't wonder whose screams he'd heard as the cabin burned to the ground. He didn't see how it mattered.

CHAPTER FORTY-ONE

It was two days before Yakabuski got a phone call from Fraser Newton, telling him he needed to come to the French Line and have a look at something. The remains of a cabin fire. Newton was already there.

A cabin burning down on the French Line wasn't that uncommon. The logs on some of the homes on the colony road were nearly two hundred years old, and every last cabin was heated by an airtight stove, which wasn't much different, from a design point of view, from an oil drum burning in the middle of your living room.

People living on the French Line weren't known for their home improvement skills, either. None of the cabins had rooms added to them, or skylights put into the roof, what you saw on settler cabins in places like Buckham's Bay and the suburbs west of Springfield. French Line cabins were what they were the day they'd been built. And a lot of those cabins burned when the tin-pipe chimney clogged and the airtight exploded.

Newton was apologetic when Yakabuski got there. About as much as the major crimes detective had ever seen him. Newton didn't like to make mistakes, and it was obvious to Yakabuski that he'd just made one. Just as obvious that he didn't know yet how bad a mistake he'd made, although a mistake of the falling-off-a-cliff variety must have struck him as a possibility.

"We missed it, Yak," he said. "I should have come myself, but with everything that's going on right now, I sent someone else. An old man dying in a French Line cabin fire — it didn't set off any bells."

"Who was it?"

"Pinot Degrasse. Seventy-two years old. Worked for the city on a paving crew for forty-two years. We're having trouble finding next of kin."

"He was connected to Morrissey somehow?"

"No, nothing like that. Degrasse is exactly what he seems. Near as we can see so far, anyway."

"So what did you miss, Newt?"

"This." Newton reached into his coat pocket to bring out a plastic evidence bag. He handed it to Yakabuski. Some burnt metal about the size of a teaspoon head, blue and green wires sticking out from it, on the metal some stamped numbers and a couple of words in a language that wasn't English.

"Do you know what that is, Yak?"

"A detonator cap. Looks Czech-made. Maybe a BS-8."

"Exactly that," Newton said. "The officer I sent out, he walked into my office this morning with that in his hand, asking if I knew what it was."

"In his hand?"

"In his freakin' hand."

"Shit."

"I know."

"The cabin was never taped off?"

"That's right. Jump ahead and imagine the worst, Yak, because that's what we have. A completely contaminated crime scene."

Yakabuski looked at the pile of ashes and singed timbers, no snow anywhere near it, nothing but mud and pooled water, some shards of ice on the north shore of the pile, where there wouldn't be much sun.

"You need to tape this off right now, Newt. Twenty-yard perimeter from the edge of the burn. No one gets inside until you talk to me."

"You got it, Yak. I am so sorry."

"Save it until we know how bad it is. Any idea what shoe size your officer would be?"

"Uhh, he's not a big man. Nine. Nine-and-a-half maybe. I'll check. I'm a nine."

"All right, stand back. Get that tape up and give me a few minutes."

❖ ❖ ❖

Yakabuski picked his spot and went to it, careful where he was stepping, as straight a line as he could manage. The spot was ten yards in front of where the door to the cabin would have been, and when he got there Yakabuski stood and looked around, casually at first, getting an impression of the land: he saw the creek running behind it, the mixed-wood forest, how the sun would have risen and fallen, and where the prevailing winds would have come. After that he pushed his feet tight together and started his sweep, rotating his feet in a complete circle, never un-clinching them, doing it on the back of his heels and stopping at each forty-five-degree angle to inspect the ground that fell within the plane.

When he had done the full three-sixty, he went back to the second forty-five-degree plane. The ambulance gurney had been there. It was easy to spot the four circular holes in the mud spaced just right. He walked up to the holes and studied the boot-prints. Quickly had the boots worn by the paramedics. They would have been issued to them by the city. He knew the boot. Sorels with the anti-shock, anti-slip sole.

He studied the pattern of boot-prints again and found the nine-and-a-half boot that landed next to the paramedics so often it must have been the Ident cop. He took a long look at the pattern, closed his eyes, removed all the prints he had identified. Saw what was left.

Still a mess. He backed up, took a wide sweep around the burn area, and headed to the creek. Once there he did another full-circle, rotating sweep, checking each forty-five-degree plane. He walked down the shoreline and picked away pine needles from a set of boot prints. Walked the shoreline fifty metres in either direction. Then he walked back to the gurney holes and shouted, "Got any numbers, Newt?"

"In my car."

"Go get 'em."

Yakabuski stayed in place while Newton ran to his car and came back cradling some plastic bags. Inside were numbered pieces of plastic, bent in the shape of a lean-to.

"Going to need two colours."

"I was hoping you'd say that. Any preference?"

"Not at all. Toss 'em over."

Newton tossed two plastic bags, and Yakabuski began to work.

He had had a feeling that creek was going to help him.

❖ ❖ ❖

An hour later he had it all laid out. One attacker and one person in the cabin who managed to get out. Yakabuski had seventeen good prints for the attacker and twenty-eight for the man who fled. They were colour-coded and numbered, and it was easy to see what had happened.

"He would have launched his attack from that rise." Yakabuski pointed to a nearly melted clump of snow that now sat inside a band of crime-scene tape, a yellow fold-out card with the number one sitting atop it. "You'll want to search that area thoroughly, Newt. He would have been positioned there for a while."

"Only position?"

"I think so. He may have scouted some others, but this is the one he chose. The man he was after got out the back of the cabin, right over there."

They walked to the other side of the pile of rubble, stood over a red fold-out card with the number one on it. "Good tracks for this man all the way to the creek, and about twenty metres heading up."

The two men stared at the trail Yakabuski had marked out in the mud and water and last-remnant snow. A zig-zagging line of red and yellow fold-out cards.

"Were they chasing each other?"

"There's no sign of gunfire. No blood. And this isn't a chase pattern. No, someone in that cabin got out, and the attacker found out about it later. Looks like he was going to follow him down the creek and changed his mind. He couldn't have missed him by much."

"Who do you think we're talking about, Yak?"

"The people you think we're talking about, Newt."

"Bobby Bangs out on the French Line. If I tell my wife that, she won't sleep for a week. Was he the one in the cabin?"

"I don't think so."

"You know those cabins don't have doors or windows in the back, right?"

"I know that."

"So how did anyone get out?"

"I'm not sure, Newt. Let's go catch the bastards and we'll ask them."

CHAPTER
FORTY-TWO

Bangles needed rest and figured he had time for it. When you firebombed a belligerent out of their hidey-hole, it took a day or two for them to regroup and circle back. He went to the apartment on Derry Street where he had been living since arriving in Springfield, one of the three apartments and two motel rooms he had under rent or lease. He rotated through on a non-repeating pattern, careful never to sleep in the same bed for three consecutive nights.

He slept for twenty-six hours. When he awoke, he took a full-kit duffle bag and left the apartment. He got new clips for his Uzi from a Shiner he met in an underground parking garage in Cork's Town, the Shiner popping the trunk of his Cadillac and never leaving the car. Got pouches of dehydrated food and salt pills from Foster's Sporting Goods. Money from an ATM in the French Quarter. When he finished his errands, he drove to the North Shore.

Bangles wasn't sure if he would see her. He knew she was under police protection, but that could mean many things. He'd been told she was still living in her apartment. Hadn't been moved. Patrol cars permanently positioned in front and back of Building C. A female cop that walked her to and from school.

He sat in the back stairwell of Building D, drinking a takeout coffee and looking out the window at the trail cutting through the woods, leading from Filion's Field to Northwest Elementary School. The leaves on the birch and poplar had only just started to bud, so the trail was easy to see. It still had patches of snow showing, as the North Shore Escarpment was one of the last places in Springfield to give up its snow.

He saw her at 3:23. Because of a dip in the trail, it was her head he saw first. A red toque, her black hair in braids hanging below the hat's earflaps. She climbed up the trail, and he saw her parka, unzipped and fanning out slightly in the slow wind. A second later, twenty feet behind her, he saw the head of the female police officer.

The girl's walk was jaunty. A skip almost. Her head turned from side to side, observing what there was to observe, a new day in a new season, a young girl wanting to explore that. You could see it in her stride. She was ready for adventure.

She bent her head to get through an opening cut in the chain-link fence, and when she was through she looked up and her eyes seemed to settle for a minute on the window of the stairwell. The sightline was perfect for it. Bangles watched her stare up at the window, take her hand and hold it to block the sun from her eyes; after that a questioning look, then a smile that appeared and disappeared so quickly he might have imagined it. She raised her left hand, a gesture that might have been a wave, might have been anything else, and then she lowered her head and walked into the back door of her apartment building.

He never saw her speak to the police officer. He wondered if she didn't like her guard, or thought her presence an infringement on her freedom. He suspected the latter. In a few years, maybe less, there would be few people on this planet capable of putting a claim on that girl. She would change or not change as it pleased her. No different than the weather.

Bangles finished his coffee, walked down the back stairs of Building D, and made his way to his pickup truck. He didn't notice the car parked nearby. Didn't notice the man behind the wheel in the Texas A&M cap. Didn't know the risk he had just taken, for only a glimpse of her.

CHAPTER
FORTY-THREE

Bangles sat on the roof of the warehouse on Ladoucer Street, his kit bag beside him. He had provisions for two nights, couldn't see it taking longer than that. Cambino would assume it was the Popeyes who had come after him at the cottage, in retaliation for what he'd done in the French Quarter. And he was not the sort of man to let his problems linger, to deal with them at some future date, the way most people did. Cambino Cortez did not see the sense in delaying the inevitable, nor in sharing the planet with an enemy.

He would be coming for the bikers. And this time, Bangles would be more direct, more personal. He would shoot Cambino the second he saw him, didn't matter where he was standing, didn't matter who else was around. Then he would stand over his body and fire two more into his head. A verified kill from two feet away. That's how this was going to end.

He watched the sun rise and chase away the shadows on Ladoucer, the red-brick buildings and auto yards appearing as though curtains were slowly being drawn open. The overnight mechanics drove away with the shadows. The 85 bus rolled down the street at 5:45 for its first run of the day. Two dumpsters pulled out of Levesque's Cartage at exactly 6:00. An hour later, cars were filling the parking lots around the warehouses and lights had been turned on in most of the buildings.

By 8:30 a.m., Ladoucer Street was crowded with dumpsters and cargo vans and ring-line buses. By midmorning the chip trucks arrived, and they stayed until midafternoon, men and women in work overalls and delivery uniforms lined up before them. Schoolchildren walked down the street shortly after 3 p.m., and cars started to pull out of parking lots at exactly 4:00. The streetlights turned on just before 7:00, and the shadows crept back shortly after.

The Popeyes clubhouse was not as busy as it had been a month earlier. There were still men in expensive suits arriving for midmorning meetings. Still a half-dozen bikers living in the clubhouse full-time, judging by his visual sweeps of the bedrooms and offices on the second floor. Still girls from the strip clubs in the French Quarter arriving just before midnight. But everything had been tamped down. Not as many visitors. Not as many girls.

Bangles had eyes on every person who entered the clubhouse that day and night. Eyes on the two black sedans that left the garage as dusk fell, to take up positions at either end of the street, a new security feature for the Popeyes. He took his no-snooze pills and kept vigil. Not only on the clubhouse, but the neighbourhood around it, looking for someone who might also be keeping vigil that night.

When the sun rose the following morning, he knew something was wrong.

❖ ❖ ❖

Bangles's phone rang shortly before noon of the second day. It was encrypted, and only one person had the number. He took the phone out of his kit bag and looked at it. Not the number it should have been. He answered, but didn't speak. In a few seconds he heard a man's voice say, "Bobby, are you there?"

Morrissey's lawyer.

"I'm here."

"I have a message for you," said the lawyer, sounding more scared than Bangles would have liked. "Your apartment on Derry was firebombed two hours ago. Police are on scene. The person who has asked me to call wants to know if there is anything in the apartment that can come back to him."

"No."

"And to you?"

"No."

"I will tell him. He has also asked that I give you a message. He wants you to know that you've just been tagged. Do you understand what this means?"

"I do."

Tyler Lawson sat in his office wondering if he was supposed to say "good luck," or something like that. While he was trying to decide, the phone clicked off.

◈ ◈ ◈

Bangles started putting his kit bag together. Burn down my hidey-hole, I'll burn down yours. Tag, you're it. He cursed himself for underestimating the man he was hunting, a man who seemed to have no weakness, no moments of situational confusion, who stayed a move or two ahead of the game even when he was the one being hunted.

He had never known a man with that skill set. To be elusive, yes. Deadly when cornered, yes. But to stay ahead of the game, never be deceived, never be trapped, he had never seen it. How do you fight an enemy like that? Planning was as close to useless as you could get.

Maybe he couldn't plan with this guy. Maybe he just had to get close to him, pull his weapon, and take his chances. A balls-out showdown with the luckiest man winning. He was sitting on the roof of the boarded-up Stedman's warehouse, packing his kit bag and thinking about that, when the first bullet hit him.

◈ ◈ ◈

The pain was instantaneous. The realization he had just been played almost as fast. Bangles fell to his knees, but rolled when he hit the ground. The second bullet struck where his face would have been if he hadn't rolled. He grabbed his kit bag and held it in front of his face, heard the soft "poof-poof" sound of two more bullets hitting the bag.

He kept rolling until he was behind an air-vent chimney. Bullets ripped into the chimney, throwing red-hot shards of aluminum onto his head. He slapped the shards away. Opened his kit bag and took out the sniper rifle he had just taken apart. Not the weapon he would have liked, but he had a good idea where the shooter was positioned. He dropped a round into the chamber, flipped off the scope, and rolled out. Fired three quick shots at the stairwell on the building behind the warehouse and rolled back behind the chimney.

A fragment from the second bullet had hit his shoulder, and there was blood seeping through his parka. The first bullet had pierced his upper thigh, which could be good news, or could be the worst of news. It depended on whether his femoral artery had been hit. If it had, he would bleed out on this roof. Less than twenty minutes probably. He looked at the blood pumping out of his leg, and couldn't decide if it was enough to worry about.

He lay on his back, his rifle quartered in both hands, arms pulled tight to his chest, and after he counted to five he rolled back out.

Two quick shots at the stairwell this time, Bangles taking time to aim between the fourth and fifth floors, where he figured the angle was right. Didn't roll back behind the chimney right away. Stayed rock still until he had counted to ten, and then he rolled back.

He started dressing his wound. He ripped apart a shirt from his kit bag, fashioning the strips into a tourniquet, but he still wasn't sure how badly he'd been hit. He did a good job with the tourniquet, knowing his luck may have already turned bad and maybe it was a waste of time, but labouring without knowing if it mattered was how you spent every workday in Burk's Falls, so he didn't wonder about it much.

As soon as the tourniquet was cinched, he repacked the kit bag and made his way to the fire escape on the east side of the warehouse. He stuck his rifle over the edge of the roof and fired without showing his head, without looking, then he rose quickly and swept the alleyway.

No one down there.

He half climbed, half slid down the fire escape, gritting his teeth in pain when he landed on the ground. He pulled his hoodie over his head as he walked down the alleyway, shifting the kit bag from his right hand to his left, leaving his right arm free to swing up and down with his stride, each up-stroke bringing his fingers within an inch of the butt of the Uzi hidden beneath his coat.

He needed to get off the street. Get deep underground for a few hours to take care of his wounds. After that — and he didn't care if half of Springfield needed to burn through the night to make it happen — he was going to find that son of a bitch, and they were going to settle this.

FORTY-FOUR

Donna Griffin's voice inflected down at the end of her sentences, which told Yakabuski there was a problem. Knew it before she got around to talking about it. Her normal speaking tone was one of excitement. Not enthused, because it was more than that, and not excitable, because that would be different. Donna Griffin was the sort of person who didn't need inspirational coffee cups telling her to seize the day. She was going to spend her life seizing every moment, eyes and arms spread wide. Yakabuski admired people like that.

So it was obvious to him she had a problem and he interrupted two minutes into her sitrep.

"Donna, why don't you jump ahead and tell me what I need to know."

"You don't want the full report?"

"I don't need the Jeep's complete route right now. Just tell me how long you had the vehicle and where it went."

"Right. We had it for seventeen minutes, eleven seconds. It went onto Highway 7 and took the Centretown exit. We actually caught it on the cameras here at the detachment. It passed us at 2:23 that morning. The last camera was a good one, a private sector camera at Edelson's Jewellers on Water Street. Camera caught the rear of the Jeep full-frame. You can see the licence plate number is covered over with mud. Best shot we have of that. Might be able to pull some numbers. Newt is looking into it."

"You're still not telling me what the problem is."

"You think there's a problem?"

"I do," he said into his cellphone.

"Right. Well, there is. I don't really know how to tell you this, Yak, but that Jeep was pulling into a parking garage when the Edelson's camera caught it. It's an Imperial garage, directly across the street from the jewellery store."

"Another parking garage?"

"Yes. And Yak, this one is a killer. The Jeep entered the garage at 2:47 a.m. and never came out. We found it this morning, in a long-term-parking section on the top floor. Newton has a team going through it. The licence plates were gone. Owner says that's not unheard of, for a long-term lot. Also says it was a cash transaction, last November. Signature on the contract is illegible."

Yakabuski didn't say anything. He was beginning to understand the problem.

"We're searching the Jeep, searching the garage, but nothing so far," continued Griffin. "Newton figures the odds of finding any diamonds there are zero to nada. He asked that I include that in my sitrep. Zero to nada."

"He's probably being optimistic."

"I think he is. Yak, we can't recover from this. I've spent all day thinking about the math, and it's impossible. That Jeep has been sitting there for seven months. Thousands of cars have gone in and out of that garage. Even if you make assumptions — the thief wouldn't have wanted to stay in the garage long — we can't make it work. As soon as three cars leave that garage, you've got an infinite number of possibilities. That's all it would take."

"Three cars?"

"We might be dead with just two. I haven't finished the math on that, but three, yeah, that's a deal breaker. And not that it matters, but to give you some idea how ugly this is, between 2:47 and 6:00 the morning of the heist, twenty-seven vehicles went in and out of that parking garage."

Her voice was falling so low, Yakabuski had trouble hearing the last sentence. Twenty-seven? Was that what she said?

"Were you able to get any sort of visual on the driver of the Jeep?"

"No. You never do with night cameras. Person looks to be wearing a parka. Looks to be a fair size, but it's a parka, so who knows? We can't even tell if it's a man or a woman. It's a dead end, Yak. I'm sorry, but we're right back to the day we started. We don't have a clue where those diamonds might be."

"You said twenty-seven vehicles?"

"That's right."

"Anyone walk in or out of that garage?"

"Camera didn't catch anyone. Yak, I'm not sure if I'm making myself clear here. There are too many vehicles. We can never figure this out."

"What if you were just looking for one?"

"One vehicle? How would that work?"

"Give me a minute."

Yakabuski closed his eyes. He hated to see good work wasted. Hated to hear Donna Griffin sounding as though she wanted to quit. It was a long shot, but the more he thought about it, the more there seemed a logic to it. He kept his eyes closed, trying to recall the numbers on a licence plate he once followed through the rain. When he opened his eyes he said, "Do you have a pen and paper?"

"I have my computer called up."

"Take this down — KZL 135."

"A licence plate number?"

"Your Hail Mary pass. Check that number against those twenty-seven vehicles. If you don't get a hit, check it against every vehicle until 9 a.m. That probably won't take long, right?"

"Shouldn't."

"Call me when you're done."

❖ ❖ ❖

Yakabuski went to a coffee shop next to the detachment and got a medium coffee to go. The girl behind the counter asked if he meant venti and he said no, medium. When she asked him if he wanted decaf, he laughed. Then he felt bad for laughing and left a dollar tip.

His desk phone was ringing when he walked back into his office.

"It was the fifth car," said Griffin. "I've already pulled the registration, and I have to say — holy fuck! What do you want me to do?"

"Follow the car."

CHAPTER
FORTY-FIVE

Bangles stared across the street at the motel office, knowing there was no way to avoid it. He had spent most of the day in a boatyard in the French Quarter, knowing a boatyard would have an emergency medical kit, which he found in one of the work bays. There was more in it than he had hoped. Iodine and saline, glass hypodermic needles, good heavy gauze, and better tape. He took the kit, along with some water bottles from a lunchroom fridge, and hid in the forward cabin of a forty-four-foot SeaRay sitting on blocks. He treated his wounds and even managed to sleep a few hours, the police sirens racing through the French Quarter and up and down Ladoucer Street not disturbing him.

It had not been the femoral artery. A lucky break. But as he looked at the motel office, he knew the lucky break had been cancelled out by the bad break that followed it. Why was it always that pattern? Just once he wished the rhythm would change. He gave his head a shake. He was wasting time.

It wasn't until he was a block from the motel that he realized what had happened. Went to get his room key from his kit bag, and it wasn't there. Stopped him dead in his tracks. A sign of just how bad not finding that key was, because when you were on the ground in search of an enemy who had already attacked, you didn't stop.

The key must have fallen out during the attack on the roof. How could he have missed it? He looked at the flashing red neon *open* sign in the office window of the Concorde Motel. The room in the Concorde was where he had his bug-out kit. Room 17, ground floor of the east wing, end unit.

He could have broken in easily enough, but he might be noticed by the night clerk; a young man with a perfect sightline on the room every night from where he sat, behind the front desk watching television. Bangles looked at the motel office and ran through his options one more time. After a few minutes, he shouldered his kit bag, stepped out of the shadows, and crossed the street to the motel.

He needed to ask the night clerk for the spare key. It put him out in the open for a few minutes, but it was the safest option.

❖ ❖ ❖

The office did not have its main light on. Just a green-shaded lamp on the front desk and a fourteen-inch colour television on a nightstand behind the desk that threw off a bit of light. Bangles pushed open the door and walked in.

The night clerk got an annoyed look on his face, turned

away from the television, and said, "Good evening and welcome to the Concorde . . . oh, it's you, Mr. Bishop."

The clerk was in his early twenties, had greasy black hair and a face full of pimples. He'd asked Bangles once about his tattoos. Said he'd always wanted a neck tattoo, just wasn't sure about it.

"Hello, Matt. Hate to trouble you, but I've lost my room key. I'm going to need the spare tonight."

"Sure, Mr. Bishop. Not a problem."

The clerk got up and walked to a wooden board, where keys were suspended from eyelet hooks, each key having a red plastic sticker with the words *Concorde Motel* written on it. The clerk grabbed the key for room 17 and came back to the desk.

"Here you go," and he pushed the key across the desk. As Bangles reached for it, the clerk said, "Hey, you're bleeding."

Bangles looked at the drops of blood that had fallen on the desk.

"Cut my hand earlier today. Looks like it's time to re-tape it."

"You don't look so good, Mr. Bishop. Here, let me turn on a light."

"No. I'm good, Matt."

But the clerk turned on the light. About as bright as a strobe, a white, garish light that just exploded out of the darkness as though a meteor had landed in the office of the Concorde Motel. And then the clerk asked fumbling, earnest questions about Bangles's skin colour, saying maybe he should have that checked out, Bangles wanting to shoot the boy but figuring that would just make things worse. Finally the clerk handed him the key and he left the office.

✦ ✦ ✦

When you were in combat, you lit a person up when you were using them as bait. When you wanted to bring in a belligerent, and you had an expendable target you thought might do the trick.

Bangles took the spare key but waited ninety minutes to go to his room. He hid in the woods behind the motel and kept room 17 under surveillance. While he waited, he changed his dressing. Glassed every room around 17 with his night-vision scope. When he felt enough time had passed, he shouldered his kit bag and walked toward the room.

He swung his left leg at an angle, to keep the tourniquet from chafing. He had lost enough blood to make even a hundred-metre walk hard work. He paused for breath when he reached the room, steadied his legs and shifted his weight, used the spare key and opened the door.

When he was inside, he closed the door, leaned against it, his spine pushing up against the metal-framed notice with room rates and a map showing the escape route down the stairwells and hallways of the Concorde Motel. In case of an emergency; in case you wanted to escape in an orderly fashion. He was still taking long, deep breaths, his eyes adjusting to the darkness of the room, when he heard a man's voice say, "I thought you could crawl faster than that."

CHAPTER
FORTY-SIX

The room was dim, but he could see that Cambino was smiling. He sat on the bed, his feet gently touching the floor, his right hand holding a Glock pistol aimed at Bangles's chest.

"Drop the bag, Bobby," he said, and after Bangles had a long hard look at the gun, that's what he did.

"Kick it over here."

He shoved the bag with his good leg. Cambino raised his left arm and pointed to a chair and table by the window. "Sit there."

Bangles sat. A tourist brochure for Springfield lay atop the table, a midsummer photo of the Kettle Falls, a war canoe shooting a set of rapids. A cheap piece of overly shellacked wood lay beneath the tourism brochure. He stared at the images. None of the pieces connected up right. He wondered what had just happened.

"Do you play sporting games, Bobby? Chess? Back-gammon? Anything like that?"

Bangles could make him out a little better now. He wore a tan-coloured windbreaker, and his hair was black and slicked back, parted down the middle. He didn't look much different from the last time he'd seen him.

"It's checkmate," Cambino continued. "It's backgammon. It's whatever you want to call it, Bobby, but you are defeated. You are alive right now only because I wish it. You know this to be true. You gain nothing by denying it."

Facial features were starting to show. The hooked nose. The deep, black-pool eyes. No facial hair. No wrinkles. Bangles took another look at the table. There would be a Gideon's Bible inside the drawer. Some pizza flyers. More things that weren't connecting up right.

"Do you want to know how I found you?"

"I know how you found me."

"You think it was the key."

"I know it was the fuckin' key."

"It wasn't."

"Bullshit."

"Here, I'll prove it to you."

Now Cambino was smiling. No mistaking it. He kept the handgun pointed at Bangles's chest, as steady as though it were on a tripod, and fished in the pocket of his wind-breaker with his other hand until he pulled out a yellow piece of paper. He walked over and put the paper in Bangles's lap. Then he backed up and sat on the bed.

Bangles looked at it. A room receipt from the Concorde Motel. A cash transaction it looked like. Room 48. West wing, upper floor, end unit. Bangles had surveyed the motel several times. He looked at the receipt and realized the room would be directly across the courtyard from his, one floor up.

"I checked in the day before I shot you, Bobby. By the way — did you really think I could miss? At that distance? I am insulted."

Bangles took another look at the receipt. It was dated three days ago.

"This is some sort of fuckin' trick."

"No trick. I've been waiting for you. I knew this is where you would come after I put you on the run. It was the closest of your hiding places. And the one with the bug-out kit. That bag over there, right?"

Cambino pointed at the leather mailman's pouch with the passports, the wallets, and the money, sitting where it shouldn't be sitting. Bangles was still staring at the bag when Cambino said, "Killing you would not have solved my problem, Bobby. We need to talk."

Old emotions came flooding back to Bangles. He wasn't sure how to respond to what he'd just heard. And he always knew how to respond. He stared at Cambino, as though a young boy not understanding a magic trick; he had that look on his face when Cambino said, "It was the girl, Bobby."

◈ ◈ ◈

They sat in silence for a long while after that, the night dusk becoming more familiar to both of them, able to see most objects in the room, sense the rest, no bright colours to startle them, no electronic hiss in the background. Sitting in a dark that was no longer true dark, until Cambino said, "Grace Dumont. You gave her a diamond. Which showed

279

you care about her. Maybe you fantasize about her, or fantasize about the mother, I don't need to know the whole story. All I needed to know was that one fact — you care about that girl.

"So I waited outside her apartment. Not as long as I would have thought. Then I followed you from the apartment, and within two days I knew everything I needed to know about you. I even know the name of the last girl you fucked in this room."

Bangles was no longer trying to hide the surprise from his face. He'd already gone over the ridge, as the tough men in Billy Adams's crew used to say when they were dying in cancer wards or getting sentenced to death in a federal courtroom, not wanting to say "meet you on the other side," because everyone said that.

"How the fuck did you learn shit like this?"

"It's not difficult. The more you know about a person, the weaker they become. You were a child when you killed your first man. Almost the same age as Grace Dumont was when you kidnapped her. I don't know when you realized that, but one day you did, and that's when you started caring for her. That was your weakness. It seems no matter how many men you have killed, you are still that boy at the weigh station. A boy's kindness to a young girl. That's how I found you."

"Is she in play here?"

"Ahhh, there it is again."

"*Is she?*"

"No. Would you like me to promise?"

"Yes."

"Grace Dumont will not be touched. She is out of this, as of today."

Bangles looked relieved, and Cambino stared at him with interest.

"Do you feel better, knowing this is why you will die? Because of this rare act of kindness on your part?"

"How much time do I have to answer?"

"Bobby."

"This is how it plays out, right? No way it can go any different?" He had to ask. You never know.

"No."

He sat back and gave Cambino's question some thought. It was a good question for a time like this, and Cambino didn't rush him. Eventually Bangles straightened his back and said, "I can't see how it matters much, why you died or how you died. Dead is dead. Probably matters more how you lived."

The smile disappeared from Cambino's face, and he studied Bangles a long time, an awkward pause that ended the way many awkward silences do, with sadness and the conviction by someone that unpleasant work laid ahead and it was time to start.

"It is a shame. Sometimes it goes that way. You cannot feel good about it, you wish it could have been different, but that is all you have, right? A wish. Nothing more. Do you have a last request?" asked Cambino.

"No."

"Are you sure? I take such things seriously."

"No, we're done here."

Cambino nodded. Then he leaned forward and rummaged through the contents of Bangles's kit bag, found the twelve-inch serrated combat knife he clearly expected to find there. He kept the knife in his hand, the gun aimed steady at Bangles's chest, and rose from the bed in a difficult squat he didn't seem to notice. If Bangles didn't already know it was hopeless, that move convinced him. Cambino didn't even seem to be breathing hard.

Bangles stared at the knife and thought, *So it's going to be a knife.* He had wondered about it from time to time. A knife would not have been his first choice.

"Let's get to work, then," said Cambino. "I have a few questions about those diamonds you stole."

CHAPTER
FORTY-SEVEN

One of the many paradoxes to Tyler Lawson was he had great respect for the law. A scrupulous mob lawyer, that's what some people around the Springfield district courthouse called him, and Lawson seemed comfortable, almost oblivious, to the sarcasm. He followed the rules of allowable evidence and agreed-upon debate, thought the codified language of the legal system was a sacred text, and not once did he cut a corner, nor engage in discreditable or disingenuous behaviour in the courtroom or before another lawyer.

He did all this in the service of pitiless men, so that the law became a perversion in Lawson's hands, yet he never stopped believing in the fundamental rightness of the legal system, never gave up his passionate, advocate's belief in the underlying fairness of reasoned debate and syllogistic thought, in the supremacy and the glory of the law.

The phone call to Bobby Bangs ended the scrupulous mob lawyer fantasy. Ended the long-held belief that he'd managed to build a wall between himself and the Shiners. How could he keep believing that when he had just bought the first burner phone of his life and relayed a message to Bobby Bangs — *Bobby freakin' Bangs*, even his kids knew the song — that an assassin was on the loose looking for him.

He might as well have said "Go to your corners." He had just become a legal officiant, some sort of courtside referee, for the next murder in Springfield.

It needed to end. It should have ended a long time ago, certainly before Sean Morrissey went to jail, but he couldn't deny it any longer. That burner phone. "You've just been tagged."

It all went poof during his drive home that day — the last twenty years of his life.

❖ ❖ ❖

Trish Lawson sat at the kitchen table and looked at her husband. They had just finished supper, and the children were upstairs, doing homework — or pretending to. They often ate as a couple, Tyler getting home late from the office two or three times a week. The children were old enough that they could make their own suppers on those nights.

They rarely used the dining room table; they preferred sitting by the bank of windows in the kitchen, looking out on their backyard and the forest beyond it. The lights were turned low in the kitchen, but she couldn't see much out the windows that night but a line of birch.

"You're quiet tonight," she said.

"Lots on my mind, I'm afraid."

"Sean?"

"He's definitely part of it."

"Frank phoned me last week, the day he got out of Wentworth."

Tyler stared at her. "You never told me that."

"I wasn't sure if I was going to. He's worried about me. And you."

"I doubt your brother spends much time worrying about me."

She nodded. "He said we were in danger. Said Sean was in danger too."

"You believe that?"

"Why not, Tyler? Christ, his father was murdered just last year, hung up on a fence on the North Shore like some hunted animal. Is the son invincible or something?"

"There was more to Augustus's murder than people think, Trish. Talk to your brother about that, next time he calls."

"Tyler, what is going on?"

He turned away. Stared at the television on the wall at the far end of the kitchen. Eight in the evening, still sitting in the kitchen. Any other night, that television would have been turned on.

"I think we should go away," he said, when he turned back to his wife. "I think we should take a long vacation."

"That's what Frank said too. Said we should jump on a plane and get out of here for a while."

"For once I agree with your brother."

"The kids are in school, Tyler."

He gestured, his palm upwards. "Take them out. A couple of weeks in the sun, it would do all of us a world of good."

"Justin has hockey. Sarah has a dance competition in two weeks. When were you thinking of doing this, Tyler?"

"I think we should do it soon. As soon as possible . . . as soon as we . . . yes, a few things will need attending to . . . but if we . . ." and then he stopped talking. Not sure what day would work.

His wife looked at him sadly. "You can't go until Sean has done something with those diamonds, can you? You're a player in all this. No better than if you'd stolen them yourself."

"That's unfair, Trish."

"But is it untrue? My God, Tyler, you used to be a lawyer."

It was the first time she'd said it. They had agreed not to discuss his work, not even agreed, as it was something that was never discussed, just understood — Tyler did legal work for the Shiners, and we don't talk about that.

He didn't know how to respond. Found himself stalling. A familiar fall-back position for Tyler Lawson.

"Trish, this is awkward," he said. "You must know that. I'm not sure what the best course of action is at the moment. Anything I do might just make things worse."

"It's a bit more than *awkward*, wouldn't you say, Tyler? Do you know this guy that's in town looking for Sean? The one who killed Gabriel Dumont?"

"I've heard of him. Exaggerated stories. Folk tales, almost."

"But he's real?"

"Yes, he's real."

"Frank thinks Sean is in trouble with this guy. Serious trouble. You don't think that?"

"I don't know, Trish. I would never think it wise, betting against Sean Morrissey. This time . . . I'm not sure anymore."

Trish Lawson pushed a strand of hair away from her face and looked at her husband with an anger that soon turned to pity, or if not pity then something kind and more invested. She rubbed the back of her hand across his cheek.

"Fuck Tyler, is it *that bad*?"

He came around to her side of the table and held her tightly. In a minute they both started crying, and when Julie walked into the kitchen and asked what had happened, Trish said an aunt of Tyler's had died. In Savannah, where most of Tyler's family still lived, and they all might need to go there for the funeral. After that they went upstairs to their bedroom, where they talked for most of the night.

CHAPTER
FORTY-EIGHT

Yakabuski was looking at another nighttime video, another car moving in and out of shadows and shimmering pools of chemical-green light. It was beginning to feel claustrophobic to him, having to sit in a room and watch these.

O'Toole was with them this time. Standing beside Yakabuski as Griffin got the video rolling, her laptop sitting on the table in the conference room on the third floor. The chief had booked the room. He didn't want anyone walking into Yakabuski's office while it was being played. Didn't want anyone arriving at his door, either, as O'Toole also had an open-door policy.

"We have it for fifty-three minutes," said Griffin. "That's longer than it needed to be. The car pulled over to the side of the road once and stayed there for nearly twenty minutes. Right by the Mission Road off-ramp to Highway 7. Camera there had him the whole time."

"What do you think he was doing?" asked O'Toole.

"No way of knowing. Tinted windows on the car. We never saw the driver."

"Phone call?"

"Perhaps. We can get cell-tower feeds for that area if we need them. But he might have just been sitting in the car, too, looking at what he had and going, 'Holy shit!'"

"You can fast-forward it, Donna. We don't need to see the entire route," said O'Toole.

Griffin hit another key on her laptop and the video sped up. In fast-forward the video looked like an oil spill coming out the back of a two-stroke boat engine. When she stopped the feed she turned away from the computer screen and said, "This is so ironic I'm not sure where to begin. The last camera to catch our car was the same last camera that caught the Econoline the night of the robbery. Both vehicles disappeared at the exact same spot."

She hit play, and the car appeared again on her laptop. Moving down a two-lane country highway with hard-mud ridges on the shoulders, lined by hardwood trees that had lost their leaves, cedars that blew in a strong wind, casting shadows across the road that looked like people falling. The headlights cast a strong beam through the darkness for six seconds, and then the car was gone.

"The exact same spot," Griffin said one more time, not making any attempt to hide her wonder. "After everything we've been doing, all these months, all that work, we're right back where we started."

Neither O'Toole nor Yakabuski said anything. They were older. It didn't seem as surprising to them.

"Don't think there's anything else we can find out," said Griffin, turning to look at Yakabuski.

"She's right, Yak," said O'Toole. "We have enough evidence to pick him up. What do you want to do?"

"I'll go get him."

"I should send a couple officers with you."

"I'd prefer if you didn't."

O'Toole opened his mouth and started to speak, then closed it and looked at Yakabuski a few seconds before saying, "I'll be here waiting for you. Call me on your way back."

CHAPTER
FORTY-NINE

Sean Morrissey sat in his office, wishing he could see those diamonds one more time. If he could, he might think it had all been worth it.

He'd thought of taking a photo of them when he had them and wished now he had. At the time it had seemed a foolish risk and he'd resisted the urge. How do you ever know? That was the time he should have given in to temptation.

He *remembered* how those diamonds looked. Like every good dream he'd ever had, all rolled into one, all the open space and pastel colours, nothing dark or linear. He'd put his hand deep in the storage crates, past his elbow, and stirred the diamonds, made them shimmer and wink at him — purple, orange, yellow, blue — the colours running over his hands like water in a creek.

The most beautiful thing he had ever seen. If he had those diamonds sitting on his desk right then, it would seem worth it to him. He was almost convinced of it.

It had been twenty-four hours since he last heard from Bangles, and he knew what that meant. He was to report in every twelve hours with a sitrep. Same time. Same burner phones. He might miss one. He wouldn't miss two.

Bobby Bangs. He'd begun to think the boy might grow to be greater than Tommy, a thought that seemed sacrilege when it first came to him, but which had grown more certain with time. Now they were both gone, and he guessed that was one more thing he'd been wrong about. He missed them. Same way he was missing his mother. Although she had been gone a long time, burying her last year just made it seem more recent. And he missed Lucy Whiteduck, surprised when that emotion came to him, but it hadn't been that long for Lucy, so maybe he was allowed.

He had become sentimental almost overnight, and he knew what that meant. The fight had gone out of him. It had fled like a thief in the night, right after Bangles missed his second sitrep. He'd thought his will to compete would last forever. Now he was a man who no longer had family or friends, and lonely men make poor warriors. It was why history felt it necessary to invent countries and flags. So the dead could belong to something.

Shortly before 7 p.m., he heard the first gunshots. They came from the back entrance of the club, and he thought that was smart. He had his best men positioned in front, and Cambino would have spotted the difference. He heard return fire, but not for long. Then he heard footsteps running through the club, heading toward the back.

There was a moment of silence. Then more gunfire. Inside the club now, and much louder, rolling thunder that had snuck indoors. When the gunfire stopped, there was the sound of large objects falling to the floor. Glass breaking. More gunfire. After that, silence.

A moment later there was a knock on the office door. Morrissey remained seated at his desk, remembering how those diamonds looked, wondering if he was actually supposed to say "Come in."

◆ ◆ ◆

Yakabuski spent the car ride debating whether he should have caught it. A game of hindsight he normally didn't play, not seeing the advantage to it, but some things were harder than others to put in the rear-view mirror.

He had had parts of it figured right. Major parts. He needed to remember that. Those diamonds had never left town. Morrissey had stashed them just like he figured a Shiner would do. The police department hadn't wasted any time at all talking to Interpol, or going through airline manifestos, overseas bank transactions. They had never been duped about that one, and as the search dragged on, the people who thought the diamonds were in the wind had begun to outnumber the people who thought they were still in Springfield.

Yakabuski wasn't even wrong about Mission Road. You could argue that one, but at no point in the investigation was he standing way out in left field. Always pretty close.

Only in horseshoes. Yakabuski smiled, thinking of what his dad would say right then if he were sitting in the Jeep with him. Close, but not standing on the right spot, and no police investigation ever got solved that way.

There were bad things that might have happened but never did, and those were things you needed to remember when playing the game of hindsight — the pieces that never got on the board. The Travellers had stayed out of it; maybe they were always going to do that, but knowing that's what Rachel Dumont wanted, and having that conversation with Linus Desjardins, he didn't think it hurt. The squatters' camp never devolved into anarchy, either, and anarchy was about as common in squatters' camps as head lice. The morning patrols and constant police presence had done the trick.

As for the violence that did occur, he wasn't sure it could have been avoided. People in Springfield were already saying a fever had overcome the city, some sort of crazy lust or bug-eyed greed. Something unnatural. People were always ready to do that: deny the violence around them.

The first winter in Quebec City, the oldest city in the country, heads were sitting on pikes by the front gates. Traitors who had plotted to kill Champlain. That's how far back betrayal and violence went around here. But no one remembers the story. No one was ever taught it. The heads on the pikes weren't even the worst part of that winter; it was a long and unrelenting one that saw twenty-seven of Champlain's original settlers die of starvation and Mi'kmaq gathered in the frozen riverbed before the fort. The game had disappeared and they also were starving, out on that frozen plain, dying by the dozens, carrion birds further darkening a sky in which the sun had not been seen for weeks.

That was the first winter. Yakabuski didn't think the season had improved much since. But when he told people the story of Quebec City they looked at him like he was a little off, like he had just given them an early sign of coming dementia. He didn't care. He couldn't pretend violence was anything but what it was — a human act so routine it was about as shocking as watching a man drink a cup of coffee.

What had been happening in Springfield wasn't unnatural. It was one thing leading to the next, the way Benjamin Chee taught him. But it was still hard for Yakabuski to avoid the obvious. He had missed something.

"Who would Sean Morrissey trust with the biggest score of his life?"

It was a good question. He should have come up with the right answer.

❖ ❖ ❖

The guard at the gate waved him through, and Yakabuski drove down tree-lined streets with houses set far back from the road. Hockey nets sat in front of three-car garages, and portable basketball hoops were already at the end of many driveways.

It had been an indifferent spring, nothing you could warm up to, but summer was on its way. He took a turn onto a cul-de-sac, and the houses became bigger. The garages no longer attached, but set aside like carriage houses. When he came to a bend in the street, he turned in to a driveway. There were no streets behind this house, just woods that ran almost to Findlay Creek. He parked his Jeep and walked to the front door. In the backyard were boards for a hockey rink that had still not been taken down. He rang the bell and waited.

The door was answered in only a few seconds. The light from inside the house backlit the man's head, so the blond hair stuck out strangely, like the corn hair you'd see on old rag dolls. Tyler Lawson extended his hand and said, "That was quick. I sent you the email just a few minutes ago."

CHAPTER FIFTY

They sat at the kitchen table, Yakabuski, his sister, and his brother-in-law. It had taken a few minutes of confused conversation for Tyler Lawson to realize Yakabuski never got his email. A few seconds more to realize what that meant.

"How long have you known?"

"Since yesterday."

"Why didn't you come right away?"

"I needed to confirm it." Yakabuski turned to his sister after he said it. She looked shell-shocked. The same look he saw on people sitting in hospital corridors late at night.

"How long have *you* known?" he asked.

"Two days," his sister answered.

"Would have been nice if you'd told me."

"We needed to get some things organized, Frank. I'm sorry."

"Where are the kids?"

"They flew out this afternoon. They're with Tyler's mother in Savannah."

"That was smart," Yakabuski said.

"It was hard to see them leave, Frank. I don't know if they'll ever be coming home. Don't know if they'll ever want to. It's hard knowing a thing like that, when your children don't."

"This is still their home, Trish. Dad and I will make sure of that."

"Oh, Frank," she said, and then she started crying. Lawson looked as though he was going to come over and try to comfort her, was rising from his chair, when he hesitated. After standing awkwardly for a second, he sat down.

It was obvious there was nothing he could do to comfort her. He was smart enough to know that. Yakabuski turned to his brother-in-law and said, "You might as well go get them."

◆ ◆ ◆

They fit into four full-kit duffle bags. Yakabuski had done the math months ago and figured you could do it in four. No more than five.

Lawson brought them up one by one from the basement, while Yakabuski sat with his sister. After the second bag arrived, Trish moved closer to him and lay her head against his chest.

"What are we going to do, Frank?"

"You already know the answer, Trish."

"Keep on keeping on. I know. Not sure if I can do it this time."

"You never do."

When the four bags were on the table, Lawson sat down

and wiped his forehead. "Heavy," he said with a smile, but when no one smiled back he looked away.

"Were you in on it right from the start?"

"No. Sean phoned me that night and told me to meet him in the parking garage. He didn't say why."

"Is it common to meet one of your clients in a parking garage at two in the morning?"

"No."

"So you knew something wasn't right. Why didn't you stay home, Tyler?"

"I didn't think I had that option."

"Did he threaten you?"

"The exact opposite. He promised me."

"What?"

"My freedom. Sean said if I hid the diamonds until he could come and collect them, I could walk away. From the Shiners. From Springfield, if I wanted. I would be free and clear. Just this one last thing."

"You believed him?"

"I wanted to."

Yakabuski shook his head. That's all it took. As good as the truth to a desperate person — Here's your way out. His brother-in-law had been played like a two-bit crook sitting in the holding cells. The best criminal defence lawyer in Springfield.

Yakabuski stood up and opened one of the bags. The diamonds twinkled and shone in the dim light of the kitchen, so many of them it looked like he had revealed a small fire when he unzipped the duffle bag. It had the colours of a small fire too: the purples and burgundies and vermillions of long-burning embers, the yellows and blues of a flame. They were uncut, without the full brilliance that would come later, but they were good diamonds — the colours were there all right — it was a sight.

But when Yakabuski looked at the diamonds, he didn't see the beauty. He saw the terrified eyes of Brady Dekker. And Jason McAllister laid out like a fallen sentry by the shores of a half-frozen lake. Another young man lying nearby, his tattooed body brutalized; an ugly death, the worst thing to ever happen to him certainly, although when you looked at that body you suspected maybe not by a country mile.

Yakabuski looked at those diamonds and saw greed and misery to rival all the fabled calamities of history, the holiest of holy crusades, the most vainglorious of quests.

He zipped up the duffle bag and sat back down. Looked at his brother-in-law.

"Do you realize what you've done?" he asked.

◆ ◆ ◆

Tyler Lawson was talking. A prepared speech, it seemed to Yakabuski. How his fiduciary duty to Sean Morrissey had ended when he was unable to reach him that afternoon, after sending him an email earlier in the day notifying him he was going to be surrendering to the police. Not that it was going to matter much, as he was going to be disbarred; attorney-client privilege would be broken if he was to make a complete atonement, which he was prepared to do. He was going to serve time.

"I've discussed it with Trish, but not the children yet," he said. "I know what's coming, and I'm prepared for the consequences. I'm prepared to pay my debt to society."

It was a very fine speech, and when he was finished Yakabuski said, "You know what's coming?"

"Utter ruination. Yes, I know what's coming. Know any good lawyers?"

Yakabuski didn't answer. He looked at his brother-in-law, who did a reasonably good job of holding his stare. After a while he said, "You haven't been able to reach Sean?"

"No . . . I . . . I haven't." Lawson stumbled. It was not the question he was expecting after his grand confession. Yakabuski pulled his cellphone from his pocket and stared at it. Then he stood up and walked to the landline on the kitchen island. Picked that up and heard the hollow silence he was hoping not to hear. Lawson had taken his own cellphone from his pocket and was looking at it strangely. Trish looked back and forth between them and said, "What is going on?"

"I think your husband has made a slight miscalculation on what's coming next," said Yakabuski.

CHAPTER
FIFTY-ONE

Lawson looked up from his cellphone and the look on his face was part wonder, part horror, the look young kids have when they board a roller coaster for the first time. He was sweating profusely, several strands of wheat-blond hair already pasted to his forehead.

"Is someone jamming the signal?"

"Someone? You're going to pretend you don't know who?"

Lawson shot Yakabuski a wounded look. Then he looked back at his phone and his gaze turned to something vacant, no recognizable emotion to it, some sort of free fall. Trish looked at her husband, then at her brother, went back and forth like that a few times and said quietly, "He's outside our house? Is that what you're saying?"

"We don't know," said Lawson.

"Yes," said Yakabuski.

Trish's hands flew to her mouth and she started to tremble. Lawson looked surprised and hurt by her reaction. Yakabuski wondered if he was going to make an issue of it. Right here, right now. Trish believing her brother, instead of her husband.

But he didn't. Instead, he walked to his wife and hugged her. Then they both started to tremble and choke back sobs, making a miserable mawing sound that reminded Yakabuski of what you hear when you walk by an old barn late at night.

◈ ◈ ◈

The Lawson house was built with as many windows as walls. The south wall of the main floor was nothing but glass. The front of the house was about half windows. Upstairs there was a great room and a master bedroom, both with cathedral ceilings and floor-to-ceiling windows, and there were banks of windows in the other three bedrooms. Even on a moon-less night, with every electric light turned off, you could walk around this house easily, move from pool of grey shadow to pool of grey shadow, down hallways lit by the dull glow of a streetlight shining through a distant bay window. You lost depth of field in the evening, but you could still make out most objects. A little one-dimensional, a little distorted — it reminded Yakabuski of late-afternoon snow cover when you were downhill skiing — but you could make everything out all right.

Which made it the worst possible place to defend. A glass house.

They had not left the kitchen, sat on the floor behind the island, away from the windows. Yakabuski had good situational awareness, as Rachel Dumont had said, and he had been sizing up the house, the backyard, making calculations on distance and likely points of attack for nearly five minutes.

The house couldn't be defended. The size of it, the number of windows and wings, the possible lines of attack and egress, it was crazy. They also had only two firearms. Maybe. Yakabuski had his service pistol, and Lawson had a skeet gun in the basement, one he bought years ago and never used. Yakabuski thought it unlikely that the rifle worked, or that Lawson had any ammunition. He asked about it, but Lawson couldn't remember having stored boxes in the gun cabinet he'd bought when he got the skeet gun.

"I remember the sales clerk showing me how to load it. There could still be bullets in it. Should I get it?"

"No."

Selling a man a loaded rifle? The day that started happening, Yakabuski was heading up north and never coming back. That skeet gun was useless. Certainly not worth dying for, and Yakabuski was beginning to think that was what would happen if they tried to move out of the kitchen.

They couldn't leave the room without passing a bank of south-facing windows. Their cellphones were jammed, which probably meant an intruder no more than two hundred metres away, and the woods behind the house were a lot closer than that. It would be an insane risk, trying to move out right then.

It could be a long night. Yakabuski had seen them before, nights hunkered down in some building, a company of soldiers under siege and each one hoping they'll see the sun rise one more time. You get hallucinogenic dreams near dawn, after too many hours staring at the colour black waiting for it to turn grey.

Although maybe it wouldn't be a long night. Cambino Cortez had been decisive when he needed to be during his road trip across the United States He had the advantage and would know it. Gaining access to the house would be easy. Everything after that would be easier still.

Yakabuski figured he was in the northwest corner of the woods behind the house. He would know their position because he would have been watching them through field glasses when he killed the signal. He'd have a night scope, so turning off the lights, as they had done right away, had been pointless. Even without night-vision, he'd have had their position when the lights went out, and he knew they hadn't moved.

Outside the house there was the cooing of mourning doves getting ready to nest for the night. There was no wind. No car coming down the road. Just the sound of the doves when Yakabuski heard a man shout — "Do you believe in fate, Detective Yakabuski?"

CHAPTER FIFTY-TWO

The voice came from the northwest corner of the backyard, by the woods, where Yakabuski figured he'd be standing. Good sightlines on the kitchen and the hallway. A five-step perimeter march would give him the back door as well.

He looked over at Trish and Tyler, whose face looked sickly and pale, like golden root you'd find in a forest on a starless night, some frail thing that didn't belong there. Yakabuski closed his eyes and went through the furniture in the living room one more time, remembering how the room was laid out, picking the best possible route if it came to that, a head-down, desperate run though the living room when the shooting started. He was about to go through it one more time when the voice shouted out, "Perhaps fate is too strong a word."

A little farther to the east. Cambino was going to stay a moving target, give nothing away, even when there was nothing to give away.

"Yes, too strong a word," he continued. "Let's start again. Do you believe, Detective Yakabuski, that certain things in life are meant to happen? That there are people you were always destined to meet, places you were always going to see? Have you ever walked into a room, sat down, and realized you were in the exact right spot at the exact right time, and it was always going to be that way? Do you believe such things are possible?"

Yakabuski listened with his eyes closed. It seemed like Cortez repositioned every ten seconds. He was that methodical. After thinking it through a few seconds, and seeing no advantage to staying silent, he shouted, "I was wondering when you might show up."

"And here I am. That is my point exactly. We have never met, Detective Yakabuski, but what history we share, what stories. I believe this night was always coming for us."

"I don't know if it's all that grand. I meet whack-jobs like you all the time."

"Ah, Detective Yakabuski, there is no need for that. If you do not wish to answer my question, I will ask another. You have had nearly fifteen minutes to think about it. What is your sitrep?"

"At the moment, I think it works out to me pissing in your mouth in about twenty minutes."

"You promised to do that once before, as I remember. Here is my sitrep, Detective: You and your family, your sister, your brother-in-law — you are the walking dead. You are alive only because I wish it. No other reason. You are all dead the minute I no longer wish it. What do you think of my report?"

Yakabuski didn't shout anything back. It would be foolish to deny what Cambino had just said. A sign of weakness. He waited, and after a minute had passed he heard what he was expecting.

"Come out of the house, Detective Yakabuski. It is time we met."

❖ ❖ ❖

Yakabuski approached the line of birch that bordered the backyard. In the darkness of that starless night, the trees seemed as bright and large as dinner candles. The wind had vanished, and crickets were chirping from the short grass near the entrance to the forest.

He judged Cambino to be well under six feet, five-nine or -ten probably, no more than 170 pounds; a slight man, although Yakabuski had seen the build before. The legendary street fighters from the French Quarter all had that build. So did the best Voyageurs, because big men were useless on long canoe trips. What worked best was a body of gristle and sinew. His clothing was not quite what he had been expecting either — tan windbreaker, baggy jeans, white sneakers — it was the comfortable attire of old men enjoying their retirement years.

Except he was holding a Glock 17 in his right hand, and he didn't look that old. He was sitting in a wrought iron chair from the patio set in the backyard. They normally weren't this far back on the property, and he suspected Cambino had moved them. He would want to be as close to the woods as possible. He motioned for Yakabuski to sit in another of the chairs he had dragged to the edge of the woods.

Yakabuski sat and continued his examination. Cambino was clean-shaven with no visible tattoos. No rings on his fingers. No bracelets or earrings. He wore a collared shirt buttoned to his Adam's apple, and his eyes could not be seen in the darkness, sometimes not his hands either.

"Been here long?" he asked.

"A few hours. It's pleasant. No mosquitos. No blackflies. Your sister must spray."

"What do you want?"

"You know what I want. And I have been told it is inside this house."

"Where did you hear a crazy story like that?"

"From a man I trust."

"You don't strike me as the trusting type."

"I'm not. It was the man's circumstances that convinced me."

Yakabuski looked at Cambino and he knew Sean Morrissey was dead. That he died a torturous death. And Yakabuski could not decide, right then, if that was right, or just, if it was what Morrissey deserved. He was a thief who had to become a gangster, because that was what he was born into, the family business, but the bloodletting stuff never seemed as natural for him as it did his father. And he had been kind, once, to that girl, Lucy, in Ragged Lake. He had overreached. A simple story that got complicated. Yakabuski wasn't sure what sort of fate a man like that deserved.

"You asked me if I believe in fate," he said, looking out on the woods. "Two strangers meeting on a path who were always supposed to meet. I suppose I do. Don't know what you'd call it — maybe fate sounds a bit grand — but I'd be a liar if I said this moment doesn't seem like one that was always coming."

"I *knew* it. Have you seen what comes next?"

"No," Yakabuski said.

"Nor have I. That is unusual for me. What about you?"

"I normally know what's coming next."

"But not this time. Does that worry you?"

"Yes. We don't know whose moment this is."

"Well said. It always matters more to one person, doesn't it? One person's lost love is another person's forgotten conversation. The two people destined to meet? Maybe only one walks away knowing it. Yes — whose moment is this?"

Cambino kept the gun pointed at Yakabuski's chest, as steady as though it were clamped in a vice. He stared out on the woods, the moonless sky, the house behind them. After a while, he said, "I have a proposal for you."

"I thought you might."

"Bring me those diamonds. Put them right on this table. I take them and go away. You walk back into that house and have dinner with your family. We will resolve this matter between us another day, when we are further down the road. There is much to be said for patience, even on matters of fate. People say you cannot run from your fate, but it is not true. You can run a long time."

Yakabuski didn't wait long to give his answer. He thought of Piers Grund walking away from those diamonds; Jason McAllister lying beside McGregor Lake all winter; his sister hiding by the back door of her house, more fear in her eyes than he'd ever seen; his niece and nephew sitting in a strange bedroom in Savannah wondering what just happened to them.

"We can make that work," he said. "Give me ten minutes."

Less than ten minutes later, the four duffle bags were sitting on the patio table. Cambino opened one of the bags and looked inside. He didn't open the others.

"The bounty of the land," he said, when he sat back down. "Who do you think has the right to claim it, Detective Yakabuski?"

"The one who's living on it, I suppose."

"A good answer. And close to the truth, I think. Only the Lord can decide who gets the bounty of the land. Problem is, the Lord keeps changing His mind."

Yakabuski didn't know what to say to that. They sat in silence for a few seconds, and then he said, "Are we done here?"

"Almost. As you can see, four bags will be too much for me to carry. I will need your sister to help me."

"That wasn't part of our deal."

"It was not *discussed*, but I am afraid it must be part of our deal. I need the help, and I do not trust you. It would be better for everyone if your sister came with me. She will be released unharmed within twenty-four hours. You have my word."

"Your word?"

"Yes. Let's write the next chapter in our story another day."

"There's no way you're taking my sister," Yakabuski said.

"No way?"

"No way."

"Ahh, I thought you might feel that way. Well, the decision was yours." And with that Cambino raised his arm and shot him.

CHAPTER
FIFTY-THREE

Yakabuski was speeding through a dark tunnel and flying out the other end, light exploding around him. Spinning and falling, bright, dazzling fragments of light, then back in the tunnel and it goes on forever this time, a hard cylinder of blackness he rolls and spirals through, shooting out an opening he hadn't seen before, not kaleidoscope lights this time, but a multi-screen cinema, filled with images from the past. Lake Dore in late fall, the hardwood trees a perfect patch of burnished reds and dark purples. A full-patch biker hanging upside down from a balcony in Laval, his face dangling beneath Yakabuski, the mouth open in a silent scream. Papa Paquette laughing and ordering a round for the table, slapping Yakabuski on the back and calling him brother. His father being shot in the toy aisle of a Stedman's department store, My Little Pony toys bouncing down the linoleum floors, the coloured horses landing in a pool of blood.

Lying on hard ground and the cinema is gone.

His sister is screaming. He can almost make out the words. It's his name. It's his name, right? He rescued his sister once from a gang of wannabe Shiners in High River, boys not that much older than she. When Yakabuski had extricated her, she wanted to go back and beat the boy who had taken her. Hardest part wasn't rescuing Trish. It was bringing her home.

More kaleidoscope lights, then darkness. Tyler Lawson is standing on a hill, so far away it looks Biblical, some heavenly summit, clouds circling the peak, Lawson holding what looks like a metal spear, shouting, can't hear the words, the spear flies over his head, and Lawson falls from the mountain. The clouds become thicker, the mountaintop gone, dark clouds coming down, his sister screaming again . . . what is she screaming? A last flash of kaleidoscope light, and then the tunnel reappears, back inside, voices singing somewhere, a downward spiral, all colour bleeding away, all worlds vanquished, falling and spinning in a darkness without end.

◈ ◈ ◈

The room was as neutral as neutral gets. Walls that were either a light brown or a dirty white colour, maybe some colour in between. Beige blinds on a two-pane window. Machines that made sounds like hot-water radiators hissing. A bouquet of flowers that had dried, sitting by the window.

His sister was curled in a chair, sleeping. Yakabuski looked at her and said, "What day is it?"

She gave a start and opened her eyes. Looked at her brother and saw him looking back at her. She jumped from the chair and ran to his bed.

"Frank! Frankie, it is so good . . . so good . . ." but she couldn't finish the sentence, just hugged him and started crying. Before long there was a nurse in the room gently pulling her off, and a few seconds after that some more nurses and then a doctor. The doctor shone a penlight in Yakabuski's eyes and asked, "How are you feeling, Detective?"

"I've felt better."

"I would think so."

"What day is it?"

"Wednesday. A little after four in the afternoon. You've been here nine days."

"Nine?"

"In a coma for seven of them. We had to induce you after the surgery. We stopped giving you the chemicals this morning. You came out rather quickly."

"How bad was it?"

"Pretty bad. I'll tell you about it one day. Right now what you need is rest."

"Haven't I just been doing that?"

"Detective, I don't expect arguments from people whose lives I've just saved. Does that seem fair to you?"

"That seems fair."

"Then I want you to get some rest. Your sister hasn't left this room, so it's time she got some as well. I'll give you a few minutes, but when I come back this room is cleared, and you're back to sleep."

It took several minutes for Trish to stop crying. Yakabuski had questions, but he waited. He wished he could return her hugs, but there were IV tubes in both his arms.

"You and Dad," she said, when she finally stopped. "You're both so damn big the bullets can't make it through."

"He shot me?"

"Yes."

"How many times?"

"Just once. The bullet nicked the bottom of your pulmonary vein." Trish pointed two fingers to the left side of her heart. "He shot low. Just like those crooks did to Dad in Stedman's. If you were average size, you'd be dead, Frankie."

She started crying again. When she was finished, Yakabuski said, "It doesn't make sense, him shooting me only once. What else happened?"

"You knocked over the table when you were shot. Those duffle bags went flying. One of them was open, so diamonds scattered all over the place. When I heard the shot, I came running out of the house, and that man . . . that man was bent over, trying to get the diamonds back into the bag. I jumped on his back. It all happened so quickly, Frank, I thought you were dead and I was so angry. I had a pretty good grip on him and I was going for his eyes. I was really going after him."

He noticed her usually long manicured nails had been trimmed round. She must have broken a few.

"That's my girl."

"It wasn't going to be enough, Frank. He threw me off, and he started kicking me. I was curled up like a baby, my arms around my head, and when he stopped, I raised my head to look at him, the way you told me once a person should do. Never look away and make it easy for the bastards. That's what you said."

"I remember."

"I think it surprised him, because he hesitated. He had the gun in his hand and was standing over me and he gave me a funny look. That's when Tyler showed up. He'd gone down to the basement to get the skeet gun."

"Tyler shot him?"

"No," and this time his sister had a good long cry. Got up from the chair halfway through and gave her brother another hug, Yakabuski managing to raise his right arm and put it over her. It stung like getting nicked with razor blades, but he would have left it there all day.

When she had stopped crying and sat up she dabbed her eyes with a balled-up tissue and said, "That man shot Tyler as soon as he saw him. Turned the gun away from me and fired. Didn't say a word. Didn't even seem to aim. I saw it, Frank. The whole thing. My husband standing right behind me, and then blood is shooting out his shoulders and he's gone. Just like that. Gone."

"Trish, I'm . . ."

"He saved my life, Frank. Last thing he ever did. I know you never cared for him, but that's the last thing Tyler ever did."

Yakabuski didn't say anything for a few minutes.

"I still don't understand."

A smile broke through Trish's tears. The briefest of smiles, but it was there for a second, and then she said, "The skeet gun went off when it hit the ground. Every pellet hit that man in the face. O'Toole told me it was a perfect shot."

"An accident?"

"Yes, Frank — a gun that never should have fired and never should have had a round in it gets dropped on the ground and that man is dead. Tyler sort of saved your life too."

Yakabuski was still thinking about that when the doctor came back and told Trish she needed to go home. *An accident.* He thought about it the rest of the day, the next, and more or less, off and on, sometimes just a feeling that overcame him at random moments, every day since.

CHAPTER
FIFTY-FOUR

The diamonds stayed in the evidence room of the Centretown detachment for nearly three months before De Kirk came back to collect them. During that time, Yakabuski read business stories about the company being concerned its share price would plummet if it retrieved the diamonds. Apparently, the share price had spiked after the heist because more than a billion dollars in diamonds had been taken off the market. Supply and demand. It was how oil companies became rich after refinery fires.

Only the threat of legal action by Great North Insurance brought the company back to Springfield. It was Grund who oversaw the pick-up, arriving in front of the detachment in an armoured truck with a police escort, leaving right after for the Springfield Airport, where a cargo plane with a four-person security detail was waiting for him. Grund saw Yakabuski on the street when the armoured truck arrived but never came to speak to him. As the truck drove away, Yakabuski thought he saw him through the tinted bullet-proof glass, giving everyone on the street the finger.

When the plane was in the air, it occurred to Yakabuski it had been a nine-month layover. Everything that had happened in Springfield, out on the Mission Road, it added up to nothing more than a nine-month layover for those diamonds. The share price for De Kirk fell ten percent the next day, but by the end of the month it was back where it had started.

The funeral for Sean Morrissey was held at St. Bridget's Basilica, just as his father's had been the previous year, but unlike Augustus Morrissey's, which had brought gangsters and bandits from across North America to pay last respects, the son's funeral was a quiet affair. Mostly locals. The gangsters who had flown into town nine months earlier sent floral arrangements this time.

Tyler Lawson's funeral was held two days after Morrissey's, and it was what Yakabuski had expected for the funeral of a once prominent lawyer who died in scandal. Poorly attended. Awkward and stilted. The people on the steps of the church were uncertain what to say to Trish or the children, and so they said little. People sat in pews and didn't talk or whisper, no longer sure if this was a life worth celebrating. Tyler Lawson was dead, so it would never make a difference to him, but the shunning had begun.

The body of Bobby Bangs was never found. The cops searched for ten days along the Mission Road, in Cork's Town, down the French Line where the cabin fire had been, but they never found him. There seemed little doubt he was dead, but it looked like his body was going to be one of those the police found on the Northern Divide only when the land thought it was time. Yakabuski noticed "The Ballad of Bobby Bangs" was added to the playlist of a local FM radio station that autumn, and it became a regional hit for a second time.

After the short, cold winter and the on-and-off-again spring, summer along the Northern Divide was spectacular that year. Most days the sky was the colour of bleached-out denim, with little wind and only high cumulus clouds that seemed to stay parked day after day. There wasn't the bad humidity that normally came with summer, and the black-flies were gone by mid-May. The forest was cool all season and had the scent of spruce gum and cedar most of the day, the pine needles thick and rubbery and you knew it would be late autumn, perhaps winter, before any of them fell. It was a season about as pleasant and unchallenging as can be had on the Northern Divide.

Rachel Dumont phoned a few days after Labour Day weekend, asking Yakabuski to come and see her.

❖ ❖ ❖

When he was crossing the North Shore Bridge it occurred to Yakabuski he would never be on this bridge again without remembering the past three years. Tete Fontaine. Grace and Rachel Dumont. Filion's Field and the bodies that once hung on the southeast fence. The oil drums that burned up and down Tache Boulevard. The bridge had been one thing to him once; now it was another. It's what happened to material objects once they got tangled up with a person's memory. *Closest humanity has ever come to building a reliable, functioning time machine*, he thought.

He drove down Tache Boulevard, the sun hitting the windshield of his Jeep, and parked in the rear of Building C so he could get a look at Filion's Field before going to the apartment. He stared at the chain-link fence and the shadows on the soccer pitch. In all his time coming there, he had yet to see any children on that soccer pitch. He got out of his Jeep and walked through the back entrance.

When he reached the apartment, he found the door open. He entered, closing the door behind him, and walked through the living room into the kitchen. Rachel Dumont was sitting at the table, drinking from a teacup. There was a teapot in front of her and an empty teacup in front of the chair opposite. In the middle of the table sat a large FedEx box.

Yakabuski sat down and poured himself a cup of tea. Sweet Cedar. As he suspected it would be. After a while he said, "Grace not back from school yet?"

"She has band practice today."

"When did you get the package?"

"Start of the summer."

"You should have phoned me."

"I wasn't sure what to do."

"You are now?"

"Not really. I was hoping you could help me with that."

"Who sent it?"

"Your brother-in-law."

❖ ❖ ❖

Yakabuski looked at the letter. Written on Lawson and Associates letterhead. The cursive writing was large, precise, and almost rhythmic in the way it flowed across the paper.

Three pages. No covers or attachments. He read it for a second time:

Ms. Dumont,

My name is Tyler Lawson. We have never met, but until recently I was chief legal counsel for Sean Morrissey.

I was not sure how to begin this letter, how to introduce myself, but from what little I have just written, you know everything you need to know about me. My employer was a gangster, a man responsible for the kidnapping of your daughter and the killing of your father. His arrogance and greed brought much misery to your family, to this city, and I was complicit in all his crimes.

For many years I pretended I was not complicit, but I was a liar. You were never deceived the way I was. How brave you were, to have left your father's home when no more than a child, to say no to life as a Traveller, to a life as a criminal.

Yes, I have researched you, Ms. Dumont. I know you made the tough choices I never did. It saddens me to realize just how much of my life has been spent rationalizing what I always knew to be wrong, until so many crimes had accumulated it would have been the height of insincerity, almost foppery, to go out and try to do the right thing.

On the night Sean Morrissey and your father stole those diamonds, they were given to me and have been in my custody since. Tomorrow my wife and children will go into hiding; I will surrender to the police, and turn over the diamonds.

What you have in this package are the diamonds I will not be giving the police. They represent ten per cent of what was stolen.

The diamonds are uncut and, as I'm sure you know, untraceable. The market value for what I have sent you is $120 million.

Knowing a little about corporate financing, and how the criminal investigation has proceeded, I am quite confident in advising you that no one will come looking for these diamonds. They belong to you now, to do with as you wish.

I have made this decision for many reasons, but chief among them is that I am tired of seeing the bounty of the land go to those who do not deserve it. Bounty is never a reward given to those who put in the hard work, who make the investment, who are diligent and honourable. It always goes to people like Sean Morrisey, to the most cunning and boldest of fortune seekers, to the plunderers.

I wish that to end. I believe your father, and the Travellers, have legitimate grievances, and had I been a better lawyer, and a more principled man, perhaps theirs would have been a cause I defended. You deserve this money, Ms. Dumont.

You also belong to this strange country that my wife and children love so much. I have never belonged here. Some days the Northern Divide seems like a fable to me, an enchanted place where the prettiest of flowers can kill you and the calmest of waters will drown you. How I have missed Georgia, with its deltas and its tame forests. But my wife is a child of this place. I see it in her eyes. See it in our children's eyes. The way they anticipate the changing of the seasons, the way they walk through the forest. They belong here. It is a gift I was never given. Or never had the grace to accept.

Whatever will be done with these diamonds now, I want it done by a person of courage, who calls this land their home. I choose you.

I hope this package does not cause you further problems, Ms. Dumont, and that you can forgive me this foolish attempt at atonement. I know it is not coming for me. I hope one day to make my peace with that.

Please do not try to contact me. As much as I would enjoy meeting you, this letter and the contents of the package must remain our secret.

With great respect and affection,
Tyler Lawson

❖ ❖ ❖

For a long time, neither of them spoke. After a while, Yakabuski opened the box. In the dimness of the room the stones glowed like a late-night cook-fire. Not a bright or glaring white, but burnished yellows and reds, molten blues, dancing purples. When he shook the box, the colours roiled and shimmered. There were hundreds of stones. He couldn't guess how many there might be. Finally, Dumont said, "Your brother-in-law is dead, right?"

"Yes."

"Did you know he was doing this?"

"No. He kept it a secret, like he said in the letter."

"I've read the letter a hundred times. I'm still not sure why he sent them to me."

"Because he wanted to do one good thing before he died."

"He was that bad?"

"No, pretty typical in many ways. And he loved my sister. I always knew he did. I tried to deny it plenty of times, but I always knew he did."

324

"Why not give them to her, then?"

"They don't belong to her."

Rachel's spine straightened. "They don't belong to me either."

"They belong to you more than anyone else Tyler could think of. He was a smart man. He was probably right about that."

"Shouldn't they be returned to De Kirk? They own them, right?"

Yakabuski reached out and touched one of the stones. "Who should own the bounty of the land? A man of great evil asked me that once. He said it was an unanswerable question because only the Lord can decide, and the Lord keeps changing His mind."

"You believe that? You don't strike me as a religious man."

"I don't believe it was religion he was talking about."

He closed the lid of the box and stood up.

"So what are you going to do?"

EPILOGUE

Yakabuski picked them up one Sunday afternoon, and they drove to Mission Road. It was a warm day, with the sun high in the sky and only a few clouds drifting overhead. Daylight Savings Time had ended two weeks earlier, but autumn was taking its time about leaving.

They walked down the trail for nearly an hour, the sun casting filigreed shadows on the ground before them. The old colony road was as firm and dry as it ever gets, and it was easy walking. When they reached the La Vase Basin, they cut off the trail and started climbing a ridge, following a path that cut sharply to the north and took them, after another thirty minutes' hiking, to Brenna's Hill, the highest peak of land on the south shore.

They stood on a windswept bluff of gneiss and granite and looked out over the Springfield River. Dark green moss covered most of the rock. They stood beneath an old-growth white pine, the sun hitting the tallest branches at just the right angle to make the needles shimmer and turn golden. It was that late-afternoon glow you get sometimes in mixed-wood forests, when even the shadows look lucid and airy, moving across the ground as though slow-spinning cutouts on a child's mobile.

They could see down the river for miles in either direction. Yakabuski could see boats trolling for muskie in Warren's Bay, and beyond that the ferry cable between Masson and Farrleton, such a clear day you could see the wire suspended above the water. He heard the splash of terns diving in some distant channel. The cry of grey jays and the honking of geese starting their southern migration.

Rachel had removed her packsack and placed it by her feet. She reached down and undid the front flaps. They gathered around the pack, and it was Grace who put her hands in first, then Rachel, then Yakabuski. When they were all standing by the cliffs with a handful of diamonds, they began to throw.

Yakabuski figures he is one of only three people in all of history to have seen such a sight. Hundreds of diamonds thrown to the wind above a great river, a yawning blue sky, a gold-green foreground, the colours of a busted kaleidoscope spinning before them. Blue. Red. Burgundy. Yellow bright as butter. Purple dark as eggplant. After spinning in the wind, the diamonds started to fall, get smaller. They looked like late-night embers by the time they hit the river. The colours faded beneath the waves, but the smaller stones took their time about sinking, so that after a while it appeared as though a rainbow had been cast from beneath the Springfield River.

Yakabuski can't tell you how long it took. He lost track of time, standing on that bluff flinging diamonds into the river, shards of colour that slipped from his fingers as though he were some mad alchemist flinging his failed creations back to the physical world, where they spun and shone and passed through every spectrum of beauty before disappearing beneath the waves.

When they were finished they stood on the bluff for several minutes until Dumont retied the flaps to her pack, hoisted it, and headed back toward the trailhead. As Yakabuski followed mother and daughter down Mission Road it occurred to him that you take your rewards in this world the way they are offered to you. No different than the bad things. It was the first time the thought had occurred to Yakabuski.